W9-BXN-567

Desert Rider

OTHER FIVE STAR WESTERN TITLES BY RAY HOGAN:

Soldier in Buckskin (1996)
Legend of a Badman (1997)
Guns of Freedom (1999)
Stonebreaker's Ridge (2000)
The Red Eagle (2001)
Drifter's End (2002)
Valley of the Wandering River (2003)
Truth at Gunpoint (2004)
The Cuchillo Plains (2005)
Outlaw's Promise (2006)
Fire Valley (2007)
Panhandle Gunman (2008)
Range Feud (2009)
Land of Strangers (2010)

Desert Rider

A Western Duo

Ray Hogan

FIVE STAR
A part of Gale, Cengage Learning

Detroit • New York • San Francisco • New Haven, Conn • Waterville, Maine • London

Copyright © 2011 by Gwynn Hogan Henline.
Five Star Publishing, a part of Gale, Cengage Learning.

ALL RIGHTS RESERVED

No part of this work covered by the copyright herein may be reproduced, transmitted, stored, or used in any form or by any means graphic, electronic, or mechanical, including but not limited to photocopying, recording, scanning, digitizing, taping, Web distribution, information networks, or information storage and retrieval systems, except as permitted under Section 107 or 108 of the 1976 United States Copyright Act, without the prior written permission of the publisher.

The publisher bears no responsibility for the quality of information provided through author or third-party Web sites and does not have any control over, nor assume any responsibility for, information contained in these sites. Providing these sites should not be construed as an endorsement or approval by the publisher of these organizations or of the positions they may take on various issues.

Set in 11 pt. Plantin.

LIBRARY OF CONGRESS CATALOGING-IN-PUBLICATION DATA

Hogan, Ray, 1908–1998.
[Outside gun]
Desert rider : a western duo / by Ray Hogan. — 1st ed.
p. cm.
ISBN-13: 978-1-59414-938-2 (hardcover)
ISBN-10: 1-59414-938-0 (hardcover)
I. Hogan, Ray, 1908-1998 Outside gun. II. Title.
PS3558.O3473093 2011
813′.54—dc22 2010051984

First Edition. First Printing: April 2011.
Published in 2011 in conjunction with Golden West Literary Agency.

Printed in Mexico
2 3 4 5 6 7 15 14 13 12 11

CONTENTS

★ ★ ★ ★ ★

The Outside Gun

★ ★ ★ ★ ★

I

This was Big Bill Krask's town. Dan Wade pulled the roan to a halt on the crest of the ridge and looked down upon the T-shaped collection of buildings and houses. The sun was beginning to lower beyond the hills to the west and he allowed his eyes to travel up the darkening cañon that lay between the twin rows of high, false-fronted structures.

Lights were coming on in the windows of several stores and in most of the homes scattered across the land behind the commercial buildings where the supper hour would be at hand. It would be hot in the kitchens, Dan thought, studying the trickles of smoke snaking upward into the night sky. The day had been a scorcher, but there was no answer to the problem. Women must still feed their men, their families.

It had been eight years since he had left Burnt Springs. It appeared to have grown little in the intervening time. The same signs on the front of the buildings, the same names, the same owners were also in evidence. Yet there had been one change. It had brought him all the way across Texas and half the distance that spanned New Mexico Territory. He thought of that, of the letter folded and tucked away inside his shirt pocket. It had caught up with him in Abilene and immediately set the wheels of memory and curiosity to turning within his mind.

Dear Friend Dan:

If you can find time to ride by, I'll be much obligated. Find

myself in considerable trouble and could sure use your help.
Yours truly,
Wm. Krask, Marshal

Two things in the letter had startled and amazed him—that Big Bill would ever ask anyone for help, and that he had become a lawman. Krask had been, or was, the owner of the vast Double K spread, a magnificent ranch lying deep in the broad, grassy depths of the Cloud River Valley. Undisputable king of that part of the territory, he was wealthy, successful, and never in need of anything or anybody. Why he should become a lawman, a marshal of a town he figuratively owned, was difficult to understand. But Big Bill had been a friend, the first man to give Dan a job when the war was over and jobs were hard to come by. He was a widower, his wife having died soon after their son Little Bill, as he had become known, was born. Krask lived only for his son, building his future, his life, the ranch—everything—about him.

Someday Little Bill would inherit and take over the Double K. He would instantly be the biggest man in the territory, the most important figure in the entire Southwest. Big Bill had great plans for his only son and he never permitted him, or anyone else, to forget it. Little Bill had been about sixteen, Dan recalled, when he had decided to quit the Double K and ride on: a big, good-looking boy, the image of his father but inclined to wildness and with a broad streak of reckless irresponsibility running through his nature. Big Bill spent a considerable amount of time and money getting him out of scrapes. And always the cattleman had laughed it off, brushed it aside as a normal and natural thing for a high-spirited boy.

Little Bill had never become involved in anything serious. Generally it was nothing more than a combination of too much freedom, an oversupply of money resulting in a tremendous amount of mischief. There was never a time, so far as Dan knew, when anyone was maliciously injured. But apparently something had finally happened. Little Bill had gotten himself into a pocket so critical that the elder Krask had felt the need for help. This did not explain the lawman angle, however. Why would Big Bill, important, wealthy, a man more likely to be governor of the territory, assume the thankless task of a town marshal?

Dan Wade stirred impatiently. He removed his hat, ran a hand through his thick shock of light brown hair. He disliked unanswered questions, unsolved problems. It disturbed him when he could not find the solutions.

A gunshot sounded in the settlement, hollow and distant as it echoed through the lush, low hills and across the frothy green swales. He stiffened, his wide shoulders silhouetted against the dark sky, head thrust forward. He probed the shadowy street and buildings with sharp, pale eyes, but the distance was too great, the night too near. He could make out nothing.

He reached down, touched the heavy and worn Colt .44 hanging at his hip. His long fingers lifted it slightly in its oiled holster, let it fall again into place. What lay ahead in Burnt Springs was uncertain. Soon he would know.

He pressed the roan gelding gently with his spurs, starting him down the slope. The horse was tired. It had been a long, sweltering ride from Mesilla but he responded instantly, taking the steep trail of the grade with careful, sure-footed steps.

They reached the bottom, swung into the ankle-deep dust of the road that led on to El Paso, Mexico, and points farther south. Dan remembered it well. It had been the route he had followed that day when the urge to move on had eventually overwhelmed him. It seemed like a long, long time ago.

He came into town, his glance flipping from side to side as he approached the end of the street. There had been no more gunshots. He could hear men yelling, laughing, the faint strains of piano music. Somewhere beyond the Rainbow Saloon and Dance Hall, which sprawled at the opposite end of the settlement on the one cross street, thus forming a dead end, the sudden hammering of hoofs told of a horse breaking away and into a hard, quick run.

To his immediate left the first building, which had once housed a small, rag-ag saloon, was vacant. Next to it Joe Kingsford's hardware store was still doing business, its windows piled high with washtubs, buckets, brooms, and the like. Then came a ladies' dress and millinery shop, owned, Dan recalled, by prim and prudish Miss Agatha Hillard. A doctor and a lawyer maintained offices in the succeeding building, all of which were dark.

Beyond the professional men's quarters and in direct sequence was a barbershop, another small saloon, a second-rate hotel called the Star of Texas, and then the largest general store in the area, one belonging to Tom Hotchkiss. Burnt Springs' one cross street intersected there, brought an end to the line of structures. On the opposite side there came first a small store of some sort, groceries and meats it appeared to Dan. There was no sign on the dusty window or above the door and he could not be sure. A clothing store was beside it, followed by the marshal's office and jail, the Chicago Café, Abner Dawson's Cattleman's Bank, and the tall, two-storied bulk of the Great Western Hotel.

Wade halted the roan in front of Kingsford's, momentarily undecided whether to go first to the marshal's office, or to the Great Western and procure a room. There were few people on the street and those were down near the Rainbow. Glancing at them, he noted that a man named Garvey still operated the stable that lay directly to the east of the saloon. He could not tell who occupied the store buildings at its opposite shoulder. There had been a printer there formerly, a small, wizened man who endeavored, without much success, to produce a weekly newspaper.

There was a light in the marshal's office. The Chicago Café also was open for business. The saloon next to the Texas Star was bright but all the remaining buildings were dark except, of course, the Great Western Hotel and the Rainbow, which blazed with lamps and resounded with the racket created by its boisterous patrons.

He decided he would go first to the hotel, to its stable in the rear. The roan deserved a stall along with the care and rest that went with it. And he could use a bit of freshening up himself. Another thirty minutes would make little difference.

He put the gelding into motion, resumed his slow progress down the dark avenue, his eyes again roving the faces of the structures, probing the black passageways that lay between. He looked carefully at the marshal's office, endeavored to see behind its dusty window. There was no one sitting at the desk. Likely Big Bill was having his supper at that hour.

He drew abreast the Chicago Café. He could use a good meal himself, particularly some strong, black coffee. It had been early morning since he had eaten. After he cleaned up, he would pay a call on the café. There would be ample time. Down in front of the Rainbow a man shouted, a woman laughed in a high-pitched, almost hysterical way. He swung his attention to that point. Somewhere back off among the houses a church bell tolled the faithful to prayer meeting and a dog barked in a slow, measured beat.

It was the same—yet there was change. Dan Wade could feel it in the hot, breathless air, in the silence, in the deserted street. Burnt Springs was a trouble town. He had ridden into too many not to recognize the signs. That apparently was the reason. He stiffened on the saddle, small stabs of warning jabbing suddenly at his consciousness. He became aware of two shadows sliding from the darkness along the south wall of the Texas Star. He drew up slowly, his hand easing toward the pistol at his hip. A voice, arrogant with whiskey, sliced through the night.

"Just where you think you're goin', mister?"

II

A third man, standing unseen a few paces to the side, spoke up: "Don't go reachin' for that iron! Could be right unhealthy."

Dan settled back on his saddle. Tension and a bright flow of anger simmered through him but he held his peace, keeping himself in check. He waited out the moments in dead silence. He watched the men move in nearer, saw the dull glitter of dim lamplight seeping through the streaky glass of the Texas Star's window, as it touched the gun in the speaker's hand. One of the trio swaggered to the head of the gelding; the other two ranged up on either side.

Wade said: "What's this all about?"

The man in front of him cocked his head to one side. He was a squat, husky individual and wore his broad-brimmed hat well back. Even in the poor light his hair showed brick red.

"Like I said before, where you think you're goin'?"

"Happens to be my business but I was headed for the hotel. You got objections?"

The rider on the right laughed. "You hear that, Cully?" he said, speaking to the redhead. "He's wantin' to know do we have objections."

Cully adjusted the position of his headgear. "Might just say we do, seein' as how we own this town. You lookin' for somebody special?"

Wade stirred. He was a man with a low boiling point and the moment was dangerously near. "Also my business," he replied coolly.

The redhead spat. "Maybe it's mine, too. Reckon you'd better climb down off that horse."

Dan stared at the man. He made no effort to comply, simply remained motionless.

"You heard him," the rider to his left said. "Get off that saddle quick unless you want me to yank you off!"

"Never mind, Carl," Cully murmured, drawing his pistol. The hammer clicked loudly as he drew it back. "Looks like he's the wise kind. It's goin' to take a mite of persuadin'."

Wade glanced at the leveled revolver in the redhead's hand, shifted his eyes to that held by the other man. He looked toward the marshal's office. There was no sign of Krask yet. A sudden worry flooded into his mind. Perhaps this was why Big Bill had sent for him—to help wrest the town from men such as these—and he had arrived too late.

"You gettin' down?" Cully's hard, pressing question drove into his thoughts.

Wade shrugged. It would be wise to play out the hand, at least until he knew what it was all about. "Sure, why not?"

"Now that's bein' co-operative," the cowboy to his left said. "Just move away from that horse. And keep your hands up around your ears."

Dan felt the solid ground under his feet. He took a short step toward Cully.

"Pull his iron, Levi," the redhead said. "Don't want him gettin' no ideas."

Wade was aware of a lessening of weight on his hip as the gun was drawn from its holster, tossed off to one side. He squared himself as Cully put away his own weapon, stepped closer.

"Now we'll do that talkin', mister. What's your name?"

A fresh burst of yelling broke out near the Rainbow. A fight had begun and the hot, night air was suddenly filled with shouts and cursing. The redhead did not turn to look but gazed steadily at Dan.

"Means nothing to you," Wade said. "I could tell you it was Jones and you'd never know the difference."

"He sure is a cute one, ain't he, Cully?" Levi exclaimed. "Maybe I ought to teach him some manners."

The redhead waved him back. "Time enough for that when I'm done talkin'. Ross wants to know all about anybody that rides in. You, Mister Jones"—he added, facing Dan again—"where you headed for besides the hotel?"

"Maybe no place . . . and maybe for some other town where people don't get so nosy."

Cully shook his head slowly. "Levi, I'm thinkin' you're right. This jasper could use a lesson or two. Then he ought to be ready to talk."

Wade felt Levi crowd in on him from behind, saw the man's hand reach for his wrist. Anger roared through him, exploded. He spun fast, caught the cowboy by the arm. Using all his strength, he whipped Levi about, released his grip, sent him crashing into Cully.

Carl yelled in startled surprise as the two men collided, went down into the dust in a tangle of squirming bodies. Wade sprang, was upon him before he could draw his gun. He locked his arms about the smaller man, pinned his hands to his sides. He leaned forward, threw Carl off balance, and then rushed him head-on into the solid, unyielding wall of the Texas Star.

Breath left the cowboy's lungs in a strangled gasp. He went limp in Dan's arms and sank to the ground. Wade whirled. Levi and Cully were scrambling to their feet. He lunged across the intervening space that separated him from them. Levi grabbed frantically for his pistol. Dan's rock-hard fist swung wide, caught him flush on the jaw. It lifted the rider off the ground and laid him flat in the dust.

Cully was on his hands and knees searching about for his weapon that had fallen when Levi had crashed into him. Wade caught the glitter of it, half buried in the loose dirt. He kicked it aside, crossed quickly to where his own gun had been tossed, and scooped it up. He turned to face the redhead. His body still trembled from the violence of his anger and he was sucking deeply for wind. He watched Cully get to his feet.

"Any more questions you want to ask?" he demanded in a low, savage voice.

Cully stared at him. He was plastered with dust and a smear of blood marked the corner of his mouth. "Go to hell," he muttered, pure hatred seething through the words. He pivoted, started off down the street.

"Not so fast!" Wade's voice was like a crackling whip.

The redhead paused, came slowly around. "Yeah?"

"You're forgetting a couple of things . . . your friends there. Take them along."

Cully glanced at Levi. The rider was sitting up, rubbing his jaw painfully. Carl still lay near the saloon. Cully walked to his side, nudged him roughly with the toe of his boot. "Come on, let's go," he said.

Carl stirred to a sitting position. He looked around dazedly. The redhead reached down, took his hand, and pulled him to his feet. Carl focused his eyes on Wade. He swore feelingly.

"That damn' drifter. . . ."

Cully said: "Forget it. Let's go get a drink."

Levi was upright, legs spread, shoulders hunched forward. "I ain't about to . . . not until I've worked this jasper over good."

"And him standin' there with a gun in his hand?" Cully said scornfully. "You help yourself. I'll pick me another time."

Levi relaxed. After a moment he moved over and joined his two friends. "Sure. Always another day."

"Now is as good a time as any," Wade said.

The redhead shrugged. "I'll do the choosin'. Don't be forgettin' that."

"I'll be looking forward to it," Dan said, and watched the three men shamble off down the street for the Rainbow.

He turned to the roan, noted he was almost directly in front of the marshal's office. He gave that a moment's thought, and then led the weary horse to the hitch rack that fronted the building. That no one was inside the lawman's office was evident; the fracas with the three cowpunchers would have brought Krask, or his deputy, into the open, that was certain.

He decided he would leave a note, let the lawman know he had arrived and was at the hotel. It would be just as well and a deal more comfortable to wait in his room. Besides, he felt the need to wash up, to stretch his body across a bed for a few minutes.

He pushed open the door of the office and stepped inside. The room was close with stifling heat, only dimly lit by a single lamp that had been turned low. He walked to the battered desk, twisted the flame higher. He found a sheet of yellowed paper, and procured a snub of pencil from his own pocket. At that exact moment he heard a groan.

He straightened up, senses suddenly alert. The sound had come from the adjoining room, from one of the cells that apparently lay behind a partition. It could be a prisoner, he reasoned, some cowboy who had gotten into a scrap or drunk too much and had been locked inside the cage until he got over it. But Dan Wade's mind refused to accept the explanation.

He thrust the pencil back into his pocket, moved toward the open door that led to the rear of the building. It was dark in the narrow corridor where he found himself and he paused to strike a match. He held it above his head in order better to see. There were two cells and both their doors were open. On a cot in the first a man lay, face down.

Wade stepped inside. The match went out abruptly, scorching his fingers. He swore softly, struck another. Holding it in his left hand, he rolled the man on the cot to his back. There was the sharp glint of metal on his breast as the feeble light reflected against something metallic. Dan bent forward for a better look. It was the five-pointed star of a town marshal. He drew back as the tiny flame again died. Someone had knocked the lawman unconscious and thrown him into his own jail! But the figure on the cot didn't look like Big Bill. Still, in a way. . . .

He fired a third match, again leaned down, this time holding the light nearer the man's face. A gasp of surprise escaped Dan Wade's lips. It was a Krask, all right, but not the one he had expected. The marshal of Burnt Springs was Little Bill.

III

Wade wheeled swiftly, returned to the office. He dipped a cupful of water from the bucket that stood in a corner of the room. Taking also the lamp, he hurried back to the cell. Finding no cloth of any sort available, he sloshed a quantity of the liquid onto Little Bill's face.

The young lawman stirred. Wade stepped back, placing the lamp on a table at the end of the cot. He looked more closely at Little Bill. There was no blood on him, no evidence of a fight. Apparently he had been hit from behind. After a moment he struggled to a sitting position. His hand went to the back of his head, probing gingerly. Abruptly he stiffened, as though realizing something. He glanced about, brought his eyes to a halt on Wade.

"Who are you . . . ?" he began, and stopped. A wry grin crossed his face. "Dan!" he exclaimed, reaching out his hand. "Sure glad to see you!"

Wade closed the lawman's fingers in his own. "Looks like I got here a little late."

Krask frowned. "You mean finding me here like this? Not the first time. It's Pa's idea of a joke."

"Big Bill . . . he hit you over the head and threw you in here?"

"Some of his boys did. Happened twice before."

Dan shook his head, perplexed. "I don't think I understand," he said slowly. "When I got the letter, I figured it was Big Bill who'd sent it. Now I find it was you and that your Pa's doing all the hell raising."

"Long story," the lawman said, rising to his feet. "Let's go up front where we can sit down. I'll try to explain."

He started for the door, staggered slightly. Dan caught him by the arm, steadied him. "You sure you're not bad hurt?"

Young Krask nodded. "I'm all right. Takes me a few minutes to get my legs back under me."

Wade picked up the lamp and led the way back to the office. Little Bill, now a man well over six feet, sank into his swivel chair. Dan dragged another up to the desk. He glanced at the young lawman. He had changed considerably since he had last seen him. The wildness was gone from his dark eyes and he had filled out to some extent. He was every bit as large as his father, and just as dark and good-looking—handsome, Dan guessed he could be termed. And he had that same stubborn set to his chin that distinguished Big Bill.

"Thought you'd be running the Double K by now," he said, opening the conversation. "Surprises me no end seeing you wearing a star."

"Cause of all the trouble," Little Bill replied, drawing tobacco and papers from the top drawer of the desk. He offered them to Wade who shook his head. He began to roll a smoke for himself. "Pa was set on me taking over."

"I remember, he had big plans for you."

"I know, but I never liked ranching. Had some ideas of my own. Pa had my life all worked out for me, the way he wanted it. I couldn't see it."

It had been Big Bill's dream, Dan knew. It was all the cattleman had lived for. Everything he did was for his son who one day would assume command of the huge Double K and carry on the Krask tradition. "Reckon that was a big disappointment to him."

Little Bill completed his cigarette, thrust the slim brown cylinder of tobacco between his lips. "More than that," he said ruefully. "Seems more like it unhinged his mind, the way he began acting."

There was a sudden drumming of horse's hoofs down the street in the direction of the Rainbow. Little Bill rose to his feet, walked to the door, and glanced out. "They're leaving," he said, more to himself than to Dan. "Guess the town can get some sleep now."

He returned to his chair, leaned back wearily. "Last time you saw me, I expect I was one of the worst mavericks you ever came across."

"For a fact," Wade said honestly.

"Couldn't make myself settle down. Didn't like cattle raising and did about everything I could to keep from it. Did a pretty fair job of dodging it, too, I guess. There's hardly a jail in the territory and in West Texas that I haven't spent at least one night in. But Pa always came along and got me out. Then one day I woke up. I met a girl, first one that I ever wanted to marry. Pa was crowding me hard to cut out the foolishness and take over the ranch about that time and all of a sudden I knew I had to make up my mind about things. I screwed up enough guts to tell him ranching wasn't for me, and that I was going to get married and shove off on my own. Saying one to him was bad enough, but hitting him with both really fired him off. He raved for days about it."

"He didn't like this girl you wanted to marry?"

Little Bill shook his head. "He didn't even know Hannah, never had seen her. She lived up Silver City way, the daughter of a rancher who runs a little starve-out spread. He said she wasn't good enough for a Krask, that I could do better. Guess he would have got over that, though, if I'd taken over the ranch. But I couldn't make myself do it. If I had, I would have messed things up right, run the place straight into the ground in no time, and ruined it for all of us. Anyway, I'd set my mind to standing on my own feet . . . and that's just what I did. Hannah and I got married. I worked around a couple of places but didn't do much good at it. About the only jobs in this country are on a ranch and that's what I didn't want. Then this town marshal job opened up. I heard about it, and, when I asked for it, they gave it to me."

"What about Big Bill . . . your pa?"

"Day I pulled out and got married, he sort of went loco. That's a little over a year ago now. He quit trying to make the ranch the biggest thing in the territory and started in . . . well, started in doing his best to become the champion hell-raiser of all time."

"Big Bill?"

"I know that's hard for you to believe, Dan, but it's the gospel truth. He's a changed man. You never saw anything like him. You think I was wild . . . you ought to take a look at him and his doings. Whiskey, women, stunts that would blunt the horns on a longhorn steer."

Big Bill Krask had apparently done a complete reversal; when he saw his fondest hopes and dreams crumble into the dust before his eyes, something within him had rebelled and broken free.

"Hard to believe," Wade murmured, thinking of the staid, dignified man he had known.

"You'll find the ranch some different, too. He's got rid of

most all the old hands that had been with him for years. About the only one left is Amos Kincaid. He was riding fence for Pa when I was born . . . and my mother died. The rest quit or else were fired by him. Or were run off by his foreman. He's got a bunch of hardcases out there now, tough boys that never do a nickel's worth of work but spend their time either here in town getting drunk or else at the ranch sobering up so's they can have another go at bucking the tiger."

"Expect I met three of them tonight when I rode in," Wade said.

"That so? Catch their names?"

"A redhead they called Cully. The others were named Levi and Carl."

"They all work for Pa," Little Bill said. "Cully Brown . . . or Red, Carl Jackson, and Levi Ferrel. Blew in here from up north somewhere. Got a hunch they're the ones who hit me across the head and dumped me in that cell, but I'm not sure. Didn't see any of them. They give you much trouble?"

"Nothing serious," Dan said. "One of them mentioned a Ross. Who's he?"

"Ross Oliver, Pa's foreman. He's the headman of the bunch . . . in more ways than one."

"You said something about them jumping you before. Sounds like a regular habit."

Little Bill shook his head. "Pa makes it rough as he can for me. There's some of his crew around here every night. Then he comes in himself a couple of times a week. It's a standing order of his for the bunch to raise as much hell and create all the trouble they can. Things are getting out of hand and bound to take a bad turn, Dan. That's why I sent that letter to you."

"If he's doing it because of you, why not move on? You could find another job somewhere else?"

Little Bill's jaw was set. "And let him think he'd run me off?

No! That's not the answer, anyway."

Wade studied the young lawman; he was like his father in one respect, bull-headed as a bogged-down yearling. "Kind of puts me in a crossways bind," Dan said then, "knowing the both of you like I do. What do you figure I can do about it?"

Little Bill sat forward on his chair. "Talk to Pa," he said earnestly. "He always liked you, respected you. And he knows you've been around. See if you can't make him show some sense. I've sort of side-stepped the problem ever since it started because he is my pa and I knew he was pulling it to spite me. But it can't go on much longer. I can't keep the townspeople pacified . . . they want him and his bunch kept out. So, sooner or later, there'll have to come a showdown and I don't want that, Dan . . . not with my own pa."

Wade said: "I see what you mean. But I doubt if he'll pay any mind to me."

"He just might. If there's one man alive he would listen to . . . it's you. Maybe this sounds selfish to you, but it's not only for my sake I'm asking. It's for him, too. At the rate he's going, he'll be dead in another year. A man his age, and not being used to it, can't pull what he's doing and stay alive. If the whiskey and women and hell-raising don't kill him, one of those hardcases will."

Dan looked up quickly. "Is he having trouble with some of them?"

"Not particularly, that I know of. But when they're all liquored up, some of them get plenty mean. Anything could happen."

Wade sat in silence for a long minute. Finally he nodded. "All right. I'll ride out to the ranch in the morning and see him. I'm not much of a talker when it comes to something like this, and I don't make any promise that it will do any good. I figure a man has a right to do what he pleases as long as he's willing to foot the bill."

"Bound to help," the young lawman said, showing his relief. "I'm betting he'll listen to you."

"Knowing Big Bill, I doubt if he's changed much that way, but. . . ."

The dry scuff of boot heels on the wooden landing in front of the jail halted Dan Wade's words. He saw Krask glance to the door, heard the heavy sigh that passed through his lips.

"Who is it?" Dan asked.

Little Bill shrugged. "Should have expected it," he said. "It's the citizens' delegation again."

IV

They filed quietly into the breathlessly hot room. Five men, all with drawn, serious faces. Wade immediately recognized two of their number: Kingsford who ran the hardware supply company and Tom Hotchkiss, the general merchandise store owner. They came to a halt before Little Bill's desk. Wade felt their eyes rake him, curious and wondering. He nodded briefly to them.

Krask said: "Pull up a bench, gentlemen. Make yourself comfortable."

"Won't be here long enough for that, Marshal," Hotchkiss snapped. "What we've got to say will be short and to the point."

"Figured that," Little Bill said dryly. "However, first I'd like you to meet a friend of mine. Maybe some of you already know him . . . Dan Wade."

Dan rose to his feet, extended his hand to the man nearest, Hotchkiss.

"Haven't I met you before?" the merchant asked, looking more closely into Wade's face.

"Used to work for Big Bill, on the Double K. It was several years ago."

Hotchkiss bobbed his head several times. "Sure, I recollect

you now. You did a lot of riding for him."

"You probably know Mister Kingsford, too," Little Bill continued. Both Wade and the hardware store man nodded.

"Next gentlemen there is Herman Wall. Runs a hay and grain and stable place next to the Rainbow."

Wall was a squat, heavy-set person who wore blue, bib overalls and a white shirt, complete, oddly enough, with necktie. He said—"How do."—in a flat Midwestern voice.

"George Calloway," Krask said, shifting his attention to the fourth man, a tall, well-dressed, elderly individual with small, shoe-button eyes and a full, white mustache. "He's the owner of the hotel . . . the Great Western. He's the mayor, too."

"My pleasure," Wade said, taking the man's hand. "You must have bought out Harry Miller. He ran the hotel when I was here before."

"Several years ago . . . ," Calloway murmured, and stopped.

"Aaron Leslie," the lawman concluded, coming to the last townsman. "Our lawyer and real estate agent."

Leslie was small, slight, with iron-gray hair and pale blue eyes that were sharp and probing. He shook Dan's hand with firm pressure and said nothing.

"You just riding through?" Hotchkiss asked, when the introductions were over.

Wade caught the hidden meaning in the question. The merchant just as well could have said: You interested in the marshal's job?

He smiled, returned to his chair. "No plans. Not looking for work, either. Still a few places I haven't seen yet."

Hotchkiss said: "I see." He swiveled his eyes to Calloway. "Go ahead, George. Let's get this over and done with."

The mayor of Burnt Springs cleared his throat. "Fact is, Marshal, we came to talk about that wild bunch of your father's. They about wrecked the town again."

"Where were you when it was going on?" Herman Wall demanded. "Kept waiting for you to show up. Maybe you could have stopped them."

Little Bill looked down at his hands. "Got tied up," he said in a low voice. "Anybody hurt?"

"Roughed that hostler that works for Garvey considerable," Hotchkiss said. "Nothing he won't live through. But something's got to be done about that crowd."

"We hired you to keep the peace around here," Calloway said. "We figured you'd be able to do it. Now, I hate to say this, Marshal, but we're wondering if we made a mistake. Maybe you're not man enough to handle the job."

"We know you got sort of a special problem," the stableman, Wall, added, "your pa being mixed up in it like he is. But that don't change things none. Either this town is law-abiding or it ain't."

"Burnt Springs is getting a bad reputation," Calloway said, picking up the conversation. "First thing you know we'll have a bunch of outlaws and drifters hanging around here, all figuring the town is a good place to hang out. We sure can't have that, Marshal. Not only would it hurt business, but it will ruin our chances for getting that other stage-line stop."

"And it will put an end to the government handling that Fort Glade payroll transfer through here, too," Wall said. "They won't be taking no chances on fifty or sixty thousand dollars gold being picked off by a gang of outlaws roosting around the town."

"Is there some talk of that?" Aaron Leslie, speaking for the first time, asked quickly.

"Not yet," Calloway admitted, "but it's bound to crop up. And if they quit sending the shipments through here, we'll stand to lose a lot of business. All those soldiers trading with our local businessmen mean plenty of extra cash changing hands. What's worse, once the word got out that the Army didn't figure Burnt

Springs was a safe and law-abiding community, we'd be dead. People would avoid us like the plague. It would not only spoil our chances for the new stage stop but cause us to lose the old one as well."

A silence fell after that. The five townsmen stood before Little Bill, seemingly waiting for some statement from him. The young lawman stirred.

"I've been doing the best I could," he said, "and without any help from the town or anybody else. Little hard to get much done when you don't have some backing. And, as you said, I've had a special problem to deal with."

"Man has to put his personal troubles to one side," Wall said. "Either that or move on. Time comes when he's got to rope or brand . . . because he sure can't do the both. There's no standing still, smack in the middle."

Krask nodded. "I'm not making excuses. I think you'll agree that I've done my job most of the time, except maybe where Pa was concerned."

Calloway shook his head impatiently. "Maybe it looks that way to you, but I've got to be honest . . . we don't agree. You've got to look at this thing from the top, take an overall view. And it boils down to this. Things are getting out of hand around here. The town's going to get hurt, and, either you put a stop to it, regardless of who you tromp on, or we hire on somebody who will. We're asking you flat out if you're willing to do it or do you want us to find another man?"

Again there was silence in the stifling room. Down the street, in the Rainbow, the piano tinkled on through the muted sounds of confusion. The roan, still at the hitch rail, blew and stamped wearily. Dan waited to hear Little Bill's reply.

"I can take care of it," the young lawman said.

Wall said: "Fine. You say you can take care of it. Now we want to know how . . . and when. So far we ain't seen much sign of you enforcing the law. Like tonight. You should have been out there, dragging those hardcases off that poor boy of Garvey's."

"I would have been there," Little Bill began, suddenly very angry, "only. . . ."

"Only what?" Calloway pressed gently.

Dan Wade could understand Little Bill's reluctance to continue the explanation—to tell how he had been attacked in the darkness, overcome, and thrown into a cell in his own jail. It would be a humiliating admission.

"Like I said, I got held up. When I did get the chance, it was too late. The Double K bunch was riding out."

Calloway shrugged. "Don't know what it was that delayed you and you don't seem anxious to talk about it, but it seems to me, Marshal, your job ought to come first, before everything else. Anyway, that's the way it has to be from here on out. We'll be expecting it."

"It's what you'll get."

"Good. Glad we understand each other now. You said you could take care of things but you never did answer Herman's question . . . how and when?"

"Beginning right now," Little Bill said. "That covers the second part." He half turned, ducked his head at Wade. "He's the how of it."

Calloway swung his attention to Dan. Interest at once broke across the faces of Hotchkiss and Joe Kingsford.

"You hiring him on as a deputy?" the hardware store man asked quickly.

Wade felt the eyes of the men drilling into him. He didn't appreciate the position into which he had been suddenly thrust, that of an outside gun being brought in to clean up a wild town. Quick denial sprang to his lips but Little Bill spoke first.

"Not exactly a deputy," he explained, "but as a friend. My pa always thought a heap of Dan. I've asked him to go talk things over with Pa, see if he couldn't settle him down a bit and make his riders behave. I think he can do it."

Disappointment was evident on the faces of the merchants. Calloway, however, did not give up. "We can use a deputy here, Wade. Any chance of you being interested?"

Dan said—"No."—immediately and firmly. "I'll leave the badge-wearing to the men who've got a liking for it. But I'll help," he added, glancing at Little Bill. "I figure to ride out and pay a call in the morning."

Calloway lifted his hands, allowed them to fall to his sides. "Well, something sure has got to be done. We can't let things go on the way they have. And, Marshal, only fair I warn you that unless you can straighten all this out, we'll be asking you for your resignation. Nothing personal, you understand, we simply have to have a man who can run things."

"I know what you mean," Little Bill said. "Don't worry about it. Things will start changing around here tomorrow."

"Hope so," the mayor said. He swung to Dan. "Glad to have met you, Wade. And good luck tomorrow when you see Krask."

Dan nodded. He shook hands all around again, watched the townsmen walk across the room and file through the doorway. Behind him he heard the young lawman sigh thankfully and murmur: "That's over with. Dan, if you fail me tomorrow, I'm finished."

V

Dan Wade wheeled slowly. It was the Little Bill Krask of the past speaking, the humored, spoiled son of an indulgent father leaning on someone else, depending upon another to bail him out of his trouble.

"Don't bank much on me," Dan said sharply. "This is your problem and you'd better face up to it. I'll do what I can to help, but I doubt if I'll have much luck."

"Pa will listen to you," the young lawman said confidently. "He's just got to."

"What if he doesn't?"

Little Bill got to his feet, spread his hands in a gesture of hopeless resignation. "Then . . . then I guess I don't know what happens. One sure thing, I can't have a showdown with him."

"Can't or won't?" Dan asked softly,

Krask turned to him, his face pulled into a dark frown. "What's that mean?"

"Big difference in the words. Either you can't or you won't . . . which is it?"

The lawman's shoulders went down. "Maybe a little of both, Dan. Point is, it would come to gun play. The way Pa is acting, I wouldn't put it past him to draw on me. And I won't let it go that far. I can't. One thing I did learn good while I was out rousting around was how to handle a gun. Pa is good but he'd have no chance against me if I was forced to pull on him."

Dan Wade nodded thoughtfully. "I see what you're driving at," he said. He was getting a better idea of Little Bill's problem now, but it was difficult to believe there would ever come gun play between the two Krasks—between father and son.

"Past supper time," the lawman said as if suddenly aware of that fact. "Hannah will be waiting for me. How about coming along? You just rode in, so I know you haven't eaten yet."

Wade hesitated. "I'm afraid that would put your wife to a lot of bother."

"Not in the least. Besides, I want you to meet her, Dan. And you might just as well spend the night with us."

"No, I'll get a room at the Great Western," Wade said. "It'd be better for me. But I'll take you up on that supper invitation. It's been a long time since I had a good, home-cooked meal."

"Fine. Let's go then. We can walk. It's only a short way."

"Walk?" Dan echoed, having a saddleman's usual aversion to it. But he gave it a second thought, decided it wouldn't be a bad idea, if not far. The roan was tired, needed feeding. He should be in a stable.

"It'll help work up your appetite," Little Bill said cheerfully, the visit from the townsmen, the problem with his father, apparently gone from his mind. "Mite of exercise never hurt nobody."

"Couple of things I sure don't need," Wade grumbled as they passed through the doorway, "exercise and something to whet my appetite. We'll have to take this horse of mine to the stable first. He needs care worse than me."

With Little Bill at his side he led the gelding to the livery barn behind the hotel and turned him over to the hostler. After arranging for his keep, he followed Krask back into the street. They strode along through the darkness, crossed a vacant lot, and arrived at a small, white house.

It was neat and well-tended. Wild yellow roses grew thick in the front yard along with lilacs, now past their blooming but still standing, full and green. A garden, lush with growing vegetables, was visible along the south side of the building and partly across the rear. Fragrant honeysuckle trailed up the well house and other vines climbed over other small outbuildings.

"Hannah did all this," Little Bill said proudly. "It was no more than a run-down shack when we moved in. She's a real wonder when it comes to making a home."

"A man couldn't ask for a finer-looking place," Wade said.

They turned up a stone walk bordered with rows of the small purple flowers that grew on the prairies, and mounted the porch. At the sound of their boot heels on the dry boards, the door swung in.

Hannah Krask was tall, gracefully formed. She had dark hair and eyes and her skin, under the shaded lamplight, had a soft, creamy look. She was wearing a white, nicely fitting dress over which she had drawn a lace-edged apron. She smiled, moved into the circle of Little Bill's arms, and kissed him unabashedly. After a moment she turned her head, looked squarely at Dan, her eyes calm and questioning.

"The name's Wade, ma'am . . . Dan Wade," he said, removing his hat.

Krask pulled away quickly from his wife. "Oh, Hannah . . . I'm sorry. This is the friend I've told you about, the one I wrote to."

She extended her hand to Dan. "I'm happy to meet you," she said in a low, quiet voice. "Bill has told me so much about you I feel we're already friends."

"I hope we are," Dan said. "I'd sure not want it any other way."

She smiled at him, stepped back into the room. "Supper is ready. Just give me time to set another plate."

"Don't go to any trouble . . . ," Dan began.

"No trouble at all," she broke in. "If you'd care to wash up, Bill will show you where, on the back porch."

The lawman led Dan to the rear of the house where he removed the dust and sweat of the trail and made himself more presentable. As he brushed down his hair with the stiff bristle that was handy, Little Bill leaned nearer to him.

"I'd be obliged to you if you don't say anything to Hannah about me getting rapped over the head. Or about the mayor and the others paying me a call. She does enough worrying over me."

Dan said: "Sure, however you want it."

He waited while the lawman attended to his own needs. Finished, they returned to the kitchen. The meal was ready and they sat down to the table.

It was a supper Dan Wade would not soon forget. Steak, fried tender and juicy, hot biscuits and honey, sweet corn on the cob flavored with fresh butter, wilted lettuce salad, strong coffee, and steaming apple pie buttressed with crushed nuts. Hannah Krask was as adept and proficient within her home as she was outside. She blushed at the compliment.

"Now if you men will go into the parlor, I'll clean up my dishes," she said when the final cup of coffee had been drunk.

"Can't you let them go . . . at least for a while?" Little Bill asked.

"Only take me a minute," she replied. "I never like to think of dirty dishes, waiting in a pan."

Dan trailed Krask into the front part of the house, sank into one of the rocking chairs. "Haven't eaten like that in years," he said. "Your wife has a way with vittles."

"She has a way with everything," Little Bill said. "I'm a right lucky man."

"For a fact."

"Big reason why I've got to straighten things up around here. I want to keep my job so we can stay here in Burnt Springs."

"Then make up your mind to it," Dan said. "Don't let anybody force you to do something you're set against."

"Meaning Pa?"

"Him or anybody else. Most men spend a lifetime hunting for what they want. Appears to me you've already found it. Now all you've got to do is fight to hold it."

"But against my own pa. . . ."

"It's a choice you'll have to make. It will either be Hannah and your life, or knuckling under to Big Bill and doing what he says, his way. It's a hard thing to decide, but you'll have to do it."

"I never looked at it quite that way, but I reckon you're right."

"I know I'm right," Dan said. He pulled himself up from the comfort of the chair. "Guess this won't show off my manners as any great shakes, but I'd best be getting back to the hotel. I'd hate to fall asleep here where I'm sitting. I've been in the saddle since before sunrise and I'm beginning to feel the miles."

"It's all right. I understand."

Dan rose to his feet. "I'll say my thanks to your wife again, and a good night." He walked to the kitchen, paused in the doorway. "I'll be going, Missus Krask."

She turned, gave him her smile. "Please call me Hannah, Dan. And you're welcome. I heard what you said. It always pleases me to see a man enjoy his food." She wiped her hands on the apron, moved nearer to him. "I want to thank you for the things you said to Bill. About his father, I mean. It's his biggest problem . . . and perhaps his greatest fault."

"He'll work it out," Dan murmured. "I'll help."

"I hope you can," she said. "I love him very much and he's a fine man. If only. . . ."

"If only what?"

"If he could just learn to stand on his own feet, depend on himself. He has the ability, but somehow he can't seem to find himself."

"I know what you mean," Wade said. "But worrying about it won't help any."

"I know that, and I sha'n't . . . now that you're here. But, in a way, I'm sorry you came."

"Sorry?"

"Yes. Now he can depend on you. Maybe, if you hadn't received that letter of his, he would have found a way to meet his troubles himself."

"I wouldn't worry about that much, either," Dan said. "If I know Big Bill, he won't listen much to what I've got to say. I doubt if it'll make the slightest difference to him."

Hannah's eyes clouded. "Don't you really think so? Bill is planning so strongly on it."

Wade stared at her, momentarily speechless. The paradoxical

stream of her thoughts, of woman's logic almost halted him in his tracks. In one breath the practical Hannah was hoping the man she loved would stand on his own feet, face his own problems; in the next she was expressing her fears that outside aid would not be of benefit to him. He shook his head.

"I expect there's no point in stewing about it now. I'm going to see Big Bill tomorrow and we'll know then for certain. Thank you again, Hannah, for the fine meal and your hospitality."

"You're more than welcome, Dan. Please come often."

He made his farewell to Little Bill, promising to meet him as soon as he returned from his visit to the Double K, and started back through the warm darkness for the hotel. He was considering his own problems now, what had to be done if Big Bill refused to mend his ways, or even talk about it, which would likely prove the case. What course could he then follow?

He was standing squarely in the middle of the controversy—a position he disliked intensely—and he was almost to the point of echoing Hannah Krask's wish that he had never received Little Bill's letter. But he had, and now his sense of obligation would not permit him to brush it aside, wash his hands of the trouble, and ride on.

He reached the rear of Kingsford's place, walked up the narrow weed- and trash-filled passageway that lay between it and the adjoining structure, the ladies' dress shop. Little Bill and Hannah had their personal rights, their license to live as they wished, and it should be respected by everyone, including Big Bill. But he could sympathize with the elder Krask, even partially understand his determination to punish, in some way, his son. That was wrong, of course, and Big Bill should be made to see it.

He gained the street, deserted now, and swung toward the Great Western. The Rainbow was still going strong, all windows ablaze with light, music blaring from the doorway, loud talking and laughing seeping through the walls. He considered, briefly, the need for a drink—it might drive the stiffness from his bones, loosen his muscles—and then dismissed it. A bed was what he really desired. After the long day and the fine meal Hannah had placed before him, he. . . .

He heard the sharp, wicked crack of a pistol, the dull thud of a bullet smash into the wall only inches from his head. For an instant he remained motionless, startled, completely taken off guard. Then it drove into his mind; someone was shooting at him. He hit the ground in a quick, flat drive.

VI

He rolled into the black shadows along the front of the dress shop, straining his eyes to locate the ambusher. The shot had apparently gone unnoticed, for the piano in the Rainbow hammered on relentlessly and no one came through the batwings to investigate. It was understandable. The sound of a single pistol report was no uncommon thing; only a flurry of shots would be likely to draw attention.

He had not the vaguest notion where the bullet had been fired from—or who could have sent it searching for his life. He had no enemies in Burnt Springs, at least none of whom he was aware. And during the short time he had been in the settlement that day he had met only five merchants. That one of them should want to kill him was scarcely logical. The trio of cowpunchers who had jumped him. He had forgotten them—the redhead, Cully Brown, and his friends, Carl and Levi. It had to be one of them. Most likely it was Cully. He again searched the street for some sign of the man, concentrating particularly on that area to the right of the Rainbow. There was a passageway between that hulking building and its neighbor, Garvey's Livery Stable. Such a place would be ideal for a man to hide and maintain a close view of the street.

He could do no good lying there in the dark. And if he got to his feet, the hidden marksman, if he were still nearby, could pick him off with ease. But the angry impatience of the man would not permit him to remain there in the dust indefinitely. Gun in hand, and still prone, he began to work his way backward. Keeping close to the wall of the dress shop, he watched the street as he labored through the loose, yellowish powder that sucked into his throat and nostrils, threatening to choke him. Finally he was abreast the passageway. Still flat on his belly, he twisted about and crawled into its black depths.

He rose to his feet quickly, ran swiftly to the rear of the buildings, his shoulders slamming alternately against Kingsford's and the dress shop's walls as he plunged heedlessly on. He turned right at the end of the dark corridor, hurried along the alleyway that cut across the backs of the structures, until he came to where it ended, in intersection with the cross street. He was at the northwest corner of Hotchkiss's store at this point, with the Rainbow, Garvey's, and the other small places just opposite.

There he halted. He should continue on, he knew, circle the Rainbow and come up behind the stable. But the instant he moved out of the shadows back of the Hotchkiss building, he would be fully exposed. He stood there in the night, smoldering and disturbed, debating the question. And then abruptly it was solved for him. Beyond Garvey's he heard the quick rush of a horse getting away fast. Dan stood perfectly quiet for several moments and listened to the rapid hammering of hoof beats striking north. He realized then the ambusher had given it up.

He walked into the open, convinced but still on the alert. There was no blast of gunfire from the passageway next to the Rainbow, or from any other position of advantage; there was only the racket from the saloon and in that he found no interest. He continued on to the Great Western, going first to the stable for his saddlebags and to check on the roan. The big gelding was enjoying his rest and Dan crossed the yard and entered the hotel by its rear door. A middle-aged clerk with black, patent-leather hair parted exactly in the center greeted him sourly at the desk and assigned him to Room 5.

He undressed and went immediately to bed, his thoughts swirling about the two Krasks, about Hannah, and about the man in the night who had fired a bullet at him. He was still convinced it was one of the three cowpunchers he had encountered earlier in the evening, with the red-headed Cully Brown being the most logical suspect. In any event, Cully was due to supply some answers.

He awakened early, shaved, bathed as best he could from the tin wash pan and china pitcher of water, and pulled on clean clothing. He went down into the street and turned left for the Chicago Café. The owner-cook-waiter served him bacon, eggs, and coffee in the grumpy silence of a man who had risen too early, too often, and then left him entirely alone. Dan ate slowly, far from hungry after the huge meal he had enjoyed that previous night at the Krasks'.

That over, he returned to the Great Western and cut around to its rear to the stable. He sought out the roan and looked him over carefully. The hostler had done a good job on the horse, currying and brushing him down until his coat was sleek and smooth. The grain and fresh hay Wade had ordered and the night's rest had put him in top condition.

Dan was throwing on his gear when the stableman appeared. He watched for a few moments, then finally spoke.

"Be right glad to do that for you, mister, but I'd guess you're a man who likes to do his own saddling up."

"You'd be right," Wade said. "The roan's got touchy withers. The saddle has to set just so."

"Be no change in the price, your doin' your own hostlin'."

"Suits me," Dan said, and went on with his chore. A thought

struck him. "You happen to be around here last night, say about nine o'clock?"

"Reckon I was. Why?"

"Hear some shooting? One shot. Sounded like it came from across the way, maybe that passage between Garvey's and the Rainbow."

"Sure, I heard it."

Wade paused. "See who it was?"

The stableman shrugged. "Didn't bother to look. Shootin' like that goes on around here all the time. Drunks, mostly, blowin' off steam. Wonder more people don't get hurt. It bother you?"

Dan resumed his task. He had the saddle on to his and the roan's satisfaction, turned now to the silver-mounted bridle. "No reason. Just wondered what it was all about."

"One of that crowd from the Double K, I'd reckon. Rode north when he left. You pullin' out today."

"No, I'll be around for a spell. You want your money now or when I settle up with the hotel?"

The hostler studied Wade for a time. Then: "Guess you might as well wait. You don't look like a man who'd beat a stable bill."

"Thanks," Dan said dryly and swung up onto the roan. He wheeled the big horse about, trotted him down the runway, and out into the street. He turned right, rounded the corner, and pointed north. It was a two-hour ride to the Double K but with the gelding feeling as he did, they likely would make it in less.

Familiar sights began to greet him as he rode steadily along through the sweet, early morning freshness. The stand of red buttes off to the right, the long, twisting band of green cottonwood trees that grew on the ragged banks of Copper Mine Creek. He crossed the deep wash where once he had killed a cougar just after it had struck down a calf, climbed the rocky slope where he had been thrown by a balky mustang and sustained a broken arm. At the top was the gnarled, brushy cedar where he had seen Big Bill shoot down a rustler.

Other places came before him, passed on as he followed the well-traveled road, and he fell to wondering just how things might have been with him had he stayed with Krask and not ridden on that spring morning when the urge to drift had gotten so strong he could no longer deny it. Probably he would have been the foreman of the Double K by now—or he could have gained nothing. When the break between father and son had come, he would have been hard put to hold his tongue with Big Bill.

The miles wore on as the heat increased. He reached the last long grade to the ridge and began the gentle but steady climb. The roan scarcely slowed when he started up but continued on in that easy, rocking lope that covered distance so efficiently. From the top Dan would look down upon the broad, green valley in which the ranch lay, a fine, beautiful sight that fairly took a man's breath away. He had sat there often in the old days, just drinking in the view. There had been times when he had thought of finding such a valley and claiming it for his own. He would build himself a ranch, find a woman he could love and who loved him, and settle down. But it had never come to pass; he had never discovered the valley or the woman, either, and thus had wandered on through the years, happy, he supposed, with his way of life, often lonely, especially after seeing the luck others, like Little Bill, had been fortunate enough to encounter. But he was never completely satisfied with himself. Deep in his mind he knew the answer, the cure for it all, yet he could never bring himself to accepting and following it to its conclusion. What he did not know was the reason why, and in that lay his fears.

He gained the summit, halted. Magnificent Cloud River Valley unfurled below him, rolling endlessly out to all sides in a pale green sea of sweet, tender grass, but there was something wrong, something strange in the picture. He considered it in silence for a time, and then realized what was missing—there were no cattle, no grazing herds scattered here and there over the land.

Pondering that singularity, he put the roan into motion and started down into the valley. A few minutes later he heard hoof beats and again drew to a stop, listening. Several riders were coming toward him. He wheeled the gelding off the road and into a stand of brush to wait, not afraid, simply curious.

It was Cully Brown and the same two who had been with him the night before, Levi Ferrel and Carl Jackson. They were obviously heading for Burnt Springs, and Little Bill's remark relative to the amount of work his father's cowpunchers did on the Double K flipped back into Dan Wade's mind. But he had other thoughts about these three. He waited until they were just past him and then rode out into the center of the lane.

"Hold it!" he barked, drawing his gun. "Raise your hands high and turn around . . . slow."

They obeyed instantly, finding the cold tone of his voice entirely convincing. When they saw Wade, their surprise was evident. Apparently whoever had fired the shot in the dark had assumed he had hit his target and had so informed his friends. Wade, his face set in hard, humorless lines, pushed up nearer.

"One of you bushwhackers took a shot at me last night," he said. "The bullet missed. I figure I ought to give whichever one of you it was another try."

There was no answer.

Wade said: "Ought to be easier. Man can see better . . . and it's three to one. How about you, redhead?"

"Who said it was me?" Cully demanded, instantly aroused.

"Nobody . . . yet," Dan replied coolly. "Was it?"

"You don't know who it was," Levi said, relaxing in his

saddle. "You're just guessin', runnin' a bluff, tryin' to find out which. . . ."

"Shut up!" Cully broke in, grinding out the words. "Keep your lip buttoned."

"He's right, redhead," Dan said. "I'm just fishing, but I know it was one of you. When I find out which, that man's getting his second chance whether he wants it or not. Nobody takes a shot at me without I get my turn, too. Now, head back for the ranch. I want Big Bill to know all about this before it happens."

Cully Brown stared at Wade blankly for a long moment, then he grinned faintly. "Sure. Whatever you want," he said, and moved off down the road. The others followed immediately.

They descended the long slope, the three abreast with Dan, gun in hand, behind a few paces. They crossed the quarter mile of open flats and turned into the yard, riding through the familiar high gate with its two interlocked Ks still hanging by chains from the crosspiece.

"Pull up in front of the house," Wade said, motioning with his weapon.

The three riders obediently angled across the hard pack, halted at the hitch rail that stood before the long, low, rambling structure.

"Just sit easy," Dan said, "while I. . . ."

"While you do what, friend?" a harsh voice demanded from the far end of the building.

Wade swung his glance to that point, watched a small, thin-faced man with leveled rifle bearing straight at his breast ease into view. There was soft sounds at the opposite corner. Two more men, guns glinting in the sunlight, showed themselves. Beyond them, coming from the bunkhouse, were three others. The Double K was an armed camp.

"One thing you'd sure better do," the man with the rifle said, "is drop that pistol. You make one wrong move with it and we'll blow you clean off that saddle!"

VII

Dan Wade let the .44 fall to the ground. He heard Cully laugh, saw the redhead twist about. "Was hopin' you'd see us comin', Ross," he said. "This here's that drifter we told you about."

Ross—Ross Oliver. This was Big Bill's foreman. He looked more like a gunman gambler, of the kind who frequented the saloons along the cattle trails.

"Sure goin' to have me some fun now," Cully said, his face evil and expectant. "You all just stand around and do the watchin'. I got a score to settle."

The men with the drawn weapons closed in from either side. Dan remained still, waited out the tight moments. Cully swung down from his horse, made a great show of looping his reins about the rail. Carl and Levi followed. Ross Oliver came to a quiet stop a dozen paces away.

"You didn't do so good last night," the foreman said, looking at the redhead. "And you had plenty of help."

"Grabbed me when I wasn't watchin'. Be another story out here."

"Maybe. Who is he?"

"Nobody much. Just some drifter. Was hangin' around the kid."

Oliver shifted his expressionless face to Dan. "You got a name?" he demanded in a harsh, brittle way.

Wade nodded. "Most men do. Call Big Bill out here and let him tell it to you."

"You know the old man?"

"He'll answer that, too."

Oliver hesitated momentarily. He nodded to Carl. "Go get him. He's inside."

Jackson swung obediently for the house. He entered, slammed

the screen door behind him.

From where he stood near the hitch rack, Cully said: "You just remember, Ross, this jasper belongs to me. Few things I'm goin' to learn him."

The foreman said—"Sure, sure."—in a patient way. "You'll have to do better than you did last night, howsoever."

"Told you he jumped me when I wasn't lookin'."

"Not the way I heard it."

The screen banged again. Dan threw his glance toward the house. Two men were on the gallery that ran the full width of the house—Carl and a large, heavily built man dressed in ill-fitting, wrinkled clothing. His hair was long, badly needing the attentions of a barber. A week's growth of beard covered his slack face and he swayed slightly as he stared vacantly at Dan.

"What's this all about? What's the trouble here, Ross?"

Even the voice was different, no longer brisk and authoritative. It now bordered on the querulous, almost plaintive. But there was no mistaking Big Bill Krask.

"Drifter crossing our land," Ross Oliver said. "Claims to be a friend of yours."

"Friend?" the cattleman echoed. "Friend of mine?"

He came off the porch, crossed the interval of yard at an unsteady shamble. Dan watched him in silence, appalled at the vast change that had taken place in the man. Krask halted at the hitch rack, focusing his eyes after some difficulty upon Wade. He jerked himself upright suddenly.

"Dan Wade! You're damn' right he's my friend!" he shouted. "Put those guns away! What the hell's wrong with all you, anyway?"

Oliver lowered his rifle slowly, reluctantly. The other men watched him closely. At his nod they, too, holstered their weapons.

"Just being careful," the foreman said.

"Hell of a note when a man's friends can't even ride by without getting throwed down on," Big Bill grumbled. "Step down, Dan! Come inside and have a drink with me!"

Wade came off the roan, scooped up his gun, and slid it back into the leather. He reached forward, took Krask's outstretched hand.

"What you doing back in this country, boy? You looking for a job? Best damn' cowhand I ever had around here," he added, throwing a side glance to Ross Oliver. "He wants work, he's hired. You understand?"

"Sure, boss, if you say so."

Krask halted abruptly, looked around the yard. "What's all these men doing here? Why ain't they out on the range where they belong? Damn it, Ross, its your job to see they keep working!"

"They're working," the foreman said, his narrow face angry. "Just happened they all dropped by at the same time. I'll get them back in the saddle, don't you worry."

"I ain't worrying," Krask said. "That's your job, Mister Oliver, running this place for me. And doing all the worrying about it. Now see they hop to it or, by God, there'll be some new hands around here! Come on, boy," he finished, grasping Wade by the arm. "No sense standing out here in this heat."

The change in Big Bill was unbelievable, and pitiful. Dan felt this heart throb as he watched the once proud man he had known stagger through the doorway, collide with one side of the frame, reel, recover, and lurch on. He led Dan through the front room, a dusty, littered parlor, into a second that served as an office. Krask collapsed into one of the several leather chairs, pointed to another.

"Set down, boy," he said, reaching for a bottle on a nearby table, "and have yourself a drink. No glasses, unless you want to trot back to the kitchen and get one."

"This suits me," Dan said, accepting the bottle. He turned it to his lips, took a swallow of the raw, fiery liquid, and handed it back to the cattleman.

Big Bill downed a hugh gulp, paused, stared at Dan. "Where you been keeping yourself, boy? Where you headed?"

"Just rode into town yesterday," Wade replied, skirting the question. "Put up at the Great Western."

"Now, why'd you do that? Why didn't you come on out here? Always got a bed waiting for an old friend."

"Hotel's all right."

Krask had fallen silent, his swollen, glazed eyes on the floor. After a moment he said: "You see Little Bill?"

Dan nodded. "Had supper with him and his wife last night. She's a fine woman."

The rancher said nothing. He took another sip of the whiskey. "Maybe, I wouldn't be knowing about that. But he sure ain't no fine son."

"You've got him all wrong," Dan said quietly. "It wasn't right to try and make him live the kind of a life you wanted. A man can't do that, and you know it."

"He should have stayed with me. This place was his, lock, stock, and tar bucket. Always was. What the hell you think I was working and slaving all those years for? Just so's he could step into my boots."

"It doesn't always turn out the way a man hopes. People are different, even fathers and sons. He didn't take a fancy to cattle raising the way you did."

"The place was for him," Krask muttered. "Damn it, he ought to appreciate it. I worked like a dog after his ma died, fixing things so's he'd always have something good. Then he turns his back on me and walks off to some piddling job."

"It's his life . . . and what he wanted."

"It was a fool thing for him to do and I'm thinking he's sorry he ever did it."

"Don't count on it," Dan said. "You're acting like it's the first time it ever happened. It's sure not, and it's no reason for you to carry on like you're doing. The way things are going, you'll be dead in a year, broke even sooner."

Krask sat up. He clamped his slack lips shut, glared at Dan. "You lecturing me, boy? You trying to tell grandma how to pick ducks?"

"I'm trying to make you see what's happening to you."

"Forget it. I know what I'm doing. Had my nose to the stone for thirty years building this place. Worked like a mule. Never had no time for anything. Then it turns out it was all for nothing. Now, I'm having myself a right good time. I'm sowing plenty of those wild oats you hear tell about. Why not? Sure ain't no reason for me to keep on grubbing away. I'm catching up on all the fun I missed while Little Bill was growing up."

"And digging your grave fast as you can."

"Maybe so. But who cares?"

"Little Bill, for one, and probably a few others, not including that foreman you've got running the spread or those hardcases he's hired on."

"You mean Ross? What's wrong with him? He's looking after things, doing what Little Bill ought to be doing. And the boys . . . they're all right. Maybe a mite on the tough side but they get the job done and they're powerful good hands to go to town with. They know how to have a good time . . . something I've had to learn."

"It could be they know a lot about other things, too, like how to steal a man blind. You getting out of cattle business?"

"Me? Hell no!"

"I sure didn't see any stock when I rode in. How many head are you running?"

Krask wagged his head. "Last tally run close to three

thousand, Ross said."

"Must all be on the north range," Dan said. "They're sure not around anywhere else. Had a good look at the valley from the ridge."

Krask moved his hand in a wide gesture. "They're somewhere. I ain't worrying about it. That's Ross Oliver's job."

"Maybe he's doing it. I'm hoping."

The rancher lapsed again into a moody silence. He offered the bottle to Dan who refused. He took a long swig, lowered the glass container, and stared at it.

"Little Bill talk about me any?"

"Some. He wanted me to do a little jawing with you."

"About what?"

"About the way you're acting, the way you and your crew keep hurrahing the town. He's going to lose out sure on that marshal job unless you quit it. Could even come to worse."

"Hope he does lose that tin star. Then maybe he'll come home where he belongs."

"No chance of that. If you cause him to fail, he's liable to pick up and move on. He's as bull-headed as you. One thing of yours he got."

"Then let him move. Let him get clean out of the country. I ain't hankering to set eyes on him . . . and you can tell him so. And while you're at it, tell him something else. Tomorrow is Saturday, my special day to howl. I'll be in with the boys and we aim to tree that town for fair. Been a lot of talking about me going on and there's a few who's about to eat their words. You tell that biggety marshal that for me, boy."

"Don't do it," Dan said. "Don't push things too far. It could mean real trouble."

"Trouble! That's something that boy ain't seen yet! Long as he keeps wearing that star, it's going to get worse and worse."

Dan rose to his feet. He turned abruptly, caught the swift

motion of shadow in the hallway. Someone had been listening, watching. He thought for a moment, came back to Big Bill.

"I'm asking you again, friend to friend, forget about coming to town tomorrow. Let it ride this time."

"Nope, we'll be there. Them dudes have a lesson coming to them and they're sure going to get it. You leaving?"

"Time to head back," Dan said, moving toward the door. "I hate to see you in such rough shape, Big Bill. It's not much like it used to be."

"Everything's changed," Krask said. "You going to be around tomorrow? I'd like to buy you a drink."

"Expect I'll be there," Wade replied. "One thing more, if you bring that redhead, Cully Brown, in with you, better tell him to watch his step."

"So? What's he up to?"

"Somebody took a shot at me in the dark last night. I figure it was him. He makes one more mistake like that he'll be looking at the business end of my forty-four."

"That danged fool," Krask muttered. "Never does show much sense. I'll jack him up a mite about it."

"Good enough," Dan said, and walked on toward the front door. The hall was empty.

VIII

Dan Wade halted when he stepped out onto the gallery. He was wary, alert for trouble. He could expect it from Ross Oliver, from Cully and the others. That he was at odds with the redhead and his pals was enough but the fact that he was an old family friend of Big Bill's and thus represented a threat to whatever was going on at the Double K heightened the probabilities. The yard was deserted. Even the horses of the three riders were gone. Only the roan stood at the hitch rack, dozing as he waited in the bright, hot sun.

Nerves fiddle-string tight, Dan stepped off the porch and crossed to the horse. He jerked the leathers free, swung onto the saddle. From somewhere within the house there was a sudden crash, a shattering of glass. Either Big Bill had dropped his bottle, likely empty, or in a fit of anger had hurled it against the wall.

He wheeled the roan about, starting for the distant slope. His back was to the ranch buildings now, prime target for anyone lurking about who had a wish to see him dead. He rode straight on, wide shoulders square against the horizon. He could feel the hair on his neck prickling, the tauntness of his singing nerves, but he did not look back.

Whoever had been hiding in the hall at Big Bill Krask's had heard all that had been said. It could have been Ross Oliver, or it might have been Cully or another of the crew. Regardless, the foreman would know now that Krask still hoped for his son's return, that despite all the loud talk and threats the cattleman still had dreamed of the day when Little Bill would take over the Double K. And he would also know that Dan Wade was a close friend, near to the problem, and one who could possibly effect a reconciliation. Thus, to Oliver's way of thinking, he would be a most unwelcome visitor to Cloud River Valley and Burnt Springs.

He reached the gate, broke onto the broad flats. Only then did he touch the roan with his spurs, send the big gelding into a long lope. After that he began to breathe easier.

To his way of thinking the visit with Big Bill had been a complete failure. He had feared it would be. He had accomplished nothing other than to verify the things the young marshal had told him had come to pass—and to add a further conviction to his fund of information. Ross Oliver and his hardcases were milking the Double K dry. And to do so they were keeping the cattleman in such a state of mind and alcoholism that he was totally unaware of what was happening. Just exactly what Oliver was doing was difficult to say at this point; it would bear looking into at the first possible moment, Dan decided. First, however, must come Little Bill's problems and his need for help. That a clash between the two was in the offing, possibly the very next day, seemed inevitable.

Dan saw movement ahead on the trail that led to the ridge. He slowed the roan, his eyes straining ahead to pick up, isolate the object. A rider. A man on a small calico horse. He studied the distant figure for some time, endeavoring to recognize the person. He was too far away, and, waiting in the dappled shade of a juniper tree, his face was indefinite. He appeared to be making no effort to hide, however. It could be a trick. Dan realized that, but there was little he could do about it. The trail was the only way out of the valley and he had not the slightest desire to turn back. He drew his pistol, thrust it into his waistband where it would be more readily available, and rode on.

When he was within a hundred yards, he recognized the rider—Amos Kincaid. He spurred the roan forward. Kincaid, according to Little Bill, was the last of the cowpunchers who had worked for Krask from the beginning. Dan had always liked the crusty old wrangler and was glad to see him. He wheeled in to the man with his arm outstretched.

"Amos, good to see a familiar face around here."

"Reckon I'm the only one," Kincaid said, wrapping his bone-like fingers around those of Wade. "Maybe you think I ain't plumb pleasured to see you."

"Didn't notice you back at the house," Dan said. "I knew you were still working. Little Bill told me."

"I keep away from that nest of polecats much as I can. Me and them don't mix-up atall. You heading for town? Reckon I'll just mosey along with you for a spell. You been talkin' to Big Bill?"

"Some. He wasn't in much shape to hear me."

"Never is no more. Stays liquored up all the time, seems."

"What's going on back there, Amos? I mean besides the way Big Bill is carrying on. That bunch he's got working for him looks more like the Hole-in-the-Wall gang than plain 'punchers."

"Just what they are. And they're stealin' him blind. Bet there ain't a thousand beeves left on the Double K. Ross and his crowd keeps sellin' them off, a jag at a time, and pocketin' the cash."

"Doesn't Krask realize that?"

"Don't know. I tried to tell him myself and got no place, except for lettin' myself in for a workin' over by that redhead, Cully."

"Big Bill wouldn't listen to you?"

The old cowpuncher cocked his head to one side. "You have any luck makin' him listen to you?"

"Not any," Dan replied.

"Reckon that's your answer. He lets Ross run the place, do as he pleases. He can sign the bills of sale and carry on the business the way he wants. And he don't cotton to nobody stickin' their nose into what he's doin'. Don't know what happened when you rode in back there, but I'm guessin' you was mighty lucky Big Bill was home."

"You're right. I had a few bad minutes while I thought I was going to have to fight Oliver and his whole crowd. You say Big Bill stays drunk like that all the time?"

"I can't hardly recollect seein' him sober since the day the boy pulled out. Broke the old man's heart sure enough, that did. But you ain't sayin' nothin' about yourself? What brung you back here?"

"I had a letter from Little Bill. He was hoping I could talk to his pa, straighten him out."

"He's a good boy," Kincaid said. "Big Bill sure ain't doin' the right thing by him. The kid weren't cut out to be no rancher, but Big Bill won't swaller it. Churnin' up to bad trouble between them I fear. Sure is a sad thing."

"It could get worse," Dan murmured. "Unless I miss my guess this thing is jockeying around into a gunfight."

Kincaid nodded slowly. "Ross'd like that. Them Krasks are just like a couple knot-head longhorns. Ain't neither one of them going to give an inch. The boy startin' to get riled?"

"Not so much that. It's the merchants. They served notice on him either to tame Big Bill and his bunch, or move on. He's made up his mind he's going to stay."

"Then we're sure pointin' for trouble," the old cowpuncher said, his long face solemn. "I can tell you this. Big Bill ain't goin' to pull in his horns none. He'll make it hard on the boy long as he can. He's got things all mixed up in his mind but he thinks he can make the boy come back if he rides him hard enough. You got any ideas what we ought to be doin' about it?"

"None," Dan said. "Little Bill's thinking is messed up, too. He won't move, yet he won't fight his pa. Don't know what he'll do when I tell him what Big Bill said. You be in town tomorrow?"

"Weren't figurin' on it. Reckon I can be if you say so."

"Might be a good idea. Could be I'll need some help and you're the only one I can trust."

"I'll be there, son," Kincaid said promptly. "If it comes to shootin', whose side we goin' to be on?"

Wade shook his head. "Nobody's, I hope. The thing we got to do is stop it before it starts."

They rode on in silence for another quarter mile. Kincaid reined in. "S'pect I'd better be cuttin' back right about here.

Supposed to be ridin' the south range . . . what for I sure don't know. Ain't no cow critters around nowhere."

Dan reached for the old cowpuncher's hand. "So long, Amos. See you tomorrow . . . and ride careful."

"Adiós," Kincaid replied. "You be doin' some of the same. The way it appears to me, you ain't so popular with Ross and his boys, either."

There was little doubt of that, Dan thought, as he put the roan to a lope. Oliver would resent any of Big Bill's old friends, knowing they would represent a threat to whatever schemes he had in mind. And it could even go deeper, he realized. Ross could be at the bottom of the continuing ill-feeling between the rancher and his son, whetting the trouble, egging Big Bill on to do something drastic. It would fit neatly into whatever plans he had.

IX

He reached Burnt Springs at noon with the hot sun drilling down with its full intensity. He went first to the hotel livery barn, stabled the gelding, then on to his room. He washed away the dust, thinking all the while on what he would tell Little Bill when he saw him. He was still undecided when he finally left the building and made his way to the lawman's office.

The marshal was not alone. A squat, heavily built man with dark hair and flat, gray eyes occupied one of the chairs. He was handsomely dressed in a broadcloth suit, fancy, handmade boots, and wore a wide-brimmed, pearl-gray hat.

Little Bill leaped to his feet as Dan entered. A smile crossed his lips and an expectant, hopeful look spread across his face.

"You see him?"

Dan nodded, halted in the center of the room.

"What happened? What did he say? You have any luck with him?"

Wade said: "None. He won't listen. Fact is, he'll be in tomorrow with his crew and they're figuring to take the town apart."

Little Bill's shoulders sagged. "Might have known it," he said in a low voice. His glance halted on the well-dressed stranger. "Oh, Dan, I'd like to have you meet Luke Grover. He's a U.S. marshal. This is Dan Wade, old friend of mine, Marshal."

Grover leaned forward, extended his hand to Wade. "Pleasure," he murmured. Then: "What's this about somebody taking the town apart? Is it something I ought to know?"

"My pa," Little Bill said, dropping back into his chair.

"Damn," Grover said under his breath. "Sure don't want that if we can help it."

Dan faced the lawman. "You here for something special, Marshal?"

"Plenty special," Grover replied.

"The Army gold shipment is due here tomorrow sometime," Little Bill explained. "Word got back to the authorities about how things here in Burnt Springs were going. They sent him to take over."

"We got a tip there might be a try at highjacking the shipment," Grover added. "Nothing definite, you understand. Only a rumor, but since there's a lot of extra cash money involved this time, they figured we'd better take no chances."

"You come alone?" Wade asked.

Grover nodded. "Didn't want to draw attention. Besides, with the marshal here and maybe one deputy, we can look after matters. Then there'll be the soldiers. I understand Major Ives usually sends a full patrol."

The federal lawman got to his feet, strolled nervously to the door, and glanced out into the street. "Hearing about your father complicates things some. With him and half a dozen of his crew tearing things wide open. . . ."

"You know about Big Bill?" Dan asked, wondering how word

of the cattleman's activities could have spread so far.

Grover shrugged. "More rumors, that's all. It got to us in a roundabout way. They said he runs with a pretty wild bunch and generally put things in an uproar. It would be a good time for a gang of outlaws to hit."

The government man was right, of course. Such a moment would be ideal for a raid. But there would have to be some prearranged plan; they would need to know the gold shipment would be in town, that Big Bill and his crew were due. He turned to the young lawman.

"Did the rest of the town hear about the shipment coming in?" he asked.

"Probably. It arrives about the same time every month. The mayor knows. He talked with Grover."

The word would spread. There was no hope now of surprise or of keeping it under cover. "I expect we'd better start getting things ready then," he said.

Little Bill, still downcast, said: "How?"

"First thing we should take a look around the town, see if there's any strangers. If there are, we'll send them packing unless they've got a good reason for being here."

"Good idea," Grover said. He looked at Dan, smiled. "You'd make a good lawman, friend. How about serving as a deputy until this is over with?"

Quick refusal leaped to Dan Wade's mind, but he held back the actual words. With matters shaping up as they were, Little Bill would need all the help he could get, and perhaps he would be in better position to do something about the elder Krask, too, if he wore a star. He glanced at the young lawman. "It's all right with me, if you want it."

Little Bill smiled. "You bet I do. Starting right now."

He reached into the top drawer of the desk and procured the badge of authority. He handed it to the tall rider. "I'm swearing you in as of this moment."

Dan pinned on the star. "I never thought I'd be wearing one of these things," he said.

Grover laughed. "There's worse things," he said. "Maybe not many, but a few." He brushed back his coat. Sunlight glinted against his own badge, touched the metal of the gun at his hip. "The heat's mighty bad around here," he said. "I think I'll head on down to the hotel. It ought to be a bit cooler there. I'll leave you two to work out the details for tomorrow."

He smiled, nodded, stepped out into the street. Little Bill waited until he was gone, then spoke.

"Pa couldn't pick a worse time to come in. Why the hell couldn't that gold shipment get here today?"

"Things just happen sometimes," Wade said. "Tell me how it works. A stage brings in the money. A patrol from Fort Glade meets it and takes it over. Is that it?"

"That's about the way it goes. Sometimes we have to hold the shipment overnight. The soldiers don't always make it here at the same time the stage arrives. Once in a while they're a day early, or a day late. When that happens, we put the gold in the bank vault."

"Where does the stage stop?"

"Goes straight to the bank. There won't be any passengers. It's a special run."

"How many guards aboard?"

"One riding shotgun with the driver. Two more inside with the money."

"That ought to be plenty of help."

"You can't figure on them. Once they unload, they're through with it. Their responsibility ends there, and they seem mighty glad of it. They usually arrive late in the afternoon and turn right around and head back toward El Paso. I figure they don't want to be on hand if anything goes wrong."

"I can understand that. They're probably acting under orders. If they were around, somebody might claim they still were in charge of the shipment, if it got lost."

"Must be something to this rumor of a hold-up, them sending Grover here."

"It looks that way," Dan agreed. "The sooner we start getting set for it, the better off we'll be. The first thing we do is drop by all the saloons and check the hotels. We want to see who's in town."

Little Bill arose. "It could wait until tonight. Might be somebody'll ride in late."

"We'll make the rounds again after dark, and a couple more times tomorrow. It's best we look behind every bush . . . and keep on looking."

"I expect you're right," the lawman said, reaching for his hat. "About Pa . . . how was he?"

Wade hesitated. Then: "Same as usual, I reckon."

"Don't hold back on me!" Little Bill exclaimed, suddenly angry. "I know what he's like. Was he bad drunk?"

"Pretty bad shape," Dan said. "Couldn't get him to make much sense. You know anything for sure about Ross Oliver, that foreman he's got? Or the rest of the bunch that works for him?"

"Only what I've told you. Ross runs the place to suit himself and Pa leaves it up to him."

"My guess is they're stealing Big Bill blind. Amos thinks so, too. Ran into him on the way back. All the time I was in the valley I never saw a steer."

"That's what I've been figuring, too. But how are you going to make Pa see it when he plain doesn't want to . . . or doesn't care?"

"That's something I can't answer," Wade said, shaking his head. "But he'd better wake up soon, or else he'll be flat broke."

Little Bill stared out through the open doorway. Small dust

devils were spinning madly in the center of the street and down near Garvey's. The blacksmith pounded on his anvil with ringing regularity.

"Maybe," he said quietly, "just maybe that would be the best thing that could happen to him."

X

They moved out into the brilliant sunlight, came to a sudden stop. Three men were bearing down upon them—Calloway, the mayor, Joe Kingsford, and Wall, the livery stable owner. Their faces were serious and they walked in a determined, purposeful way.

"More trouble," Little Bill murmured.

"None we can't handle," Dan said. "Don't let them get under your hide."

"Marshal," Calloway said before he had even come to a halt. "We just ran into that U.S. Marshal . . . Grover, or whatever his name is. He told us your father and his crew of roughnecks are coming in tomorrow, bent on tearing the town up? That true?"

Dan said: "That's what he told me. I saw him this morning."

Kingsford's eyes had noticed the star on Wade's breast. A sort of relief passed over his features. "Looks like we got us a deputy, Mayor," he said.

Calloway and Wall both took a second look. The mayor said: "Fine, fine. I've felt like we've needed a good man for a long time. But about tomorrow . . . what are you planning on doing?"

"Not much I can do, unless Pa breaks a law of some sort."

"Tearing up the town, wrecking property, fighting and scaring people half to death . . . that ain't law breaking?" Wall demanded. "Must be some kind of a law against it."

"There is," Calloway said. "And it's got to be enforced, Marshal. We can't let that Double K crowd take over things with that shipment of money coming in. Now we think you. . . ."

"Just a minute," Dan broke in quietly. "There's a little something I'd like to say. You want law and order in your town. You've hired the marshal, here, and me to get it. All right, suppose you go on about your business and let us do it. Interfering isn't going to help us one bit."

"What's that?" Calloway said sharply.

"I said that, if you will keep out of it, leave the law to us, we'll take care of things. If we have to climb over you every time we turn around, it will just make things tougher."

A slow smile broke across Kingsford's face. Calloway and Herman Wall simply stared. Finally the mayor found his voice.

"Now see here . . . we're responsible to the people. . . ."

"And we're responsible for the law. If Big Bill Krask or any of his boys get out of line tomorrow, they'll damned quick find themselves in a cell. It's as simple as that. Now, gentlemen, if you'll excuse us, we have work to do."

Wade stepped around the three men and started on down the street. Little Bill, momentarily startled by it all, grinned faintly, nodded to the merchants, and then followed. When they reached the first stop, the Great Western Hotel, Calloway and the other two men still stood where they had left them, talking among themselves.

"I think you sort of set the mayor back on his heels," the young lawman said as they entered the lobby of the hotel. "Nobody around here ever talked to him like that."

"Then I expect it was high time," Wade said. "A man like him means well, but he just gets in the road."

"You mean what you said about Pa?"

"About locking him up? Sure. He breaks the law, he goes to jail to cool off. That's all there is to it."

Little Bill wagged his head doubtfully. "It might turn out to be quite a chore, keeping him there. The crew will make a try to get him out."

"We'll skin that cat when the time comes," Dan said, halting before the hotel's desk. "I want to see your register," he said to the clerk. "I'm interested in anybody that's new in town."

The clerk grinned, ran a hand over his sleek, glossy hair. "Only two strangers, deputy. You and that U.S. marshal."

Further search around Burnt Springs that afternoon failed to turn up any other newcomers, but later that night, in the Rainbow, they discovered two riders, both of whom were familiar to Dan Wade.

"Harley Biggs and Clint Applewhite," he said, pointing the pair out to Krask. "They've been in jail more of the last ten years than they've been outside. I'd like to know what they're doing here." He began to make his way through the crowd to the table where the men sat.

Both glanced up at the approach of the lawmen. Only Applewhite registered surprise at the star on Dan Wade's vest.

"You boys are a little off your regular trail," Dan said, halting before them. "Why?"

"You're a bit off the trail, too, ain't you?" Applewhite said. "Never figured you for a badge-toter."

"Times change," Dan said dryly. "What are you doing around here?"

Biggs shrugged, slouched back into his chair. "Just passing through. Is there a law against that?"

"Passing through, no . . . staying overnight, yes. How soon will you be riding on?"

The Rainbow's piano dribbled into silence. The steady flow of talk began to fade, dropped to a whisper as the crowd became aware of the conversation between the two lawmen and the strangers.

"Can't say as we're ridin' on tonight," Biggs drawled. "You got some objections to us stayin'?"

Wade said—"Yes."—in a flat, uncompromising voice. "Finish up that whiskey and move on. If I find you around here thirty minutes from now, you'll spend a couple of days in the jug."

"Here! Wait a minute!" the bartender said, pushing through the crowd. "You got no call to be running off my customers like that!"

"I have these two," Dan said.

"Why? They've done nothing!"

"And they won't be getting the chance," Dan replied coolly. He glanced at the two drifters. "All right, pull out."

"I tell you, you can't do this!" the bartender protested, his voice rising to a shrill bleat. "It ain't right, busting in on a man's business this way. I'll go to the mayor!"

"You do that," Dan said, shouldering the sweating man aide. He stepped back, watching Biggs and Applewhite start for the door.

"Remember . . . thirty minutes," he warned.

Biggs shook his head. "Don't go workin' up a head of steam, Deputy. We'll be long gone by then. No cause for us to hang around this flea-bit town."

The bartender was trembling with rage. "I won't stand for you hurrahin' my customers like this. . . ."

"You get any more like them tonight or tomorrow, do them a favor and tell them to keep moving. This town is going to be unhealthy for their kind."

He swung about, faced the crowd, scanned it quickly. He saw no one he recognized. He glanced at Little Bill. "Do you know all of these people? Do they all belong around here?"

The marshal swept the patrons of the Rainbow with a critical eye. "No strangers," he said after a moment.

"Good. Let's take a look in the Texas Star. And I want to be sure Biggs and Applewhite kept going."

The crowd began to drift away, return to their tables or to

their places at the bar. The piano struck up again. A gaudily dressed woman, one of the saloons regulars, sauntered toward Little Bill, her lined, painted face drawn into a hard smile.

"First time I remember seeing you in here, Marshal. Where you been keeping yourself?"

"Got a job to take care of," the lawman said stiffly.

"And a Sunday school goer for a wife, too, I hear tell. You're sure not much like your pa! Now, there's a real humdinger of a man. When he takes a hold of a woman. . . ."

Little Bill's arm lashed out, slapped the woman smartly across the mouth.

"Shut up!" he snarled. "You're not fit to talk about my pa!"

The saloon girl fell back a step, came up against the end of the bar. She touched her bruised lips gingerly, stared at young Krask. Then: "We'll see about that. We'll just see what he's got to say."

Little Bill swung on his heel, started for the batwing doors. Dan glanced at the girl, studied her for several moments.

"Do us all a favor," he said, "forget this. Don't mention it to Big Bill. There's trouble enough brewing."

Her dark eyes snapped angrily. "Trouble? Deputy, you don't know what trouble is. When I get through telling Big Bill what's what, he'll be ready to hang that kid from the nearest cottonwood."

Dan Wade said nothing when he rejoined the marshal who awaited him on the porch of the Rainbow. There was little point to it now; the damage had been done. More fuel would be heaped upon the fire that raged within Big Bill Krask and his consequent reaction could be only speculation at that point.

They made the rounds of town once more before midnight, and then called it a day. Little Bill went on home to Hannah while Dan headed for the quiet loneliness of his hot, shabby room in the Great Western. He had no illusions as to what faced him and the young marshal that coming day. Not only was there the responsibility of the gold shipment, but there was small doubt Big Bill would be at his worst. The tale the saloon girl would tell him would double his enmity and he would consider the whole affair as a personal affront and insult. Dan groaned inwardly as he walked slowly down the dusty, dark street. How did he manage to get himself into such a situation? And worst of all it meant he was taking sides with a friend—against another friend. He thought of Amos Kincaid's question. Where would he stand when the shooting started? He shook his head, tried to side-step the problem, but there was no ignoring it. The saloon girl had been right, he thought, as he entered his room; the real trouble was yet to come.

XI

The stage carrying the shipment of gold and currency whirled into Burnt Springs shortly after 5:00 the next afternoon. It arrived ahead of the soldiers from Fort Glade who had not yet put in an appearance. Dan Wade, standing at the corner of Kingsford's store, watched it roll up to the bank and slide to a halt in a boil of dust.

A little farther along Little Bill Krask, shotgun in hand, had taken up a position in front of the Texas Star. Almost directly opposite him across the street, Luke Grover, his frock coat brushed back to reveal not one but two revolvers, leaned against the corner of the Chicago Café. As the stage halted in its pall of yellow powder, Dan and Krask moved in closer. The guard, sitting beside the driver, spat, looked down at Little Bill.

"Where's the soldiers?"

"You can see they're not here yet," Grover snapped before the lawman could reply. "Hurry it up. Get that money unloaded from this hack and inside."

The driver spat again, studied the government man thoughtfully. To Little Bill he said: "Just who the hell is he?"

"A U.S. marshal, Pete," Krask replied. "Sent down here to look after the shipment. They got rumors of a hold-up."

"So?" the guard exclaimed. He leaned down, slapped hard against the side of the coach. "All right, boys, unload. Soldiers ain't here, so it goes into the bank this time."

A chain rattled within the vehicle. The door swung open. Two men supporting a small, ironbound chest between them stepped into the street. In their free hands they carried cocked revolvers.

"Hurry it up!" Grover urged, repeating himself.

"Keep your shirt on," one of the guards muttered. "Goin' as fast as we can."

Dan wheeled slowly around, made a complete and thorough survey of the street and of all the buildings that stood along its edges. Two men slouched on the porch that fronted the Rainbow. A woman and a half-grown child had paused near Hotchkiss's store to watch. Otherwise Burnt Springs appeared deserted and he could see nothing suspicious or out of the ordinary.

The men carrying the money, backed now by Pete who had climbed down from the box, reached the door of the bank and entered. Grover followed to that point, halted as if to bar it to anyone else who might seek to go inside.

"Where's those damn' soldiers?" he demanded peevishly. "This is one time they ought to be here."

Little Bill shook his head. "I doubt if they'll make it today. They're usually here by noon or a bit after if they're going to be early. They'll probably show up in the morning now."

"Stinking luck," Grover said. "It means we'll have to stand a night watch."

The guards came through the doorway at that moment, their chore completed. The government man looked them up and down.

"How about sticking around until the Army comes? We could use a little help."

Pete bit a fresh chunk of tobacco off the plug he carried. "Nope, not us. We got business waitin' for us somewhere else. What'd you say your name was, Marshal?"

"Don't remember telling you, but it's Grover, Luke Grover. Why?"

"Nothin' much. Just figured it was sort of funny we didn't hear nothin' about you bein' here."

Grover shrugged. "Nothing funny about it. I'm straight out of the head office. We don't think it's necessary to tell every jerk-water way-station driver and shotgun messenger our business."

Pete grinned. "Man asks a question, he gets a answer. Ain't always a civil one but it's a answer. *Adiós,* Marshal . . . see you in church."

He swung up beside the driver. The other two men were already inside the coach. The driver popped his whip and the four-up lunged forward in the harness, surged out into the street in a tight circle. A moment later the coach was only a swirl of dust racing southward.

Luke Grover stood motionlessly, his gaze on the vanishing cloud. "Before I leave here," he said slowly, "I want the names of those four men. They're going into my report. No good reason why they couldn't have delayed overnight and given us some help."

Dan Wade was thinking of the guard's remark. It seemed strange to him also that the stage authorities had not known about Luke Grover, that, in this instance at least, they had not instructed the guards and driver to give the lawman all the co-operation he needed. On the other hand, Grover's blunt explanation could have been the exact truth. And possibly it could have been a case of having no time in which to make advance preparations.

"You could have ordered them to wait over," he said then. "Expect your authority would have covered that, being a federal man."

"Guess I could've," Grover said thoughtfully. "Don't know why I didn't think of it. But no use hashing over it now," he added, rubbing his hands together. "Too late to call them back. We've got to make plans for the night. Since the Army's not likely to show up until morning, we've got no choice but to stand guard until then. Agree?"

"Whatever you say," Little Bill replied. "I don't think there's much danger, however, with the money locked in the vault."

"Taking no chances on it," Grover said. "And I sure won't rest easy until the soldiers take over and I hand the shipment to Major Ives at the fort."

"You going back with them?" Dan asked.

"Yes, sir. My job is to see that money through right up to the moment it's put into Ives's safe at Fort Glade. My responsibility ends there, not before."

Dan said: "I understand. With them being so careful it's a wonder they didn't put you on as a sort of shotgun messenger right at the start, have you ride with the shipment from the beginning."

"About the only reason they didn't was because there wasn't time," the lawman said. "Anyway, this is where we expected the trouble."

Little Bill said: "Let's hope none comes. How do we work this? No sense in all three of us standing here in front of the bank."

"True," Grover said crisply. "I was about to suggest to you, Marshal, that one of you stay here, the other go around back. I'll just drift around town, keep my eyes peeled and my ears open for anybody or anything suspicious. That way we'll be covering everything."

Krask glanced at Dan. "Sound good to you?"

Wade nodded. "Good a plan as any."

"You think of something better?" Grover asked, almost belligerently.

"No," Dan drawled. "Like I said, it's as good a plan as any. You take the back," he said, turning to Little Bill. "Anybody shows up you don't know is all right, sing out."

The young marshal nodded, swung off toward the rear of the structure. Dan's motive reached further than the reason implied; it was just as well Little Bill be out of sight when his pa rode into town. The longer the meeting between them was delayed, the better for all concerned.

"I'll be close by," Grover said, adjusting the position of his crossed gun belts. "You want me, yell."

"I figure on it," Dan said. "But this responsibility is as much yours as ours. Don't get too far away and keep out of places where you can't hear me."

"Don't worry about that," the federal man said, "I've been through. . . ."

He checked his words abruptly. A spatter of gunshots and the hard pounding of running horses broke across the hot evening air. The racket came from beyond Garvey's. Yells lifted and another round of shooting sounded. A half a dozen or more riders swept around the corner of the Great Western, came racing down the street.

Dan Wade swore softly. Big Bill Krask and his Double K hardcases had arrived.

XII

Dan shuttered a glance at Grover. A hard smile pulled at the lawman's lips briefly, then faded. Along the side of the bank the rap of Little Bill coming up at a run could be heard. Wade lifted his arm, waved the lawman back.

"Just the Double K bunch," he said. "Stay in the alley."

He listened, hopeful Krask would accept his explanation and return to his post. A moment later he breathed easier. Little Bill had obeyed. He brought his attention back to the street. The cattleman and his riders had halted before the Rainbow, were dismounting. They had holstered their pistols, more interested at that moment, apparently, in slaking their thirst. Two of the men gathered up the reins of the horses, led them off toward Garvey's. The remainder followed Big Bill across the gallery and through the batwing doors into the saloon.

A great shout of welcome and laughter greeted the rancher and his crew. Most likely the elder Krask was a generous spender, and, while he was present, he doubtless stood for all drinks.

Grover hitched at his guns again. "I expect it would be smart to head on down that way, keep an eye on things."

"Do me a favor," Dan said. "Tell Big Bill I want him and his men to stay inside the Rainbow. They get out on the street, causing trouble, I'm locking them up."

"I'll tell him," Grover said. "You want me, just holler."

Dan watched the lawman strike off through the dust. He was an odd sort; he professed a strong interest in the need for precautions, yet was doing little himself to protect the money. Dan guessed Grover knew what he was about, but for his own self, if he were worried about the shipment, he would at that moment be either inside the bank with a shotgun across his knees, or atop the building directly across the street where he could see everything that moved. A thought moved into Dan's mind. Could it be the danger of a hold-up was far less than the government man indicated, that it was merely a plan to arouse the town, to jar it to wakefulness, and make it more aware of its responsibility? It was possible—but it was Luke Grover's affair;

he knew what he was doing. Dan brushed it all away, glanced toward the rear of the bank building.

"Everything all right back there?"

"All set," Little Bill replied. "You getting hungry?"

"No, a little early for me."

"Ought to have told Hannah. She could have fixed us up a basket of fried chicken."

"Taste mighty good," Dan admitted.

He had brought his attention back to the Rainbow. Luke Grover, following an erratic, vagrant course down the street, in and out of the passageways, appeared on the gallery fronting the saloon. He paused there for a short time, his eyes turned toward the east road; abruptly he wheeled, pushed through the swinging doors into the blare of light and noise.

An hour wore by, two. . . . Big Bill and his men were still in the saloon fortifying themselves well with whiskey, Dan assumed. He hoped Grover had passed along his warning but there was little likelihood the rancher would heed it. Big Bill was the sort who took orders from no one. And this night, he had served notice, was to be one of particular importance. There was one encouraging possibility; Luke Grover also was in the Rainbow. Perhaps he could compel Krask and his crew to stay in line.

A figure broke suddenly from the wall of darkness beyond Kingsford's. Dan came to quick attention. A moment later he saw it was a woman, her dress ghostly white in the deep shadows. He relaxed, leaned back against the wall of the bank, watched her easy, graceful approach. It was Hannah.

When she reached the center of the street, she hesitated, called softly: "Bill?"

"Over here, ma'am," Dan said, replying.

She came on at the sound of his voice. "Oh, it's you, Dan. I brought you and Bill some supper. One of our neighbors told me what you were doing."

"Bill's around back," Wade said. "And I'm obliged to you for thinking of us. Not much chance of us getting away for a bite to eat."

She removed a plate from the basket she carried, handed it to him. It was piled high with fried chicken and still warm biscuits.

"I'll take the rest to Bill," she said. "If you would like coffee, I can get it from the café."

"This will do fine," Dan murmured.

The chicken was crisp and delicious, as were the biscuits. Dan had not realized he was so hungry until it dawned upon him he had again skipped the noon meal. It was an old trail habit of a solitary rider. Usually he ate a hearty breakfast and a good supper. Halting during the noon hour to prepare food when he was on the move never occurred to him. And now, when he was within the circle of civilization, it was hard to break the pattern.

There was a shout down in front of the Rainbow. Dan threw his attention to that point. A half dozen men were on the porch, more were crowding through the doors. All were watching two cowboys, locked in each others arms as they wrestled about in the dust. Both went over, prone into the street. The smaller of the two sprang clear. He drew back his booted foot, lashed out at the other. The blow caught the man on the chin. His head snapped to the side. He hung momentarily and then fell forward, burying his face in the ankle-deep dust.

A new burst of yells went up. Several men pushed forward to slap the victor on the back. A few turned, headed back into the saloon; others came out. Dan watched narrowly. This could be the beginning, the springboard that would launch the violence he felt so certain was bound to come.

He heard the whisper of Hannah's flowing dress behind him, caught the fresh, clean smell of her perfume.

"Would you like for me to get that coffee now, Dan?" she asked, pausing at his shoulder. "I'm going after a cup for Bill."

Wade, his gaze now riveted to four men down the street, shook his head. "Best we forget it," he said, handing her his empty plate. "Obliged just the same."

"But I'm getting it for Bill. . . ."

The four men had moved away from the Rainbow, were advancing slowly along the street.

"Forget it," Dan said again. "Get away from here, Hannah. Go home . . . please."

She followed his rigid line of vision. A moment later she was running lightly toward Kingsford's, hurrying off into the darkness for the safety of her home.

"Something wrong?" Little Bill called from the rear of the bank.

"Visitors coming," Dan replied. "Four of them. Can't make out who they are. Some of the Double K bunch, I'd guess."

"Want me up there?"

"No, hold your place. Let me handle it."

"Where the hell's this Luke Grover?" the lawman wondered, his tone angry and impatient. "Thought he was going to be around, helping out."

"Last I saw of him he was going into the Rainbow," Dan said. "I was hoping he'd make your pa and his crowd stay inside. I guess he couldn't do it. No more talking, now. I'd as soon nobody knows where you are."

He watched the quartet draw up closer. They passed through a shaft of light that flared from a window of the Great Western. He recognized all four: Cully, Levi Ferrel, Carl Jackson, and the foreman, Ross Oliver. He allowed them to draw up within a dozen paces.

"Far enough!" he barked suddenly, showing himself.

They came to a quick halt. Levi, caught off balance, stumbled against the redhead, cursing fluently.

"What do you want?" Wade demanded.

There was a moment's pause, then Oliver said: "You. Old Cully here's got a score to settle with you. We aim to see he gets the chance."

Dan said: "Later. Come around tomorrow. Right now I got other things to do."

"You ain't that busy," Oliver said, his voice thick.

"Too busy to fool with you," Wade said. "Now, head on back to the saloon or I'll lock you up."

"You'll lock us up?" It was Cully. "Since when did you get to be marshal?"

"He's sure wearin' a star," Levi said. "Maybe we got us a new lawman."

"Don't make any difference," Oliver said. "We come here to help Cully. Spread out. Work in from all sides. The thing to do is grab him, hold him so's Cully. . . ."

"Don't try it," Dan warned. "First man that does, gets a bullet."

Oliver laughed. "Don't let him bluff you, boys. He can't shoot us all . . . and he's by himself."

"Not quite," Little Bill's voice broke from the darkness along the bank.

The four men froze. Levi said: "Why, that's our reg'lar marshal! Your pa's lookin' for you, kid."

"He knows where to find me," Krask said.

"Your wife know you're out here in the dark?" Oliver asked in the same bantering tone. "Young 'uns ain't supposed to be running loose this time of night."

"Move on," Dan Wade said, his words sharp. "We don't want trouble with you . . . not tonight."

"What's wrong with tonight?"

"You heard what he said," Little Bill broke in. "Get off the street . . . now!"

"You listening, boys?" Oliver said. "You better hark to what the marshal's telling you. He's real fierce."

There was a loud, metallic click in the deep shadows. It was followed immediately by a second, identical sound.

"That was the hammers on a double-barreled shotgun," the young lawman said. "It's pointed straight at your bellies. Any of you takes one step except back toward the Rainbow, I'll scatter him all over the street."

Ross Oliver had no answer to that for there was no mistaking the promise in Krask's tone. Levi wheeled carefully around.

"Come on," he said, "let's be gettin' back to the saloon. Ought to tell the old man where his kid is, anyway."

"I ain't finished my business with this smart Aleck jasper yet," Cully said, protesting mildly.

"You won't have much fun doing it with your guts strung all over hell," Oliver said scornfully. "We've got plenty of time."

They turned about, trooped off down the street.

Little Bill sighed audibly. "Close," he said. "Figured we were in for it there for a few minutes."

"We are now for sure," Dan said grimly. "Long as your pa didn't know exactly where you were, we had no problem."

He watched Oliver and the others mount the two steps to the Rainbow's porch, making their way across it and disappearing into the building. In only moments they were back, now with several other men. There was no mistaking the huge figure in the lead—Big Bill Krask.

"Here he comes," Wade said. "This is going to be a little rough, especially for you. Good chance for you to duck out if you've got the notion."

There was a long silence while Little Bill considered. Then, in a low voice, he said: "No. I reckon it might as well be here, tonight, as anywhere else."

XIII

They paused in the intersection of Burnt Spring's two streets, immediately in front of the Rainbow. In the light that streamed from the saloon Dan could distinguish Big Bill, Oliver, and several more of the Double K crew. Another dozen women and men had bailed out of the Rainbow, swelling the crowd, their voices adding to the hubbub.

After several minutes the knot of people began to flow down the dusty avenue, aiming for the bank. Four men were distinctly in the lead now: Krask, Ross Oliver, Cully, and Levi. Dan watched them draw nearer, feeling the tension rise as a deep quiet settled over the town.

"Better let me handle this!" he called to Little Bill. "Maybe I can talk your pa out of it."

Again the young marshal was silent as he thought over the suggestion. And again he declined. "No. It's my quarrel, not yours."

Dan had a momentary wish that Hannah could be somewhere close by, that she might see and realize the hour had finally come when her husband was facing up to his problem. But he quickly amended that hope. The incident could turn into a tragic affair, one better not witnessed by the girl. Hannah Krask could be proud of her man now, even as Dan Wade felt a strong lift within himself for the young marshal.

The crowd slowed as it reached the front of the hotel. Big Bill said something about another drink. A bottle was passed to him. He took a long swallow and once more they came on. Dan moved away from the dark shadows along the bank building, took a long stride deeper into the street. A dozen yards away Big Bill saw him, halted.

"That you, lawman?"

The cattleman had not called his son by name, or even recognized a relationship. He was keeping that out of his mind, stubbornly maintaining a separation of identities.

"No, it's me . . . Dan Wade."

Ross Oliver leaned toward Krask, said something to him. The rancher pushed forward another unsteady step.

"Close enough!" Dan said in a flat, warning tone.

Big Bill halted. "You taking sides with that tin star, boy? You forgetting who's your friend?"

Dan said: "No, I'm just trying to keep you from making a mistake. It's your own son, your own flesh and blood you're after."

"No son of mine. He walked out on me."

"You forced his hand. Any man has the right to choose his own life."

Ross Oliver again turned to Krask, said something to him in a quick, angry way.

"You're listening to the wrong man there," Dan said. "He's stealing you blind . . . and he's prodding this trouble between you and Little Bill. If you'd sober up for a day and take a good look around. . . ."

"Ross's all right!" Big Bill shouted, staggering a little. "He's doing what I tell him!"

"You sure? You know how many cows you got left on the range?"

"Ain't nobody's business but mine!" the elder Krask yelled. "Where's that kid . . . that tin star? Why ain't he here talking for himself?"

From the darkness beyond Wade, Little Bill said: "I'm here, Pa."

The rancher stiffened. "Hiding, eh? Come on out where I can see you."

Dan heard the thud of the lawman's heels as he moved up from his position. He threw a hard look at the crowd. Where the devil was Luke Grover? He should be there, doing his part to protect the shipment. It was risky to leave the rear of the bank unguarded. If there were outlaws lurking about now would be an ideal time for them to make their try. Everyone's attention was on the trouble in the street.

Little Bill came to a halt an arm's length to the right of Dan. "I wasn't hiding," he said calmly. "I've got a job to do and I'm trying to do it."

"I put him there," Wade said. "I was hoping I could keep you two apart but your friends spoiled that. If you didn't have such a thick head, you'd see I'm right."

"Right about what, boy?"

"That they want this trouble between you and Little Bill. They want you dead. Then they'd own everything you got. They're out to get rid of you, one way or another."

Oliver lurched forward. "That's a damn' lie!"

Dan Wade's gun was in his hand in a swift blur of motion. "Don't try it, Ross! For what you've done to Big Bill, I'd like a reason to kill you!"

The foreman halted abruptly. Krask reached out, grasped him by the shoulder, and drew him back roughly.

"Keep out of this!" he snarled. "Both of you . . . all of you! Keep your noses out of my doings. This is betwixt me and that tin star."

Little Bill said: "Forget it, Pa. Go on home. I won't fight you."

"Well, you're going to whether you want to or not! I'm going to tear that badge off you and give you the beating of your life. You got a lesson coming. You've been doing a lot of talking about me and you've been slapping my friends around, insulting them and making out like you were a real big man. Now you're going to answer to me."

"Forget it. . . ."

"And there's a few others around here that's been shooting

off their mouths. I figure they got a lesson coming, too. Soon as I'm done with you, I'm starting on them . . . me and my boys. This town's going to be sorry for what it's been saying . . . what's left of it when I'm done."

"You're drunk, Pa. Mount up and go home."

"Don't be ordering me around! You ready to step out here and face me or are you running again?"

"I'm not afraid of you," Little Bill said quietly. "Not in the way you think. Guess I never was. It was only that I wanted to dodge trouble."

"You ain't dodging no more. And I'm through jawing with you."

"What you goin' to use on him, Bill?" a voice from the crowd yelled. "A willow switch?"

Big Bill whirled around. "Switch, hell! He fancies himself with a six-gun. I aim to show him what a real hand with an iron looks like!"

An instant hush fell over the street. It was as if the persons gathered there, having goaded their man to the point of culmination all in the spirit of great fun, were startled to discover it was not great fun after all, was instead a serious and deadly situation.

"You hear me, lawman?" the rancher shouted. "I was going to use my hands on you, but I've changed my mind. You and me are going to settle things with guns. You want, you better start running now."

"I'm not running . . . and I won't fight you, Pa. Not with a gun or anything else."

"Then you're scared, no more guts than a mangy jack rabbit."

The inevitable Dan Wade had feared was at hand. The crisis he had hoped would not come, but deep in his heart knew was unavoidable, had shaped up. He took a step to the side, away from Little Bill.

"He's a better man than you'll ever be," he said, throwing the words at Krask. "I always figured you for the best. I was wrong. You're nothing but a big-mouthed drunk . . . a liar!"

The cattleman's head snapped up. "What's that you said? You talking to me, boy?"

"I'm talking to you," Dan said evenly. "And I'll back up everything I said."

"Then me and you's got some business to take care of, just as soon as I'm finished with that tin star."

"No, it's right now. I've got first call."

The sudden, shattering blast of a pistol brought everyone around. Luke Grover, with a half a dozen or so cavalrymen still on the saddle, stood in front of the Chicago Café. They had apparently come up from the south end of the street, completely unnoticed. A sigh of relief slipped through Dan Wade's lips. At least that worry was over. The responsibility for the money shipment no longer rested on his and Little Bill's shoulders.

"I want you all to move away from here," the federal officer said, his voice hard. "I don't intend to meddle in your local affairs, but I've got work to do and I'm taking no chance on interference. If you've got some fighting to do, do it down at the other end of the street."

Dan studied the waiting soldiers, a frown on his face. Something apparently had delayed them and they looked none too happy. He glanced at Grover.

"Are you loading up and pulling out tonight?"

"Why not? Army finally got here. Sooner I get this job over with, better I like it."

"Little risky traveling at night," Little Bill observed.

"Be as hard for outlaws to see us as it is for us to spot them. Works both ways. Anyway, looks like it was all just a rumor." Grover swung his eyes to the crowd. "Well, how about it? You moving on down to the other end of the street or do I call on these soldiers to step in?"

"Just you simmer down a mite," Big Bill said. "Happens this is my town. Don't go crowding me." He brought his attention back to Dan. "You was shooting off your lip plenty loud a minute ago. You still figure to back it up?"

"Any time you say," Wade replied.

"Ten minutes . . . down in front of the Rainbow," Krask snapped. "I'll be waiting. And you be there, too," he added to Little Bill. "I get this saddle tramp out of the way, I'll be ready for you."

Without waiting for an answer from either man, the cattleman wheeled about and started back for the saloon, the crowd trailing along in his wake.

Immediately the cavalrymen rode in to the hitch rack that served the bank, dismounted. Dan gave them a brief glance—a lieutenant, a sergeant, and four privates. All were tough-appearing, hardened soldiers. Major Ives had chosen a well-experienced crew to escort Grover.

"Where the hell's that banker?" the federal man wondered. "He's supposed to be here and open up for me."

"Somebody's coming now," the lieutenant said. "That him?"

"That's him," Little Bill said. "You finished with us, Marshal?"

"I am . . . and I'm much obliged. Like I said, it appears this hold-up was just talk, but we couldn't see taking any chances. Everything's safe now, with the Army here."

"Hey, drifter!" It was Ross Oliver, shouting from the crowd now gathered in front of the saloon. "We're waitin'!"

Wade nodded to Grover, started off down the street. At his shoulder Little Bill said: "You didn't fool me, Dan, getting yourself crossways with Pa. I won't let you go through with it."

Wade smiled bleakly. "Nothing you can do about it now."

XIV

They walked slowly through the powdery dust. The full import of his situation was registering on Dan Wade's consciousness in those moments, the incredible position of being forced into a gunfight with a friend he had always admired and respected—a man for whom he now felt only sorrow and pity.

"It's my doing," Little Bill murmured. "My own fight. I won't let you stand for me."

"You want to shoot it out with your own pa . . . kill him?"

"He might kill me instead."

"Not likely, not if you tried. You're better with a gun than he is. You know that."

The young lawman was silent. Dan looked ahead. The crowd in front of the Rainbow had multiplied as word of the showdown had spread.

"And he knows it," Little Bill said, taking up the conversation where it had broken off. "Same as he knows he'll be no match for you. What's the matter with him? Why does he keep pressing it?"

Wade paused, glancing back over his shoulder. Luke Grover and the soldiers were just entering the bank building. In a few more minutes they would have the shipment loaded and be on their way.

"Who knows?" he said, replying to the lawman. "Pride and stubbornness, for one thing. And the yapping Ross Oliver and the others have been doing. Mix that up with the liquor he's guzzling and maybe you've got your reason. He can't think straight. If he ever got the chance to sober up, he'd realize what was going on."

"They're the ones we ought to be throwing down on," the lawman said, his voice tight and angry. "Oliver and Cully . . . all the rest. I wouldn't mind taking on the whole bunch."

Dan Wade came to a dead stop. A glimmer of an idea, of

hope, slipped into his mind. "Maybe that's the answer," he said, his eyes on the crowd. "It could be what we're looking for."

Little Bill moved around to where he could face the tall rider. "Answer to what?"

"To your pa . . . to straightening out this mess. Do you mean what you said, that you're willing to stand up against Ross Oliver and his bunch? Odds will be maybe five or six to our two."

"A shoot-out?"

"It'll probably be just that, unless I'm figuring Ross Oliver wrong."

"And leave Pa out of it?"

"That's the idea."

"I'm ready," Little Bill said without hesitation. "What are you figuring to do?"

"First we find Amos Kincaid," Dan said. "Then I'll explain."

They moved on down the street into the crowd. Big Bill, standing a bit to one side with Oliver and several of his crew, watched Wade approach with dull interest. He ignored his son.

"You ready, boy?"

Dan shook his head. "Don't rush me. There's a couple of things I have to do."

"You getting cold feet?"

"No," Wade said, glancing over the expectant faces turned toward him. "I want to do this thing up right."

Kincaid was not in the two dozen or so persons gathered in the street. Dan motioned to Little Bill.

"Keep that scatter-gun pointed at Ross and his bunch," he said. "I'm taking a look in the saloon, and I don't fancy a bullet in my back."

The marshal nodded. "I'd like for one of them to make a wrong move. I figure I owe somebody there for a rap on the head the other night."

Dan shouldered his way across the gallery of the Rainbow

and pushed through the doors. The saloon was completely empty. Disturbed, he wheeled about. The old cowpuncher had said definitely he would be in town and Dan knew Kincaid well enough to know he would not fail. Something had happened to keep Kincaid from keeping his promise.

"Quit stallin'," Cully said, as Wade stepped back into the street. "You was talkin' mighty big a few minutes ago. You aim to weasel out now?"

Dan whirled on the man, caught him by the shirt front, jerked him forward. "I'm looking for Amos Kincaid. He was supposed to be here. You know any reason why he's not?"

Cully's flushed face paled. His eyes flared, then squeezed down to small slits. "How the hell would I know where he is?"

"He said he'd be here. And he told me you'd jumped him before."

"He's got a long nose . . . ," the redhead blurted, and stopped suddenly.

Anger rocked through Dan Wade. His free hand lashed out, slapped Cully hard across the face. "If you've laid a finger on that old man. . . ."

"What's going on here?" Big Bill demanded, shoving up behind the redhead. "What you hurrahing him for? It's you and me that's got things to settle."

"He's backin' down," Ross Oliver declared in a loud voice. "That's what he's doin'. Trying to start somethin' with somebody else so's he won't have to face you."

"Let me have him!" Cully yelled, beside himself with rage. "Been wantin' my chance with this jasper. . . ."

"Shut up," Big Bill said. "He'd blow your head off before you knew what was going on." The rancher peered at Dan. "You backing down from me? Is that what this's all about?"

"You know better. I'm trying to find out what's happened to

Amos Kincaid. I've got a hunch he's been hurt, or maybe he's dead."

"Amos?" the cattleman echoed, his voice cracking a little. "Who'd be wanting to hurt him?"

"Any of that bunch you call a crew. The redhead there beat him up once before . . . just because he was trying to look out for you."

Big Bill frowned. "Old Amos? Never heard nothing about it. Anyway, it's got nothing to do with us. I'm waiting, boy, waiting for you to get out there in the street."

"He ain't got the guts," Ross Oliver murmured, a sly grin on his face.

Dan studied the foreman's ruddy face. "Maybe you'd like to try first. It'd be a good way for me to limber up my arm."

Oliver's grin faded. "I ain't hornin' in on the boss' fun," he said, shrugging. "You're his meat."

"And you're mine," Dan said. "Remember that, Ross. I'm coming for you when this is finished."

"I'll be ready," Oliver said, and winked broadly at Cully and the others.

Dan turned about. Directly before him he saw Joe Kingsford. He motioned to the merchant, drew him off to one side. He caught Little Bill's attention, waved him over.

"Fixin' up your funeral?" Levi called. "Don't worry none about it. We'll see you're planted . . . good and deep."

The crowd roared with laughter. Cully said something else and there was another burst. Dan faced the merchant.

"Joe, we need your help. I don't want this shoot-out to go through."

"If you don't stand up to him, everybody will think you're backing down."

"It makes no difference what they think. I'm not going out there and kill Big Bill and I sure don't aim to let him kill me."

"What can I do about it?"

"Get Big Bill inside the Rainbow, away from that crowd. I don't care how you handle it . . . just so you do it."

"I've got to have some kind of reason."

Wade nodded. "I'll furnish it. The important thing is to get him away from Oliver and his bunch. Little Bill and I have some business with them that needs taking care of."

Light broke across Kingsford's features. "You two taking them on? All of them?"

Dan said: "Big Bill's in a fog. He doesn't know what's going on, they've got him that fuddled. Once we get them out of the picture, I think we can bring him to his senses."

"A hard bunch," the merchant said doubtfully. "Could be you're biting off a big chew."

"We'll take our chances," the lawman said.

The crowd was growing noisier, egged on by Oliver and his followers. Shouts for Wade to stand and draw or ride out of town, a branded coward, echoed along the street.

Dan glanced at Kingsford, at Little Bill. "We all set?"

"You call the turn," the younger Krask replied, handing the shotgun to Kingsford. "Hold this, Joe. I won't be using it."

Kingsford accepted the weapon, hung it in the crook of his arm. "All you want me to do is get Big Bill out of the crowd and into the saloon."

"That's it," Dan said. "I don't trust Oliver and his bunch. One way or another they're going to get a bullet into him. If not by me, by one of them."

"I see. All right, I'll work it somehow. You start things off."

Dan wheeled. He glanced at Big Bill Krask, flanked closely by the Double K crew. "Keep an eye on Oliver and the others," he said in a low voice to the young lawman. "Don't make a move until your pa is out of the way."

He took a step toward the center of the street, halted abruptly, his eyes reaching beyond the crowd. A riderless horse had walked into the light, a small, chunky buckskin wearing a McClellan Army saddle and a bold U.S. brand on its hip.

XV

All the small, tag ends of doubt that had been plaguing Dan Wade suddenly fused, crystallized in his mind. He knew now what it was that had disturbed him, had given life to the vague worry that had beset him as he watched the squad of soldiers from Fort Glade ride in and dismount before the bank. The horses did not wear Army brands—and the men forked stock saddles, not the conventional government issue. Major Ives, a spit and polish officer who went strictly by the book, would never permit such disregard of regulations. Somewhere between the Army post and the settlement an ambush had taken place. The killers had appropriated the cavalrymen's uniforms, but apparently had not bothered to acquire their horses also; one of the straying Army mounts had managed to find his way into town.

Wade threw a hurried look down the street. Grover and the imposters were still there. They were ready to pull out. Two had mounted; others were swinging up. The federal man was saying something to Dawson, the banker.

"Outlaws!" Dan suddenly yelled. "It's a hold-up! Those men aren't soldiers! Come on," he added to Little Bill, and started for the bank at a run. "We've got to warn Grover . . . help him!"

"Hey!" the elder Krask's voice thundered along the buildings. "What's going on? Where do you think . . . ?"

"He's runnin'!" Cully shouted. "By God, he's runnin' out on the fight!"

"Head him off! Cut him down!" It was Ross Oliver's voice. "Don't let him get away!"

Wade half turned in stride, the foreman's words sending a

stream of warning through him. He saw Cully and Levi bolt from the crowd, saw them dragging out their guns. He drew fast, snapped a shot at the redhead. Cully went to his knees as the bullet smashed into him. Levi halted uncertainly. Farther back Dan could see Kingsford clutching Big Bill Krask's arm, talking to him earnestly. Evidently the merchant thought this was the diversion he had been promised.

There was no time to stop, even to call back an explanation to the now jeering crowd. He glanced ahead, to the bank. Grover was walking to his horse, his face turned toward the street.

"Marshal . . . it's a hold-up!" Little Bill cried. "Those men aren't soldiers . . . they're outlaws!"

Grover either didn't hear or understand. He placed his foot in the stirrup, gained the saddle. The horses beyond him began to mill about.

"Watch them!" Dan yelled his warning to Little Bill, a dozen paces to his right. "They'll open up at us any second!"

"I'm ready," the lawman said grimly.

Something was happening back in front of the Rainbow. Dan could hear the confused babble of voices, of shouts. He did not look around. It could be that Oliver and the rest of the crew were following, were coming to claim vengeance for his shooting down Cully. He grinned bleakly; if so, they'd have to wait their turn.

The bank was just ahead. Dan put his attention on the government man. "Grover . . . those soldiers are fakes . . . they're outlaws! Can't you hear me?"

Luke Grover wheeled his horse about. He looked straight at Dan and Little Bill. "I hear you," he said, and drew his pistol.

Dan heard the crack of the weapon, saw the orange circle of its powder flash. He felt the breath of the bullet as it skimmed his cheek—and only then realized what it meant. Grover was no U.S. marshal—he was an outlaw! "Hit the dirt!" he howled at

Little Bill as he saw Grover's gun flame again.

He went into the ankle-deep dust, began to roll. He fired as he came onto his belly, aimed at the first and nearest target. It was one of the bogus soldiers. The man jolted from the impact of the slug, started to fall.

Little Bill opened up at that moment. The riders in front of the bank were wheeling uncertainly. A second outlaw was down, lying partly on the ground with one foot still caught in the stirrup of his saddle. Little Bill had scored, too.

A sudden hail of bullets erupted from Grover and the others. Dust spurted up around Dan, showering him with fine, dry powder. He heard the young lawman gasp, knew instantly he had been hit.

He sent an answering fire at the outlaws, a wild, sudden rage possessing him. A third rider sagged, but did not fall. Dan threw an anxious look at Little Bill. The lawman was not shooting, simply laying full length in the center of the street. He had been hit hard, possibly was dead.

Dan's pistol clicked as a spent cartridge came up. He cursed, rolled to his back. He hastily thumbed a half dozen bullets from his belt loops, punched out the empties, and shoved the fresh loads into the cylinder. He heard the hard thud of horses' hoofs, glanced up. Grover and the three men able to ride were swerving toward him. Their guns began to blaze.

He snapped the loading gate of his .44 shut, rolling frantically to one side. He had to escape not only the murderous rain of bullets they were throwing at him as they sought to break through and reach the open ground behind him, but the oncoming horses as well. He fired hastily, taking no aim, hoping only to halt the charge. A slug drove into one of the horses, dropped him to his knees. The outlaw leaped from the saddle, struck on his head and one shoulder.

Dan saw Grover in that moment, only a dozen yards away.

He twisted about for a shot, heard Little Bill's revolver blast again. Hope surged through him. The lawman was still alive. Wade leveled on Grover, saw another of the outlaws wheel straight for the wounded Krask. He prayed Little Bill was aware of the man's close presence. He saw Grover throw himself to one side, knew he had missed his shot the instant he squeezed the trigger.

"Your last try!" the false marshal yelled, his lips pulled back into a hard grin.

Wade struggled to get up, to roll to his feet, throw himself from the path of the horse. Grover was too near. Dan saw the sudden, looming shape of the outlaw's mount before him, heard the deafening crash of Grover's gun almost against his head.

In the fragment of time he felt the shocking wallop of the horse's body against him, he went backward and down into the dust, rolling over and over. Grover's voice again touched him.

"So long cowboy!"

The outlaw would kill him now; he would have an easy chore. His own gun was empty; he was flat in the street, half dazed from the collision with the running horse.

The town echoed with the blast of a shotgun, two thunderous reports. The rapid crack of a pistol followed immediately. Dan pulled himself about. Grover's horse, with no rider on the saddle, was trotting off toward the other loose animals. He sat up, his mind clearing rapidly now. Two men were upright. Joe Kingsford, carrying the shotgun the marshal had thrust upon him, and Big Bill Krask, a smoking pistol in his hand.

The cattleman moved to where his son lay. Dan watched him drop hesitantly to his knees, pause momentarily, and then reach down and gather the boy into his arms. The crowd that had trailed up from the front of the Rainbow fell silent.

"You all right?" Kingsford called to Dan through the pall of dust.

"I'll make it," Dan said. "I was lucky." He remained where he sat, finishing the chore of reloading his gun.

"That damn' Grover . . . ," Kingsford muttered. "Sure had me fooled. Looks like Little Bill's hurt bad." He turned away, started for the cattleman and his son.

Dan flung a glance at the pair. Big Bill was still on his knees. He was holding the young marshal against his chest.

"Let them be," Dan said, rising to his feet. "This is the time they both need. Somebody go after the doc?"

"Reckon you're right," the merchant said. "Yeah, Doc's on his way."

Dan walked to where Luke Grover lay. The man was dead. He had taken a charge from Kingsford's shotgun. Methodically the deputy went on to each of the other outlaws. Two were still alive. But the man Big Bill had stopped just as he was swinging in to finish off the young marshal was not one of those; the cattleman's bullet had struck him squarely between the eyes. Big Bill was still expert with a six-gun.

"Let me in here."

Dan heard the doctor's words, gentle, but firm, as he dropped beside the Krasks. George Calloway came up at a trot, glanced around briefly, and then hurried to where Dan and Kingsford stood. The crowd had pulled in closer, now formed an almost complete ring in the street.

"Don't quite understand all this," Calloway said. "You mean Grover wasn't a U.S. marshal at all? And those soldiers weren't soldiers?"

Dan nodded. "Somewhere there's a genuine marshal lying dead, I expect. Grover had to get the badge and papers somewhere. We ought to send word to Major Ives. Could be they'll find those soldiers alive. Might even be a good idea to start a party from here, backtracking to the fort."

"I'll get a posse headed out right away. What tipped you off, Wade?"

"That Army horse walking into town," Dan said. "Something about those soldiers had bothered me right from the start, but I couldn't pin it down. As far as Grover was concerned, I was a sucker for him right up to when he started shooting."

Calloway gave a low whistle. "Good thing you had your eyes open. They'd have got away with that money shipment for sure."

"More luck than anything," Dan said. "But it's all finished now."

From the deep shadows along the edge of the street Ross Oliver's harsh, threatening voice said: "Not yet, friend. Not for you."

XVI

Dan Wade wheeled about slowly. Three men were there—Oliver, Levi, and one he did not know by name. He felt his pulse quicken as the sudden press of danger again closed in upon him, then came the long, free-flowing coolness as his nerves steeled to meet the emergency.

"Out of the way, Mayor," Oliver said in that same dry tone. "You, too, storekeeper, unless you figure to use that scattergun."

"It's empty . . . ," Kingsford said, and bit off his words abruptly.

It would have made no difference if he had not spoken, Dan knew. Oliver was aware the gun was of no use, that its twin barrels had both been discharged, just as he could see that neither of the men carried a pistol.

"Move off," he said quietly. "No point in your mixing in this."

Calloway pulled back, quickly got out of the line of fire. Kingsford held his ground stubbornly. "I can't let you stand here alone . . . not against three of them."

"Nothing you can do about it," Dan murmured.

There was nothing anyone could do. The crowd would take no hand, would remain strictly aloof of the trouble. Kingsford said something under his breath, backed toward Calloway. Wade faced the foreman.

"You won't need them," the foreman replied evenly. "Levi and Deke won't be takin' a hand . . . not unless they have to. This here is between you and me."

"You can bet on it," Big Bill Krask's voice cut through the hush.

Wade turned his head slightly. The cattleman was on his feet. He had unpinned the town marshal's star from his son's vest and now wore it on his own. He walked slowly to Dan's side.

"That boy of mine is laying there almost dead," he said. "I've been playing a damned old fool and I reckon I'm to blame for what's happened. Now I'm getting a chance maybe to make it up to him a little."

"You hornin' in on this?" Ross Oliver asked, a definite note of pleasure in his tone.

"I am . . . if Dan here is willing."

It was the Big Bill that Wade remembered. Cold sober now, he stood, tall and wide-shouldered in that faintly stooped stance, lower jaw jutted outward, hat off, huge hands hanging at his hips.

"Welcome, friend," Dan murmured. "This is like the old days."

Krask nodded slightly. "I'll be asking your pardon, boy, when this is over. When a man takes it on to make a fool of himself, he can sure do a right fine job if he tries."

"Happens once to all of us," Dan said. He was watching Oliver and the two men. The foreman was a step or two ahead of the others. They were fanning out, each moving to the side.

"Keep your eyes peeled," Wade said, keeping his warning low. "You take Levi. I'll look after Ross and the other one."

"Fair enough," Big Bill murmured. "Watch that Ross. He's fast. We wait for them?"

"Their fight. That makes it their move."

Levi and Deke came to a sliding halt six feet on either side of the foreman. Their faces were slack, their eyes blank.

Dan said: "There's still time to call this off, Ross. No need for more killing. Throw down your guns and give yourself up. You'll stand trial for your thieving and get a few years in the territory pen . . . but you'll be alive."

"The hell with you," the foreman snarled and snatched at his gun.

Dan's hand flashed down and up. He fired fast, aiming for Oliver's belly. He heard Big Bill's pistol echo his shot just as he triggered off a second at the man called Deke. Their weapons flared in unison. Dan felt the searing scorch of a bullet as it smashed into his leg, spun him half around. He lunged a step to one side, whirled back for a third shot.

There was no need. Ross Oliver lay full length in the dust. Beyond him, dead, was Levi. Deke, on his knees, clutched at his chest, a strange, drawn look on his bearded face. Suddenly he stiffened, pitched forward.

A tremor shook Dan Wade. A thick wave of sickness washed through him. He swallowed hard, took firm hold of his nerves. Death, even for the worst of men, was never a pleasant thing. It was something he could not harden himself to.

Someone broke out in a cheer. That was the release that unfettered the silent, awe-struck crowd. They surged forward in a body, gathered around Dan and Big Bill, laughing, congratulating, all striving to get close.

The rancher turned to Dan. "That apology I was mentioning, I'm making it here and now before God and everybody.

I'm hoping you'll accept it and take my hand, boy."

Dan reached for the cattleman's fingers, clasped them in his own. "Forget it," he said.

"Something I won't soon be doing," Krask said.

"The marshal's going to be all right!" someone shouted from the edge of the crowd. "Doc says he's going to make it."

Dan raised his glance to the cattleman. "What about him?"

"Got some apologizing to do there, too," Big Bill said. "To him and his wife both. Maybe they'll laugh in my face when I ask them to forgive me . . . but I aim to try anyway."

"They won't laugh," Dan said. He shifted his weight. His leg, numb for several minutes, was beginning to pain.

The doctor, hatless, hair awry, pushed up to Krask's side. "They're taking the boy to my place. He'll be all right soon as I get those two bullets out of him." He turned to Dan. "Were you the one asking about Amos Kincaid?"

Wade frowned. Fear crowded into his mind again. "Yes. Is there something wrong?"

"A rancher brought him in a while ago. Found him on the road. Somebody gave him a right fierce beating. But he's all right. Amos is a tough old bird. You better come along and let me have a look at that leg."

Relief ran through Dan. "Glad to hear that," he said, adding—"I'll come in a minute."—as the physician hurried on.

"Speaking of Amos," Big Bill said. "Going to have to work myself up a new crew . . . a good one. You interested in being foreman?"

Dan Wade let his eyes drift over the street. Volunteers were moving the dead bodies of the outlaws, of Ross Oliver and his followers. Again a slight tremor racked him. He faced the cattleman.

"I'll just take that offer," he said. "I don't think I was cut out to be a lawman."

★ ★ ★ ★ ★

Desert Rider

★ ★ ★ ★ ★

I

There were four of them—four scowling, agate-eyed men with wicked, brutal faces. They rode carefully, tightly abreast, down Yucca Flats' single, dusty street that blistering July morning, their narrow, probing glances missing little. Few saw them arrive, it being that hour of the day when the heat had a lethargic effect upon the residents of the small desert settlement. Those who did see them were, from that moment, marked men. It was as though they had looked upon some 19th-Century Medusa, the result of which was to alter their lives violently, even end them.

Milo Morgan was one of those. He stood inside his general merchandise store, the largest in the area for miles around, and looked pridefully through the new, crystal-clear glass window he had recently installed. It was sixty by seventy-two inches, figures he made known to all who entered his well-stocked establishment, and this window, too, was the largest in the territory. He watched the dust-caked riders move by and wondered who they might be.

He doubted if they represented any amount of cash business. They appeared to have little, if any, money. Their clothing was old, well-worn butternut and denim, and their boots were scarred, with broken, run-down heels. Their gear was patched and needed replacing. And their horses—all four of them would not be worth a double eagle. He drew a silver monogrammed case from an inner pocket and selected a cigar. He had given up a pipe, feeling that the factory-rolled weeds were more appropriate to his position as one of the town's leading citizens. He thrust it into his mouth, rolled it to one corner, cocked it to an upward slanting angle, and studied the passing riders. No, he could expect no business from that bunch. Saddle bums seldom had money.

Abel Moss saw them. He stood in the doorway of his Desert City Bank, absorbing the faint breeze induced by opening a window in the rear of the building, and observed their slow approach while a vague disturbance arose within him. They were hardcases, little doubt of that, always meaning trouble, never doing a place any good. There really should be a law preventing such men from even riding down the street of a decent town. Where the devil was Banning, the marshal? That's what they paid him for, wasn't it—to keep such riff-raff out of Yucca Flats? He moved a step back into the shadowy depths of the building, suddenly aware of the covered, slanted glances they were sending in his direction.

And Carl Schweitzer. In truth, however, he paid less mind to the men than he did to their jaded horses. He sat in the wide, double doorway of his livery barn, his two-hundred-fifty-pound bulk filling a rocking chair to capacity, and assessed their horseflesh with a practiced eye. The animals had about run their last mile. Thin, gaunt-necked, a man could even see the slight tremble of their legs as they walked. And their eyes had the faint cloudiness that comes from being ridden too hard for too long. Schweitzer watched them haul up in front of Campion's Place and saw the riders dismount. They looped the leathers over the rail and walked inside, never glancing back at their animals that were left to stand unfed, unwatered in the withering sun. The stableman saw them gradually wilt, their heads dropping lower and lower as exhaustion claimed them. Poor beasts! A man ought to be lashed for neglecting his animals like that. Back East where he came from, people took care of their stock. Out here, where a horse was as important to a man as his left leg, they ignored them, let them suffer, and treated them like clods of dirt.

By heaven, he had a notion to walk over there and fetch them to his stable. Put them inside out of the sun, give them some fresh water and some hay and grain. It wouldn't hurt to rub them down, either. That lazy hostler wasn't doing anything, anyway. Probably back there asleep in one of the stalls. By heaven, he sure ought to do it. Only a man could not, he reminded himself soberly. Out here they looked at things differently. A man kept his nose out of other people's affairs. The four riders looked none too friendly, as it was. But those animals—they sure ought to be looked after.

Gordon Campion saw them, and was the first to feel the impact of their presence. He was behind the bar of his saloon, cleaning up the last of the previous night's glassware when they pushed through the swinging doors and stalked, like stiff-legged wolves about to converge upon a kill, to his counter. Campion, who had only recently come from the Territories to the north, took one look at them—and the terrifying thought—*My God, the Wind River bunch.*—surged through him. Throttling the nervousness such knowledge brought him, he faced them, mustering a faint smile of mercantile welcome.

"Gentlemen?"

The one in the center stared at him intently. He was a big man with broad features, deeply seamed. He had dark eyes that held no life, and his thick, brown hair was in need of cutting. Campion remembered him as Dan Groth, the head man of the gang.

"I know you?" Groth asked, his voice a low, thrusting demand.

Campion said: "Doubt it. Unless you've been here in my place before."

Groth shook his head. "First time."

"And the last," the one next to him added. They had called that one Hondo. Red hair, red mustache, and a lean, handsome sort of face. Quite a ladies' man, or so he fancied himself. "How about some beer, bartender? Little hot for whiskey."

"Beer," Campion echoed. "All around?"

"Make mine whiskey."

That was Coaley. Coaley, they had said, was not exactly right in the head. Things did not always click the way they should in his brain, but that did not prevent him from being one of the most ruthless killers that had ever drawn a six-gun. Perhaps it was the reason why.

The fourth member, much younger than the others, Campion recalled as Chick Adams, scarcely more than a kid, but wild and every bit as bad as the others. "Mine'll be beer," Adams said.

Campion, struggling to keep his nervousness from showing, drew two mugs of beer and poured a shot glass of whiskey. He set them on the counter and switched his attention back to the outlaw leader.

"You didn't order yet, Mister Groth . . . ," he began, then stopped short, realizing suddenly what he had said.

Groth smiled at him thinly. "Thought you said you didn't know me."

Campion, taking strong hold of himself, squeezed down his fluttering nerves. Why was he getting so all-fired rattled? No reason for him to be afraid of the Wind River bunch. He'd never done anything to them. "Didn't say it that way," he replied boldly. "You asked me if you knew me. I said no. And you don't. But I remember you and the others from one night in Cheyenne. Saw you there in the Trail Star saloon."

"Cheyenne," Groth repeated absently. "Must have been one, two years back."

"About two," Campion said. "Will you have a beer or some whiskey?"

"Whiskey."

Campion felt Coaley's vacant stare upon him as he poured the drink. He placed it before Groth and began to wipe at the counter with his towel, making a show of disinterest, of keeping busy at his own affairs. But he had made a dangerous error, and the mark of that lay upon him, turning his movements into quick, bird-like actions and changing the color of his face.

"Dan, how about this here jasper knowing us? You reckon that's a safe thing?" Coaley asked then.

"If he knew us in Cheyenne, I expect he knows quite a few things," Hondo observed. "Maybe enough to keep his lip buttoned."

Coaley blinked owlishly, not removing his flat eyes from Groth. He ignored Hondo's remark. "What you think, Dan?"

Campion felt fear crawling up his back, prickling at his scalp. He wished, at that moment, that John Banning would come through the swinging doors. Then he would not be alone. He would have some help. He waited out the long, dragging moments while Groth viewed his own reflection in the backbar mirror. It was a terrible thing to realize that his life depended upon one word from the outlaw leader. Groth lifted the glass and downed his liquor in a single gulp.

"No," he said, sliding the glass toward Campion, "I don't figure it's so good. We'll think about it for a spell." He lifted his gaze to Campion's shocked face and smiled genially. "Fill 'em up again, Mister Bartender."

Young Dave Culwell, fifteen and tall for his years, had seen the four men arrive. He sat now at the desk of the man he called Pa—he had lived for so long with John Banning as parent that the actual relationship of uncle and nephew was almost forgotten—and thought not at all of them. He looked up as Moss, followed by Morgan and Carl Schweitzer, entered and halted in front of him. The banker looked hot and riled.

"Where's the marshal, boy?"

"Out serving some papers," Dave replied. "I'm minding the place while he's gone."

"When will he be back?"

"Pretty soon. He was just goin' to the Austins'."

Moss turned, looking down the street to where the four horses were still standing before Campion's. There was a deep, angry frown on his pinched and narrow face. "Might have known," he said.

Morgan studied the banker for a moment. "What's this all about, Abel? You said you wanted Carl and me to go with you to talk to the marshal. All right. But what about? What's got you so worked up?"

"Those four hardcases that just rode in. We oughtn't to let them hang around here like they're doing. The marshal should keep their kind moving on."

Morgan thought for a time, scratching at the back of his head. "Well, now, Abel, I ain't so sure about that. We need that transient business, and Lord knows there's mighty little of it coming by."

"You think any of that bunch is going to spend a copper with us? Not on your life. Maybe a dollar or so at Campion's or some other saloon, but they won't be buying anything from anybody else."

"You're probably right there," Morgan agreed. "They sure didn't look very prosperous. But I'm not just thinking about them. I'm thinking about all the men who ride by here. Some of them will have a little money to spend. I don't figure we can set up any hard and fast rule about running every stranger that comes along right on through the town. Word will mighty quick get around. And, first thing you know, there won't be anybody . . . good or bad . . . coming by."

"We'd be a lot better off if their kind would stay away," Moss said stubbornly.

"Sure, their kind. I agree to that. But how're you going to tell? You can't set up a hard and fast rule. . . ."

"And they ought to have a chance to feed and bed down their animals," Schweitzer said in his slow, heavily accented voice. "Animals got to eat and rest, same as folks. Ain't no fault of theirs if the men who own. . . ."

Moss wheeled impatiently around to the boy. "When Banning gets back, tell him I want to see him. Tell him to come over to the bank, right away."

"Sure, Mister Moss," Dave replied, and watched the three men file out.

He wasn't sure just what they were talking about. Somebody or something the banker didn't like. But that was nothing new. Mr. Moss never liked anything much, it seemed to him.

He picked up the deputy marshal's star he had taken from his uncle's desk. A couple more years and he'd get to pin it on for true. Pa said he was too young now, and, besides, he wanted him to be something more than a regular lawman. Marshals and sheriffs didn't make much money. And they worked harder for what they did get than almost anybody else, except maybe a cowpuncher. But, he decided, he sure couldn't see anything wrong with being a lawman. He pinned the star to his shirt breast and eyed it admiringly. You had to be good to be a lawman. Fast with a gun and not afraid of anything. Like his pa. Everybody said he was a top lawman.

People called him mister, and they were always asking him for advice and maybe coming to him for help of some kind, like when they wanted somebody straightened out. Old Mrs. Sorenson had done that. She couldn't make her boy quit drinking so much, and he wouldn't go to work. Just laid around all the time. Pa took the kinks out of him quick. He got himself a job at Magerkurth's ranch that very next day. Maybe he still did some drinking, sort of sneaky-like, but he sure was staying on that job.

His Aunt Lucy, who he had called Ma, had died a few years after he had come to live with them; she didn't like a lawman's life, either. He remembered her saying so once. Too dangerous, she had said, too risky and for so little. People didn't really appreciate a lawman, but they always expected him to be around handy in time of trouble.

He felt a twinge of loneliness when he thought of Lucy Banning. She had been the only mother he had ever fully known, just as John Banning had been his only father. He had been very small when his real parents had been killed.

He pulled open the bottom drawer of the desk, where he knew it was kept, and took out a small daguerreotype. It bore the likeness of a young woman, one with a wealth of dark hair piled high on her head and with a round, sweet face. She had been a pretty woman, prettiest in the whole state of Tennessee, Pa had said many times. He was sitting at the scarred old desk, moving the daguerreotype to different angles, noting how the light changed the picture and even blanked it out completely if held too flat, when a burst of gunshots erupted in the street. He laid the picture down and hurried to the doorway. Three men were backing away from the bank, shooting as they did so. One of them had a pair of saddlebags slung over his shoulder.

They looked familiar. Dave thought for a moment and then remembered—they were the men who had ridden in earlier, the ones Mr. Moss and the others had been talking about. But there were four of them then. Where was the other one?

One of the men yelled, saying something Dave could not understand. He saw the fourth man then as he moved up with the horses. But he needed a better look. Their descriptions would help Pa when he started out after them. He left his place in the doorway and ran into the street. The man carrying the saddlebags whirled about to look at him, attracted either by the sudden movement or by the sun glinting sharply off the deputy marshal's star the boy wore. The outlaw fired quickly.

The heavy bullet struck Davey Culwell dead center. He never really knew what hit him.

II

Marshal John Banning had been a short quarter mile above Yucca Flats when he heard the gunshots. He had not paused to listen for more but had immediately set spurs to his chunky buckskin and moved out at a fast gallop. He was not sure if the firing had taken place within the town or somewhere beyond it. It did not matter. Gun play anywhere in or around the town was his business.

He reached the end of the street, pistol in hand, and slowed the horse to a walk. One glance told him that whatever had happened was over with now. People were running toward the bank, toward Gordon Campion's saloon, toward his own office. There were crowds before each, and these thickened quickly as more of the residents burst into the open.

He holstered his gun and pointed the buckskin for his office. He reached the hitch rail and swung down, tossing the reins over the bar. He turned about, meeting a wall of silent faces. He frowned then, his dark wide-set eyes cutting down to narrow slits.

"What's the trouble here, Ben?" he asked the man nearest him.

Ben Mitchell looked away and swallowed audibly. "Marshal, there's been some shooting. A gang robbed the bank. I'm afraid your boy. . . ."

John Banning stiffened, seeming to grow taller. His mouth settled into a hard line, and the points of his wide shoulders came back slightly.

"Davey? What about Dave?" he pressed in a level, breathless sort of way.

"He come out of your office while all the shooting was going on. Guess one of the outlaws must have figured he was the law. . . . Shot him down. . . ."

Banning suddenly pushed through the crowd into the heat-packed depths of his office. A dozen people were there, several of them women. They turned to him, their expressions set, pitying. One of the cell cots had been dragged into the center of the room. A blanket covered the figure lying upon it.

Banning pulled up short, the solid shock of what he saw stopping him like a granite wall. He had not expected this, not death. A wound, a serious injury perhaps, but not death. He stared at the shrouded shape unbelievingly.

"They shot up Abel Moss, too, Marshal. And killed Campion. And old Horace, the bank teller."

Banning stood in stunned silence. He was no stranger to death; he had seen it often, felt its presence more times than he cared to remember. But Davey, the boy—dead? It wasn't possible. It couldn't be. But there he lay, beneath a dusty, ragged blanket. Some sort of an accident. He'd heard somebody whisper that Dave had been wearing that old deputy's star; he had gone outside when the shooting started. Was that what Ben Mitchell had told him? An accident? He kept a tight grip on himself, trying to keep in the blind, unreasoning anger that was building up within him.

"Who were they?" he asked of no one in particular, his voice still taut.

" 'Fore Gordon died, he said it was the Wind River gang, from up Wyoming way. Or part of them, anyway. He knowed them from the time he was up there. Reckon that's why they wanted him shut up."

"Marshal," one of the women said then, in a voice heavy with sympathy, "if you like, I'll tend to the boy. I'll look after the burying."

At that, something seemed to break within John Banning's rigid frame. A wild, furious hatred raced through him, tightening the skin of his face, brightly firing the depths of his dark eyes. Lucy had been right—the price any man paid for being a lawman was too high. In one way or another, too much. First Lucy and now her sister's boy. A monstrous spasm of grief shook the big man, like a summer storm lashing a towering pine. He whirled about, his jaw hard-cornered.

"No, just get out of here!" he shouted. "Get out! All of you! Leave me be!"

He pushed them toward the doorway, his arms flung wide, sweeping them roughly before him. They crowded through and out into the street, halting there uncertainly. They began to mill about.

The woman who had made the offer protested mildly: "But, Marshal, I only wanted. . . ."

"Let me alone!" he cried, and savagely kicked the door shut in her face.

He stood there for a long time, the first onslaughts of grief beginning now to ebb. He turned and walked slowly to the cot, reached out, and pulled back the blanket. The sight of the boy's empty, drawn features was like the blow of a maul, but he did not look away. Rationality was gradually reclaiming him. Dave looked even younger than his fifteen years. And much like his mother, he thought. Lucy and the boy's mother had been sisters.

The glint of metal caught at his attention. He drew the blanket lower and saw the badge. He recalled how Dave had always said he wanted to be a lawman, how he had discouraged the idea. Likely he would have made a good one. He was smart, quick to learn. But that was all ended now. It was finished. He reached out, almost hesitantly, and touched the boy's dark hair. Davey had been almost a son to him.

"So long, boy," he murmured. "I'll not let them get away."

He wheeled about, his face grim, and plucked a rifle from the wall rack. He levered it sharply to check its loads, then yanked open one of the desk drawers, took up a handful of cartridges, and stuffed them into his side pocket. Then he saw the daguerreotype, lying where the boy had dropped it. He picked it up, the harsh lines of his face altering slightly as he studied it. After a moment he placed it back in the desk. Dave had loved his aunt as much as a son would love his own mother.

He strode to the door, pulled it open, and stepped out into the fiery blast of the midday sun. The crowd was still there, gathered in a silent, waiting half circle. He shouldered his way through them to his horse. He jammed the rifle into his leather boot and spun about.

"I want a posse," he said in a clipped, hard-edged voice. "You, Clinginbell, Snapp, Hartshorn, Mitchell, Valdez. Consider yourselves deputized. Get your horses. We leave from Schweitzer's livery stable in ten minutes."

"They rode west out of town," a voice somewhere in the crowd volunteered. "Headed for the desert."

Banning nodded. Milo Morgan came hurriedly up the street. He bustled importantly through the crowd and halted before the lawman.

"Marshal, we've got to get a posse after those killers. Moss says they got around fifteen thousand dollars. He wants us to bring them in."

"They killed my boy," Banning said coldly. "And Gordon Campion and the bank teller. That doesn't count with you and Abel?"

"Of course," Morgan said, glancing around the crowd in some confusion. "And I'm sure sorry. We can't let something like this go by the board, not in a town as big as ours. You want me to get a posse together?"

"It's been done," Banning said. "We'll be leaving from Schweitzer's shortly. You can tell Moss. Maybe he'll rest easier."

"Somebody else can tell him," Morgan said. "My place is in that posse. Nobody does that to my town," he added, and hurried on to his place of business.

Banning, his face a mask, turned to the woman who had spoken to him earlier inside the jail. "Missus Lee, I'm obliged to you for the offer you made. I'll appreciate your looking after Davey. See that Hoffman gives him the best. If I'm not back by noon tomorrow, go ahead with the services."

The woman drew a sharp breath. "You won't be at the funeral? Your own family?" she asked in a shocked, disbelieving way.

Banning said quietly: "I'll do everything I can to get back. But I've got to go after the men who did it."

"But it doesn't seem hardly decent. . . ."

"I'll be here, Missus Lee," he repeated, his voice going harsh again, "if I can manage it. I can't wait. I want the men who did it. Give them a full day's start and they'll get clear out of the country."

"I suppose so," the woman said. "I'm just wondering if the law is that important. So much so a person can't even attend. . . ." Her words trailed off into nothing.

"One thing more . . . tell Hoffman to leave the badge on him."

"That old deputy marshal's star?"

"Yes, I want him to wear it, pinned right where it is now. You'll find clothes at my place for him."

Abruptly he swung to the buckskin and mounted into the

saddle. He was more shaken than he appeared, and talking of the boy had not been easy. Only his ironbound will was making it possible for him to do the things that had to be done.

He pulled out into the middle of the street. A small group was clustered in front of the bank. Banning rode to that point and halted, then singled out a man from the crowd. "What's the doc say about Moss, Arthur?"

"Not much chance of him making it. They shot him up real bad, Marshal."

Banning thought for a moment. "Too bad. Meantime, you see about locking up the bank for me. Better send somebody to Pattonville. Tell the banker there what's happened. He'll know what's to be done."

"Sure, Marshal, sure. And, say . . . I'm sorry about the boy."

Banning nodded and cut back into the street. The minutes were slipping steadily away. He angled, then, for Schweitzer's stables. There were seven men in the saddle awaiting him, including the ponderous Schweitzer himself. A dozen more onlookers had gathered about. Milo Morgan rode forward to meet him.

"All ready, John," he said, adding: "except for a little doubt on the part of a couple of the boys."

Jess Clinginbell spoke up at once. "Now, wait just a damn' minute there, Milo. I didn't say nothing about backing out. All I said was maybe we ought to send for the sheriff at Pattonville. This is a mighty desperate bunch of murderers we're going up against. Ain't sure its a job for a jackleg posse like us."

Banning allowed his expressionless glance to run over the remainder of the men. "Anybody else feel the same?"

Harvey Hartshorn, who ran the feed store, stirred uncomfortably. "Well, Marshal, seems to me there's sense in what Jess's saying. We sure won't be no match for the Wind River gang."

Banning hung tightly to his temper. He needed these men; he

had to have them if he were to bring in the outlaws. It galled him to have to reason with them, even beg.

"There's only four of them, and I count eight of us," he said, faint sarcasm tingeing his voice. "Pretty good odds, no matter what kind of a fight. As far as the sheriff at Pattonville is concerned, you can forget him. It would take until noon tomorrow for him to get here. We can't wait that long."

Hartshorn said: "Guess that's right. Never thought about how long it would take."

"Now, you're all deputized and under my orders. Once we move out, there'll be no backing down. Any of you feel like you don't want to go, get out of the saddle now. Is that understood?"

There was a long moment of silence. Milo Morgan said: "Guess everybody's ready, Marshal."

"Let's go, then," Banning said, and led them out onto the road.

III

Banning estimated that the outlaws were a good thirty minutes ahead of them. With the posse pounding along behind him, they crossed the flats two miles west of Yucca Flats in short time. There, the road began to curve into a tangled band of tamarack, wild olive trees, greasewood clumps, and other such growth that had sprung up years past and now separated the desert proper from the area immediate to the town. Likely the quartet of killers would strike head-on into the breaks, considering it to be ideal country in which to hide, but they could also turn aside and swing north, hoping eventually to reach the safety of the Colorado mountains.

The prints of their horses were plain; they led up to the first outward thrusting of brush. Banning lifted his hand for a halt, swung down immediately, and began to cast back and forth until he again picked up the tracks, well inside the breaks. He had figured that was the way it would be, but John Banning was a thoroughgoing man; he took nothing for granted at such moments but relied strictly upon facts. The need to keep moving, to run down the killers, was a throbbing, insistent force within him, pushing impatiently at him, but he ignored it. First a man had to be sure. A wrong trail now and all would be lost.

"What you think, Marshal?" Mitchell asked, walking his horse up beside Banning. The man was soaking wet from sweat, and his horse was covered with lather. "You figure they're going to hole up here in the breaks?"

Banning shrugged, his face immobile and dark. "Anybody's guess. I'd keeping moving, fast, if it was me."

"They won't be moving fast for long," Schweitzer volunteered, mopping at his florid face. "Not on them animals they was riding."

Banning turned and looked inquiringly at the stableman. "Are they in bad shape, Dutch?"

"Plenty. Mighty beat and looked like they'd come a long way without no rest and dang' little feed."

"That's right," Morgan said. "I saw them myself when they rode in. The horses were about spent."

Banning considered that information in silence. If the outlaws were faced with such a problem, it was reasonable to believe they would not try to travel far. They would instead seek out a good place in the tamarack and lay over, at least until sundown. If true, it was going to be a matter of the posse beating through the bush, driving them out much as a man would flush a covey of quail.

"It leaves us one thing to do," Banning said then, and swung back to his saddle. "We'll have to roust them out before night. Once it's dark, we've lost them sure. I figure they'll be holing up somewhere here in the breaks to rest. We'll string out in a forage line, say about a hundred yards apart. Then we'll move in. Somewhere along the way we'll jump them out."

Hartshorn objected at once. "Bit risky . . . each man will sort of be by himself that way. And there's four of them, all in one bunch. If a man runs up against them. . . ."

Angry impatience surged through John Banning once again. He glared at the man. "Stay within that hundred yards and you'll be all right. And carry that gun in your hand, not in the holster. This bunch won't be letting us take them alive, so don't hold back on shooting."

Snapp spoke up then. "Hartshorn's got a point there. You figure a long line, like you say, is the best way to do it?"

Banning's voice was raw, edgy. "You got a better way?"

Posses, he reflected, forever followed the same pattern. All brave and willing to serve at the beginning, but after a short while, after the bloom of heroics had worn off and the sober reality of danger possessed them, they began to hedge and find fault and argue. If he did not need them so badly, he would send them all packing for home.

"No, reckon not," Snapp admitted, and drew his pistol.

"Then, spread out. We're working against time."

Banning remained where he was, thus choosing the most likely and, therefore, most dangerous position for himself. The outlaws would probably keep to the thickest part of the breaks, staying clear of the edges, where the growth was sparser and where searching eyes might more easily see them. Hartshorn, of course, was right. The nature of the country was such that a man, even no more than a hundred yards away, would at times be completely lost to his neighbor and, in effect, momentarily alone. But there was no other solution to the problem. The line had to be long enough to stretch across the breaks. His one hope was that any member of the posse encountering the outlaws would raise sufficient alarm to draw the men nearest him and thus balance the odds to an equal degree.

He waited for the others to find their places in the line, which seemed to take them an abnormally long time. He was struggling to keep his mind on the job that lay ahead, hoping to prevent his thoughts from dwelling upon Dave and the terrible tragedy of his death. The pressing need to find the killers, bring them to justice one way or another was driving him relentlessly. And he wanted to return to the settlement as soon as possible. The idea of having Davey cared for by others at such a time, even though they were good friends of long duration, was hard to accept. He should be there himself; he wanted to be. But he had been offered no choice. He faced a job that had to be done. The only answer was to do that job quickly and return.

He heard Jess Clinginbell sing out, far to the right. And then Morgan, followed by Joe Snapp as they, in turn, reported their positions. He was next. First to his left was Ben Mitchell, then Valdez, Hartshorn, and finally Carl Schweitzer on the end.

"All right," he said to his flankers. "Pass the word to pull out. Stay up even. And no talking."

He put the buckskin into motion, holding him down to a slow walk. He rode with the reins looped over the saddle horn, sitting erect, his arms crossed over his chest and his gun in his right hand. In such a position he would be able to see well and also bring the pistol into play quickly, should it be necessary.

The first quarter mile went by with frustrating slowness. Banning could feel the tension building up along the line. He could see it on the faces of the men when they were periodically visible to him; he could feel it in the very silence he had imposed upon them. The horses were making only a normal amount of noise, their hoofs well muted by the thick mat of dead leaves that littered the ground. There was an occasional snap of a dry limb, the thick swishing of a leafy branch as it swung back into place. Other than that, the stillness was complete.

The minutes dragged on, becoming more oppressive as the

posse drew nearer the desert. The afternoon heat was like the breath of a blast furnace. Sweat beaded Banning's dark face and smarted in his eyes. Streams of it trickled warmly down his back and along his ribs, plastering his clothing to his skin. He took up the canteen hanging from the horn and shook it speculatively. It was about half full, perhaps even less. He unscrewed the cap and took a small swallow. It might be a good idea to go easy, just in case the chase lasted longer than he anticipated. He should have taken time to refill it before he left the town.

The ragged edge of an arroyo appeared ahead, a wide, deep slash in the otherwise level floor of the breaks. A flock of white-winged doves, feeding on wild wheat, fluttered noisily away as they approached, darting and veering off to the left in their erratic way. Banning signaled a halt, staying well within the protective screen of an olive tree. He probed the sandy floor of the wash with a steady gaze, searching for those all-important tracks. He saw none, and he was considering what that could mean when the first gunshot shattered the quiet. He came quickly around.

It had come from the left, and seemingly to the rear. Hartshorn or Schweitzer. There was a sudden rush of hoof beats as Snapp and Morgan came up from the opposite end of the line.

"Who was it?" Morgan demanded, hauling up short. Banning held up his hand for silence. He shook his head. "Not sure. Seemed to be back of us."

Another blast rolled through the breaks, setting up a chain of echoes. And then Hartshorn's voice reached them.

"Over here! Over here!"

Banning spun the buckskin about and drove recklessly toward the sound of the man's urgent voice. Behind him Morgan and Snapp followed, picking up Ben Mitchell and Valdez, the *vaquero,* as they swept through the brush. They sliced across the breaks, going at right angles to the course they had pursued. The arroyo was still to the side, curving now slightly in and gradually growing shallower. Hartshorn and Schweitzer had somehow fallen behind the line. Damn them! Banning was suddenly angry. Damn the fools who couldn't mind orders!

"Down here, Marshal!"

Hartshorn's voice summoned Banning to the edge of the arroyo. He swung the buckskin to that point and rode down into the sandy bed, the others close on his heels. Hartshorn was kneeling beside Carl Schweitzer, who, round, ruddy face covered with shining sweat, was lying flat in the meager shade of a greasewood bush. His left shoulder and breast were stained with blood, and Hartshorn was working steadily with a pad of cloth at the wound. The stableman opened his eyes and grinned apologetically at the lawman.

"Guess I wasn't minding my business so well, eh, Marshal?"

Banning shrugged. A little late now for recriminations, and not much point to it. He said—"Forget it, Carl."—and dropped down beside Hartshorn. "How bad is it?"

"Bad enough," the man retorted sharply. "Bullet went all the way through. Bled quite a bit, but I about got it stopped now."

"Know how it happened?"

"Just like we tried to tell it might. They ganged up on him. Shot him out of the saddle and took his horse."

"Took his horse?" Morgan echoed.

Hartshorn nodded. "Left one of theirs." He indicated a worn-looking bay, standing hipshot off to one side. "Looks to me like he's gone lame. Probably the reason they grabbed Carl's."

"You were close enough to see all that and still couldn't help him?" Banning asked then, rising. "What were you doing all that time, Hartshorn?"

Hartshorn's face reddened. His lips began to move, but Schweitzer's voice stopped him. "Nobody's fault but mine,

Marshal. I plain wasn't watching what I was doing. Maybe I was half asleep. Don't go blaming Harvey. Reckon he didn't see much until it was all over."

"It appears to me," Banning said slowly, "if Harvey had been watching like he was supposed to be, you wouldn't be lying there now with a bullet hole in you, Carl."

Hartshorn, thoroughly aroused, said: "Don't be trying to blame me, Banning. This was your idea."

Jess Clinginbell eased in between the two men. He stared for a long moment at Schweitzer, then shook his head. "We'd better get this man to the doctor. And mighty quick."

"I think we better all go back to town," Hartshorn declared. "This is a damn' fool stunt, chasing after a bunch like that. We ain't got a show against them."

"I'm inclined to agree," Morgan said, his face drawn into a thoughtful study. "I think we're making a big mistake if we go on. How about it, Marshal?"

Banning faced them while the old impatient anger slogged through him. He knew what they wanted him to say, what they hoped for, but it was far from his mind.

"Two men can handle Schweitzer," he said dryly. "The rest of you remember this . . . you're still sworn deputies, and you're under my orders. We'll go on."

There was a silence following his speech, broken only by the rasp of the stableman's breathing and the occasional sound of some wild thing off in the breaks.

"There's no sense to this at all," Ben Mitchell said. "Marshal, I don't think you understand what you're asking us to do. I don't think you can see it because it's a family matter with you. Now, I'm wondering, if you'd be so all fired anxious to catch up with that bunch, if it wasn't."

Banning's dark face hardened. Mitchell's insulting implication lashed at him, turned him instantly furious, increased the bitterness that rankled through him. From his position on the ground Carl Schweitzer spoke.

"Ben, you know better than that."

Mitchell moved his thin shoulders in a gesture of resignation. "Well, this ain't right. Nobody can tell me any different."

Banning turned back to the stableman and knelt beside him. "Carl, I'm sorry it had to be you. But you'll be all right, soon as Doc Edmunds patches you up."

"Sure, sure. And, Marshal . . . I'm sorry about the boy. I didn't get a chance to tell you sooner. A damn' shame, a thing like that happening."

"Hard to figure," Banning said, taking the man's huge hand extended to him.

"For a fact. Now, don't you go worrying any more about me. I'll be all right."

Banning moved back to his horse. He mounted and sat there in the saddle for a brief moment, lost in thought.

"Ben," he said suddenly, "you and Hartshorn get Schweitzer back to town. The rest of you move out."

"Marshal," Milo Morgan said, walking up to the lawman. "I'm afraid I'm going to have to return, also. Some things I ought to be doing at my place. And I was just thinking . . . if Abel Moss dies, somebody will have to be looking after the bank. . . ."

"That's been taken care of," Banning snapped. He shifted his glance to Ben Mitchell and Hartshorn. They had started to get the stableman up, preparatory to putting him onto one of the horses. He glanced at the other members of the posse. They were watching, waiting, saying nothing.

"Mount up," he said brusquely. "I need you worse than you need to go back."

Banning pulled the buckskin about and crossed over the arroyo, following the tracks of the outlaw who had stolen

Schweitzer's horse. He climbed the far bank, hearing the creak of leather and the grunt of the horses as the remaining members of the party came on behind him. He stayed with the single line of tracks. The three other outlaws apparently had pulled on ahead of this one and had awaited him farther along. Things were working out well, despite the one casualty. They had the outlaws on the move, were driving them through the tangle of brush, giving them no time for rest.

They pressed on in the sapping heat, Banning somewhat ahead, keeping to the trail, the others in a small knot a few yards behind. They had not spread out, forming a line as they knew they should. He halted then to await them, while scathing words shaped themselves on his lips. And then he saw there were but three riders. Morgan had pulled out.

IV

He watched them come up in cold silence—Jess Clinginbell, Enrique Valdez, and Joe Snapp. They came to a wordless halt a dozen feet away and stared at him, sitting their saddles in a sort of weary patience as though aware of their inadequacies but determined to bear their burden nevertheless. He started to speak, to censure them angrily, and then thought better of it. Three men were better than none at all. He could not do it alone—not, at least, if he expected to come out alive.

He said—"Spread out a little. You make an easy target, bunched up like that."—and rode on.

They pushed on steadily. The afternoon hours wore on, breathlessly hot. They were riding straight into the sun, its dazzling rays striking them face on, causing them to wear their wide-brimmed hats tipped forward over their eyes. Banning, as were the others, was soaked with sweat, his skin prickling with salt-induced discomfort. The horses, too, were feeling it. They were showing the strain of the continual drive in the heat and were beginning to tire.

Banning could not forget Ben Mitchell's accusing words, and time and again he carefully searched his heart and soul, seeking to assure himself that what the man had said was untrue. It was no matter of personal revenge and satisfaction. Had Dave not been a victim of the gang's guns, he would have acted and done the same. They seemed to forget it was his job, that it was what was expected of him. Perhaps he was wrong in that he pressed the men of the posse too hard. It could be he asked too much of them. But he was asking no more of them than he had a right to expect—or thought he did. That is where he could be wrong, he concluded. None of them was a lawman or had ever had any such experience. Nor was any of them particularly adept with guns. They were merchants, clerks, businessmen. Only Valdez, who had punched cattle and done a considerable amount of knocking about, was in any way qualified to be a member of such a posse. And Valdez was no certain bet. He was a strange one, as apt to turn about and leave in the next moment as he was to continue on, caring little what anyone else thought or said.

Some of those who had begun the chase were sincere in their intentions, some were not. He thought then of Milo Morgan. The storekeeper was as transparent as that new window he had installed. All things he did were for a purpose. And they added up to one thing—the furtherance of prestige and the standing of Milo Morgan in the community. He was compelled, as one of the town's leading citizens, to be a member of the posse. It was expected of him, and he missed no opportunity to fulfill that obligation. But at the first well-presented moment he would take himself off the hook, just as he had done. His purpose had been served; he had ridden bravely out with the posse in pursuit of a bloodthirsty gang of killers, and the picture had been established in the minds of the citizenry. Therefore, the matter was closed, and it was time to return. Just how he would explain that action to the townspeople Banning was not sure. But it would be explained, and to no discredit of Milo Morgan. You could be sure of that.

They were coming again to an arroyo, one much wider but of less depth than the other. Banning rode on to the edge and there lifted his hand in a signal to stop. The wash was completely open, an ideal place for a trap. Anyone who tried to cross over would be an easy target if there were men hidden in the thick brush on the far side. Clinginbell and Snapp swung up beside him, saying nothing. A few moments later the vaquero sidled in. Snapp reached for Banning's canteen and took a short pull from it.

"We still on the trail?" he asked.

Banning said: "Back on the three men now. Lost the man who was alone." He pointed to the spread of prints in the loose sand of the arroyo.

"They split up, that it?"

"Have been ever since back there where Schweitzer was shot. The man who took his horse never has joined up with the others."

"He could be hanging back, waiting for a good chance to pot us," Clinginbell said, glancing around. "Like he did the Dutchman."

Valdez, a wisp of a brown-paper cigarette hanging from his thin lips, his rolled-brim Mexican hat pushed to the back of his head, said calmly: "*Señores,* I leave you here."

Banning had been studying the hoof prints, which followed a straight line across the sandy arroyo and entered the thick brush on the opposite side, and he heard Valdez but did not look around. He stifled the sudden lift of anger the *vaquero*'s words had aroused in him and accepted the weary, hopeless sort of resignation that took its place. There was little use, little point in trying to hold the party together now.

Clinginbell's voice said: "In other words, you're pulling out. Scared, is that it?"

"Of course," Valdez replied. "Only a fool would not be. Soon the jackals will tire of running. They will stop, will hide themselves in the brush. Then they will use their guns. It will be at such a place as this. Death comes for a man soon enough in this life, *amigos.* I have no wish to hurry it along."

"That's sure what we're doing," Snapp said morosely. "We're just asking for it."

"Then why the hell don't you pull out with him?" Banning demanded savagely, whirling about in his saddle. "About all you and the rest of this posse have done since we started is bellyache. You're supposed to be men . . . deputized lawmen, in fact . . . but you haven't got the guts of a prairie dog. You think I'm liking this any better than you? You think I'm enjoying this riding up ahead, making myself an easy target for that bunch? You're damn' well right I don't. But it's something that has to be done. Those killers have got to be caught. They've got to be shot down or hauled back to swing from a rope. And it's our job to do it whether you like it or not. Now, you make your choice. Either ride on back or stick with me."

"Nobody is going to blame us if we quit now," Snapp said. "We ain't more than a few miles from the desert. You sure don't figure to keep going then?"

"What difference does that make?"

"Plenty, to my way of thinking. We ain't got enough water, for one thing. And my horse sure ain't in no condition to try crossing it."

Banning smiled thinly. "A man can find an excuse for anything," he said, and squared back around in his saddle.

He touched the buckskin with spurs and headed off to the left, sick clear through of the constant bickering and eternal opposition. He rode slowly along the arroyo, not looking back, no longer caring. He continued on to a point where the wash narrowed, affording a safer crossing since it was not close to the trail left by the outlaws. If they were waiting on the far side, as the *vaquero* had suggested, he would be spoiling their hopes for an easy shot.

He crossed over without event and came onto the opposite bank. One thing was persistently nagging at his mind, and had bothered him for some time—where was the fourth outlaw? It was dangerous to have him off somewhere to himself; at any moment he might materialize, and Banning, bent upon following the others, could be caught unaware and be under the man's gun before he could move to defend himself. And it could be a plan, one designed to trap him in between the two factions. There had to be some reason why the man had not rejoined the others.

He walked the buckskin along the rim of the arroyo, carefully watching the ground for tracks. He was heading back to the point where he could again pick up the trail of the three riders. He had to stay with that one definite lead. This he would do, taking his chances on the fourth man.

He reached the spread of tracks, made a brief search of the brush adjacent to assure himself the outlaws were not hiding there, and moved back to the edge of the arroyo. He threw his glance across the sandy breadth, to where he had left the last of the posse. There was no one there. Lifting his gaze, he was just in time to see the three of them disappearing into the fringe of a clearing some distance beyond. They had all pulled out on him.

Banning sat there in the dappled shade of a tamarack and considered the hand that had been dealt him. A vague anger moved through him, cording the muscles of his jaw into hard, bulging lines. He guessed he had known all along it would end up this way, that in the finish he would be going it alone. Well, perhaps it was better that way. Now he could handle it as he pleased, do as he willed without the necessity of thinking about other men. Actually he preferred to work alone, but, when you were up against four such killers as the Wind River gang, you did need some help. He could forget that now, though. He was on his own. And, on his own, he would get the killers—the men who had killed Davey.

Banning mopped the sweat from his eyes with his forearm. Not long now until sundown. He moved on, keeping on the trail of the three outlaws, never once forgetting the fourth man, mysteriously separated and off somewhere by himself. The shadows were growing longer, deeper, making it more difficult to watch the surrounding areas. Alone now, he could move with greater care and much less noise.

The ground became sandier as he drew nearer the desert. The leaf brush gave way to more clumps of greasewood and brier, and the tamarack thinned out. Smoke trees began to appear, their thin limbs ghostly gray in the diminishing light.

Near full dark he pulled up for a rest. The outlaws were still ahead, moving steadily. There was little doubt they were pointing straight into the desert. He got down to examine the tracks. It was well over a hundred miles across the desert, following the route they had chosen. He wondered if they were aware of that. Endless, tortuous miles of waterless sand and badlands where nothing existed but cacti and the small animals born to the terrible heat. No man in his right mind would attempt to cross at that point. Although such a direct line to the deceivingly distant blur of mountains, visible when the haze or intermittent dust storms did not hide them, seemed the shortest trail, it was, by far, the most dangerous. Those who knew and respected the desert swung southward, bearing always toward the low hills known as the Whitetails. There water was to be had, along with a smattering of shade from scrubby trees and brush. From that halfway point, completing the journey was not too great a risk.

Remounting the buckskin, Banning took a swallow from his canteen. It was little more than a quarter full, and he wished now he had taken time back in Yucca Flats to refill it. But it was no serious matter. By carefully hoarding it, he would have enough to carry him to the water hole in the Whitetails—if he were lucky.

He sat there in the shelter of the tamaracks, his broad face quiet as he located himself and renewed his familiarity with all the major landmarks. A man had to know where he was going, where he would be hours from any given point. Lost, there was small hope of coming out of the desert alive. Finally satisfied, he rode from the entanglement onto the edge of the desert. There he again halted, lined himself with the tracks of the outlaws, and started doggedly on after them. They continued on, taking a straight line for the center of the desert. He smiled grimly in the darkness. They were going to make it easier for him than he had hoped. By this time tomorrow, unless he was badly misjudging them, they would be easy pickings. Three of them anyway, he amended. The fourth man was yet to be accounted for.

The day's drilling heat had begun to break. Banning removed his hat and allowed the faint breeze to riffle through his dark, tangled hair. He unbuttoned the top half of his shirt and permitted the welcome coolness to bathe his lean body. It felt good at the moment, but he knew that within a few hours he would be pulling on his brush jacket and thinking about a fire.

The desert played with a man as though he were a child's toy; it crisped and blistered him during the daylight hours, then chilled his blood and put ice in his bones after dark. He reached a low hill, climbed to its summit and halted. He stood up in the stirrups and threw a long, searching glance ahead. Perhaps the outlaws had halted, had built themselves a fire. He looked for some time but saw nothing. Only the vast, far-flung darkness. He pushed on.

With the complete settling of night, the breeze lifted quickly and grew in force, sharp and cold. Banning was still keeping to the trail left by the outlaws, but it was becoming increasingly difficult to follow. Not only was the darkness making the imbedded prints almost impossible to see, gradually and surely the rising wind was wiping them away, covering them over with fine, loose sand.

By midnight he gave it up. On foot for that past hour, he led the buckskin down into a shallow ravine where an escarpment of lava rock offered some protection from the stinging sand. He halted there, building no fire to ward off the cold, but settled back, his shoulders against the wall of rough, black stone. The warmth of a small blaze would have felt good, but he would take no chances. He did not want the outlaws knowing they were being pursued farther.

This should be the last night of it. Come daylight, he would again take up the trail. It was invisible now, of course, but they were plainly following a definite pattern. They were hewing to that deceptive, fatal straight line leading to the mountains beyond the desert. They would not be traveling fast. Come noon that next day, after the sun had driven its merciless fingers into them for a full morning, they would be faltering. Their tired horses would be having hell's own hard time of it, and the men themselves, no better prepared for such a journey than they reportedly were, would be seeing their visions, chewing at their lips, and fighting their clothing. He should be catching up to them about that time. And by dark he should have them in his hands.

V

Banning was awake at the first pale streaks of dawn. The air was pointed, and he wished again he might build a small fire to drive the chill from his lank frame, but better judgment prevented him from doing so. He was too close to the end of the chase, too near a success to chance the outlaws seeing a wisp of smoke, however faint, trailing up into the sky. He hugged his brush jacket tighter to him, consoling himself with the thought that within an hour or so he would be more than warm enough.

He should be hungry, but the thought of food did not appeal to him. There were some strips of jerky in his saddle bags that he could use, but they were heavily salted. To eat them would instantly arouse thirst, and he was too short of water to indulge himself in that. He put the idea of forcing himself to eat aside. Later, when he reached the water hole, perhaps.

When it was light enough to see the surrounding country, he crawled to the top of the lava butte and did his scouting. It was early, with the heat haze yet to rise, and he could look out over the savage, rugged desert for miles. A man on horseback would be easily visible. He saw no one, nothing—only the endless flats and knolls; the sparse, wind-scoured, heat-blasted vegetation; the higher, smoothly sculptured dunes; the low, dark, pool-like areas, indicating deep hollows into which sunlight had not yet seeped. Four men were out there—somewhere. Three were together, as far as he knew, and one was alone. But in the end they would likely unite in one group. The immediate problem was to locate them all. That was the next move.

Banning swung slowly about, his eyes, set deeply beneath their shelf of overhanging brows, searching across the land in a patient, persistent way. The sunlight slanted against his face at that angle, accentuating the maul-like blockiness of his jaw, making the high cheek bones of his face more pronounced.

There was a wiry, whip-like strength to John Banning, an unyielding drive that came from years of being a lawman, of hunting, and, at times, being hunted. It stamped him boldly, mirroring the stubborn determination of his soul.

The outlaws were nowhere to be seen. But they were out there somewhere, hidden now by any one of the numberless sandy ridges or deep swales. And they would be moving on into the desert, heading for the mountains they believed offered sanctuary. But they would be wrong. They would never make it.

He turned away and started back down the butte to the ravine where he had spent the night. It was warming rapidly. In another hour the day's searing heat would rise, and once again the country would become a vast, brown cauldron, glittering and breathless beneath a burnished sky. He knew he should get mounted and put a couple of hours steady riding behind him before the heat grew too intense.

He saddled the buckskin and moved out, keeping to a low-running ridge that offered easier footing for the horse. He rode steadily, slicing deeper into the desert, feeling the heat rise and become more constricting with each succeeding mile. There was no trail to follow, only his firm belief that the outlaws were maintaining a straight course for the opposite rim of the desert where the faint, bluish hills held their promise of shade and water.

Sometime after noon, with the devastating heat searing deeply into his body, he halted in the filigree shade of a smoke tree. A rattlesnake, lying beneath a small ledge of rock, buzzed its warning, but Banning ignored it. The reptile was too wise to venture into the direct sun. Outside his small square of shade he knew certain death awaited him in the blistering rays.

A cloud of dust far to the north drew his attention. He studied it thoughtfully for some time. The yellowish cloud was too large for a single rider or a wagon to make. Or the outlaws, either. Yet it was thick and bunched, not trailing out in a long streamer as it should if it were a wagon train on the move. It could hardly be anything but a large group of riders, a dozen or so. Could it be another posse, one formed and led by the sheriff from Pattonville? Was he following the wrong trail?

That question hit him like a thunderbolt. It did not seem likely—and yet. . . . He mopped at the sweat lying heavily upon his forehead and squinted his eyes to cut down the glare. The trail the outlaws had left had been plain. Three horses striking directly into the heart of the desert. It was hardly possible they could have altered their course and swung that far north in the time that had elapsed. But he was not entirely convinced. He knew from experience that desperate men can accomplish fantastic things.

He unbuttoned the rest of his shirt and pulled the tail free of his belt. It was plastered to his skin, and separating the two gave him momentary relief. He took a swallow from the canteen, mentally cursing himself again for not refilling it before he left Yucca Flats. That lack of water, eventually, was going to play an important part in his plans, he knew. He could figure on one more day. Not much beyond that, for then the need for water would have to be satisfied. It was a good thing the buckskin had taken his fill that previous morning in town, before they had pulled out. Heat such as this dried out man and beast alike.

He leveled another glance at the distant pall of dust, the uncertainty of that turning him still. He shook his head. If he were wrong, then he would just have to be wrong. It was too late to make changes. He would stand by his judgment. He started on again, heading out across the burning flats, alive only with shimmering heat devils. He should be getting nearer to the outlaws. They could be traveling no faster than he; they, too, would have been compelled to halt that previous night when the wind had risen and the sand had begun to blow. Their lead had been trimmed considerably back in the tamarack breaks. Again that nagging question pressed him—could he be on a wrong trail? Could they have swung northward?

He fought it through his mind again, clinging doggedly to his original decision. It was not reasonable for them to have turned. When you came right down to figuring it, they could have swung east or even doubled back into the breaks, planning to hide out there until matters calmed some. They could be anywhere. He decided suddenly it made little difference, for he had no choice other than to move on, to keep looking.

His thoughts shifted then to the posse, now safely back in Yucca Flats. He had no strong feeling against those men now, only a sort of pity, perhaps a faint envy that they could so easily dismiss their obligations while the selfsame demands rode him with merciless fervor. He wondered how Schweitzer had fared, and he hoped the wound had not been serious, for he considered the Dutchman a friend of his. And Moss—had the crusty old banker died? And, as before, his mind swung to his nephew Dave. Dave was dead, too. Dave was gone, just as was Lucy. He had no one left now, and whether or not he came out alive after he met the Wind River bunch no longer seemed important. All that counted was that he overtake them, capture them—or kill them, if necessary. They had to pay for what they had done. They had to pay for Davey.

He pushed on, now bearing slightly southward, in the direction of the Whitetails. Whether that was a conscious move on his part he did not know, nor did he particularly care. The scalding heat was beginning to have its way with him. His mind wavered, was slightly fogged, and his vision was blurring. His clothing had become a sodden, sticky part of his body, and inside his boots his feet were pure fire.

He took another sip from the tepid water in the canteen, vaguely aware there was scarcely any left. Through slitted eyes he looked toward the Whitetails, still invisible to the south. It was a long way; mile piled upon desolate mile, hour upon endless hour across a seething, glittering world of hot sand, brittle weeds, and blistered rock. He brushed wearily at his eyes, trying to wipe away the sweat.

Late that afternoon he was on foot, leading the faltering buckskin. Thirst had been superseded by a desire only for relief from the glaring, merciless sun. A cloud passing in front of that unrelenting disc, momentarily shutting off its white hot shafts, would be one of God's dearest gifts, a small patch of shade no less wondrous than heaven itself. And night, when it came, would be like entering another world. Never again would he complain against the chill of the dark hours.

He was barely conscious of sundown, so insensible was he when it came. He grew gradually aware of a lessening in the brilliance around him, permitting him to open more widely his cramped-down, bloodshot eyes. The heat had slackened only slightly, but the sun was gone, the pitiless, crucifying rays that had spared him nothing had vanished. It was relief enough just being beyond reach of those driving, fierce lances, which had drilled into him like pointed, white-hot blades.

He halted below the rim of a dune, ankle deep in fine, loose sand. He sank down gratefully. The buckskin, head swung low, front legs spraddled, waited nearby. For a time John Banning was motionless while he fully enjoyed the surcease of movement, the good feeling of heat slowly draining from his spent body. After a time he began to revive. He rose and took a short pull from the canteen, then replaced the cap and shook the canteen thoughtfully. Only two or three swallows left, at most.

He rubbed at his face and neck, breaking the stiff sweat crust, and looked over the buckskin. Still not in too bad a condition, but another day such as the one now behind them and the horse wouldn't be good for much. He would have to hoard the horse's strength, just as he did the precious drops of water left in the canteen.

A breeze began to lift, blowing in from the north, sweeping light puffs of powdery sand about his feet. It felt good, its cooling waves brushing the last of the packed heat from his body and clothing. But he should move. The dune was no place to be if the wind got up again, as it had that previous night. He could, most likely, find a better place farther on, where the sand, shifting downwind, would not touch them. He took up the trailing reins of the buckskin and climbed on up to the top of the dune. The rim was no more than a dozen feet away. When he reached it, he came to a surprised halt.

A lone wagon stood at the bottom of the slope.

VI

Banning started down the long incline eagerly, the thought of water and food turning him light-headed. A woman was bending over a small fire, preparing the evening meal, and, when she heard him, she straightened up. He saw she was young and well-formed, despite the shapeless dress she wore. She had black, raven's-wing hair, and her face was a pale, serious oval as she turned to look at him.

"Lucy!"

The name exploded from his lips involuntarily. In the next instant he knew it was not Lucy—that it could not be. Lucy was far away in New Mexico, lost to him along with Dave and all other things he had once held dear. His frayed mind was playing tricks on him. But she did look very much like Lucy, he was forced to admit. The way she stood there, so grave, watching him come up. The same tilt of the head, the same level, blue eyes, a blue dark as night.

"Ma'am . . . ," he began, his breath coming in long drags, "I. . . ."

A man, a young man of perhaps nineteen or twenty, blond, with huge splotches of freckles marking his face, stepped suddenly from behind the wagon. He held a cocked rifle, leveled at Banning's breast.

Banning pulled up short. For a moment he stared at the gun's muzzle, and then he managed a grin. "No need for that."

"Keep your hands up!" the cowboy ordered.

He looked vaguely familiar to Banning. Lifting his arms in compliance, he raked through his memory for some clue.

"Move away from that horse."

Banning eased off the buckskin. Someone inside the canvas-covered wagon began to cough, a dry, wracking sound in the stillness. The girl glanced toward it, her eyes filling with worry and fear.

"Hurry, Chick," she urged, turning to the man with the rifle.

The cowboy stepped to the buckskin and jerked the canteen from the saddle horn. He shook it vigorously, the small amount of liquid inside it making only a faint sloshing noise.

"About empty, Missus Simmons."

"Might be a swallow or two," Banning said. "I was hoping I could get a little from you."

The points of the girl's shoulders went down perceptibly, and a deep hopelessness swept into her eyes.

"You're welcome to what's there," Banning continued, "and without the rifle."

She nodded briefly. Taking the canteen from Chick's hand, she went at once to the wagon. Banning heard her murmuring something to the person within. The coughing ceased, and after a short while she returned to the fire.

She motioned to the rifle in the cowboy's hands. "Do we still need that?" she asked, shuddering noticeably, as though the sight of the weapon appalled her.

Chick shrugged. He glared at Banning for a moment, apparently trying to fathom the big man's purpose, and then lowered the gun.

"Thank you for the water," the girl said. "It helped him a great deal."

Banning dropped his arms and walked a few steps nearer to her. He noted the gold wedding band on her finger. She was either the wife of Chick or the man inside the wagon. The latter, he decided, remembering the way the cowboy had addressed her earlier. He glanced about the camp.

"Some trouble here?" he asked, subconsciously pushing his own grim purpose to the background. Old habits die hard. Before he could realize what he was doing, he had injected himself into another's problems.

The girl nodded wearily. "We're lost. My husband is terribly sick. And we're out of water."

Banning considered the statement for a time. "You're a long way off the main trail. How come you to be this far north of it?"

"People we were traveling with stayed over at the last town. We went on. I thought I was on the right road, but somehow I got off it."

She made no reference to Chick. He glanced to the cowboy, and she caught the question in his eyes.

"He's Chick Adams. He came walking in this morning, early. His horse broke a leg sometime yesterday, and he was lost on the desert."

"No water, either?"

She shook her head. "Only a pair of saddlebags. I gave him the first drink he said he'd had in days."

Banning looked at her closely. She was a stranger to the desert country, he could see that. "Water you needed yourself," he commented.

She moved her small shoulders resignedly. "What else could I do? He had to have some water."

Banning said: "Everything has to have a little water in this country. But a man generally looks out for himself," he added, and swung his glance to the cowboy. "Do you have any idea where you are?"

Adams shook his head, wary and sullen. "Got myself twisted around. You know where the closest water is?"

Banning nodded. "Sure. There's a water hole in the White-tails. Couple of days off. Maybe three."

Some of the hard fierceness slipped from Chick Adams's face, and an expression close to friendliness came over it. "That's good news. Sure glad you came along."

The man inside the wagon began to cough anew. The girl sighed. "I'm afraid it's no use. We can't last that long."

Banning said nothing for a moment. Then: "As long as a man's alive, I reckon he's got a chance. The main thing is to keep on trying." He stopped and grinned. "Sounds a little like I'm preachin', I expect. My name is Banning. John Banning."

"I'm Ruby Simmons," the girl said, nodding to him. "It's my husband, Will, who is sick in the wagon. Where were you going when you came into our camp?"

"Looking for four men. You happen to see anybody today? Maybe off in the desert somewhere?"

"We've seen nobody. Only Chick and now you. I don't think anything else can live in this terrible, hard land."

"Where were you headed when you got lost?"

"For Nevada."

Banning said—"Long drive."—and looked away. The coming of night was bringing its welcome coolness, and he felt better already. He watched Ruby Simmons go to her knees and stir at the pan, frying meat and potatoes. The smell of the food set up a strong hunger within him.

Without looking up she asked: "Have you been traveling all day?"

"Since sunrise. Looks like you've done about the same."

"We have, but we've not come far. It's so terribly slow."

Banning eyed the wagon critically. "It'd be better if you'd do your moving at night. Easier on the horses. On you and your husband, too. Hold over in the day while the heat is so bad."

He stepped to the side of the Simmons team, admiring them. Once they had been a fine, matched pair. Now the rigors of the land had changed them into gaunt, worn beasts, suffering badly in the dry atmosphere and heat. He looked them over carefully. With luck and a great deal of care, they might make it to the Whitetails.

"You think we ought to travel on tonight?" Ruby was at his elbow. He had not heard her approach, and he wheeled swiftly. The suddenness of his move startled her. She sprang back and her lips parted quickly, revealing even, white teeth, while her eyes spread into wide circles of alarm.

The nearness of her, the resemblance to Lucy sent a strong hunger coursing through John Banning. The terrible events of the last days were swept from his mind. He felt an almost uncontrollable urge to seize the girl, crush her in his arms, and kiss her full, sweet lips. But cold reality laid its restraint upon him, cautioning him, bringing him back to the present. "Sorry," he muttered, the tautness leaving his body slowly.

The frightened look left her face. "Are you all right, Mister Banning?"

He grinned. "Nothing wrong. I'm a little quick when I hear a sound, I reckon. And just call me John."

"You probably need something to eat," Ruby said. She turned to the fire. From the skillet she filled a plate for him, and laid a thick slice of bread along its edge. Handing it to him, she smiled.

"No coffee to go with this. One of the penalties of having no water."

He said his thanks. "This will do fine. After I'm finished, I'll look to your horses. I always like to pay my fare."

Chick Adams, silent through it all, took a share of food from the frying pan. Ruby, a third plate in her hand, entered the wagon. Banning could hear her coaxing her husband, trying to get him to eat. And he heard the man's grumbling, fretful refusal.

Glancing at Adams, Banning said: "Pretty tough on a woman."

The cowboy nodded. "Got any ideas how to help?"

"Maybe," Banning replied. He finished with the plate and set it near the fire. He reached into his shirt pocket and dug out a sack of tobacco and a fold of papers. His badge, carried there as a rule, came with it as the pin snagged the muslin bag. It fell to the ground between the two men.

Banning watched as Chick Adams's sunburned features slowly changed. He let the badge lie for a minute, then idly picked it up and returned it to his pocket.

"Smoke?" he asked, offering the makings to the cowboy.

Adams wagged his head. He placed his unfinished meal on the ground and got slowly to his feet. A tenseness had come over him, tightening his face, turning him alert and watchful.

Banning eyed him from the cover of his hat brim. Something about Chick Adams disturbed him. Something did not seem just as it should. With the fingers of his right hand, Banning spun up a thin shaft of tobacco. Moistening the edge of the paper, he smoothed it and placed it between his lips. He reached into the fire for a burning twig. Holding the small flame against the cigarette, he puffed slowly. When it glowed, he dropped the brand and took a deep drag.

Exhaling, he looked directly at the cowboy. "Adams, just

what did happen to that horse of yours?"

VII

Chick Adams snatched up the rifle he had leaned against a greasewood clump and backed hastily away. He leveled the gun at Banning.

"I'm not answering any of your questions," he said in a low voice.

At that moment Ruby Simmons came from the wagon. She hesitated, noting the crouched shape of Adams, the ready rifle in his hands, the calm, indolent figure of Banning resting on his heels near the fire.

"What . . . what is it? What's wrong?"

"This jasper's a lawman," Adams said. "Saw his badge there a minute ago."

Ruby stared blankly at the cowboy. "Suppose he is? What has that got to do with us?"

Adams's taut shape relaxed a notch. He lowered the rifle, apparently suddenly remembering that in John Banning lay his sole hope for water—and life. He forced a grin. "Reckon I'm sort of jumpy."

"Some men get jumpy real easy," Banning commented dryly. He was still trying to fit Chick Adams in somewhere. The possibility of his being one of the outlaws, the missing fourth member, had presented itself earlier. But somehow that did not seem right. He had turned up too far south. The man who had taken Carl Schweitzer's horse would have pushed on in a westerly direction, planning to join up with the other outlaws. No, he concluded after considering it, it was not likely. The fourth man would have kept on until the gang was once again all together. They would remain in a group until they crossed the desert. They would need each other. After they reached the mountains, if they did, they could be expected to split up as a means for avoiding suspicion drawn to them as a group. The answer probably was that Chick Adams was on the dodge, right enough, but for some other reason. That accounted for his seeming to be familiar; somewhere there had been a Wanted dodger on him. No, the outlaws were still out there on the desert somewhere.

Ruby Simmons broke the long silence. "I'm certain Mister Banning isn't the least interested in us, Chick."

Her voice was stiff, and Banning could detect a faint thread of resentment, as though she had decided his coming meant only more care and trouble for her, after all. He glanced at her sharply. Her nerves were whetted to a knife blade's edge, and close to the breaking point.

"That's right," Banning said, rising. "Got other things to be thinking about." He tossed his dead cigarette into the fire. "Reckon I'd better see to your horses."

"There's a little hay left in the back of the wagon," she said, turning to her dishes. "You're welcome to some for yours."

Banning said—"Obliged."—and moved off.

He unsaddled the buckskin and removed the bridle, leaving only a short length of rope trailing from the hackamore. He led the animal to where the Simmons team, still in harness, was munching at the hay. Throwing down a handful for the buckskin, he started to remove the team's leather.

Ruby walked to where he stood. "You said something about traveling at night," she reminded him. She was very cool and proper, keeping her words on a business-like level. Apparently he had been right. The incident with Adams had not pleased her. Anger stirred through John Banning.

"Now, look here, Missus Simmons . . . I don't aim to cause you any trouble. . . ."

"Of course," she cut in quickly. "Now, about traveling tonight."

Banning gave her serious face a brief glance. "No chance," he said, shaking his head. "They need some rest. Might try it tomorrow night. When a team doesn't get water, it needs more rest. It's a good thing you've got that hay. It'll help some. Is there an old sack or blanket around I can have to rub them down with?"

Ruby frowned. "Rub the horses down?"

"Sure. Get all the sweat and caked dust off them. They'll stay cooler if they're clean."

She brought him a worn, coarse blanket, and stepped aside to watch. He wadded the cloth into a pad and set himself to scrubbing the horses. After a few minutes' work their coats began to gleam dully in the half light. They had perked up perceptibly when he finished, and she noted this right away.

"My father used to do that with our horses, back in Saint Louis. I never thought about doing it out here. Always thought it was just for appearance's sake." She stepped up close to one of the blacks. "If we only had some water for them," she said, rubbing the animal's neck.

"They'll be all right for another day or so. Horses can stand a lot when they have to," Banning assured her. He had turned to the buckskin and was scrubbing him with the blanket.

"Then . . . you think we have a chance of getting through?" Her voice faltered slightly.

"Sure," he replied at once. "You'll make it."

She laid her hand on his arm, drawing his direct attention to her. "The truth, John," she insisted quietly.

He ceased his work on the buckskin. "It'll be a hard go," he admitted. "The horses aren't in too bad a shape. The problem will be your husband. Sounded to me like he was pretty bad."

"He is," she said, lowering her eyes. "We should never have gone on alone. When the Robersons were with us, they helped. We shared provisions and water, and it was sort of like a family affair. I see now it was a mistake not to wait over for them. But Will wanted to push on. I think he feels that every day counts, that he doesn't have too much time left in which to reach Nevada."

"Sick people sometimes understand more than others think," Banning said softly. "A sort of second sight."

Ruby's tone was once again friendly. Banning studied her quiet face. She was so small, so slender, yet completely self-sufficient and courageous. The memory of Lucy moved through him again. She had been much like this Ruby Simmons. The urge to help her, to share her great burden, came upon him suddenly. He should stay with her and her dying husband, guide them, at least, to the water hole in the Whitetails. Once there, they could rest and lay over until another westbound wagon came along. She could not do it alone, he knew. And it wasn't much to ask of himself.

In the next moment that selfsame recollection of Lucy brought him sharply back to his own duty, to the need for completing the job he had undertaken. Each hour he spent helping the Simmonses placed him that much farther away from the outlaws. If he waited, taking the time to guide Ruby and her husband to the water hole in the Whitetails, his chances for capturing the outlaws, and avenging Davey and the others, would steadily diminish. Time was what counted now. The outlaws had to be overtaken, brought to justice one way or another. It was his sworn duty—and his own promise to himself.

In a rough voice, he said: "I wish I could help you some, but I've got to keep moving. Come morning, I'll have to pull out."

She said—"Oh."—in a faint, despairing way.

"Were I you, I'd start early myself. Drive until it gets hot, say about noon. Then stop and rest out the day. After dark you can start up again. Do that and your team will be able to go all night."

"Go! Go where?" she cried. Her words were an exhausted drag in the quiet. "We can't make it across the desert without water. You know that."

An idea came to John Banning. He paused in his work over the buckskin. Chick Adams. He was the answer. The man could not be trusted, that was certain. But he could be forced into helping the Simmonses.

"You'll be heading for water," he said. "I'll give you a map showing you how to reach the Whitetails."

Hope sprang into her voice, but she guarded it carefully, as though fearing to believe what he had said. "You think we can make it?"

"With this man Adams driving and helping you along. And if you don't try to make it too fast. That's a fine pair of blacks, but you'll have to take it easy with them."

"And the map. . . ."

He turned to her, his face serious. "One thing you've got to understand," he said, thinking of the cowboy, "is that I'm giving *you* the map. You're to keep it to yourself. Don't let him have it. You do the looking at it."

She studied his stern features. "You don't trust Chick, do you?"

"Not at all," he said flatly. "I figure he'll stay around and help you so long as he has good reasons. Let him get his hands on the map I'll draw up and he'll steal one of your horses and light out quick."

She was shocked, and she showed it. "He wouldn't do such a terrible thing. He couldn't . . . knowing what it would do to us. Why, we'd die here, stranded without our team. Nobody could do that to someone else."

Banning gave her a twisted grin. "You're a long way from Saint Louis. A mighty long way from polite talk and kind ways and gentle sort of living. Out here a man like Chick Adams stays alive the best way he can. And, if he has to hurt somebody doing it, then it's too bad for them. He won't stop to ask what's right and decent and what's wrong."

Ruby shook her head slowly, disbelievingly. "People mostly are good. And kind."

"If it suits them. If it doesn't happen to go against their own interests."

She waited a long minute before answering. Then: "I think you've lost all faith in others, John. Whatever it was that caused it must have been a terrible thing. I'm sorry. And I'm sorry to see you leave."

"I've got a job to do," he said, strangely upset by the regret in her tone. "You'll be all right, as long as you keep Adams trailing along with you. He's on foot and needs water. He'll stick with you until he finds some."

She said: "Of course. I was wrong to hope you might come with us. I guess I had already begun to lean on you. I'm grateful, John, for the things you have done."

"Forget it," he said. "Now, get me a pencil and a piece of paper and I'll draw up that map."

They returned to the center of the camp, passing before the open front of the wagon. Banning glanced inward, but the shadows were so deep he could distinguish nothing. Ruby left him and climbed inside. He continued on to the fire and there tossed in more branches to rekindle the low flames. He glanced about for Adams. The cowboy was not around, was probably off somewhere in the night. That was good.

Ruby was back in a few moments, bringing with her a ruled writing tablet and a stub of pencil. Banning took it from her and squatted down before the fire. He began to outline a crude map of the area.

"I'll put in the landmarks I can remember for you to go by," he explained. "You sort of fix them in your mind."

She was very close to him, kneeling beside him with her shoulder touching his own. A stray wisp of her dark hair brushed against his cheek.

"You won't see those Whitetail hills until you are close to them. Don't get an idea you're lost or going in the wrong direction. They're not much more than piles of rock. But there's a good water hole and some shade you can rest in while you wait."

"I see," she murmured.

"And don't let Adams get in a hurry and push the team too hard. Rest them often. The main thing is to get there."

Banning completed the map. It was not a good one, insofar as accuracy was concerned. It had been a long time since he'd been through the country, but the map would take them to the water hole by the shortest possible route. That was the important thing. He tore the sheet from the tablet and handed it to her.

Her eyes were bright in the fire glow. "I don't know how to thank you, John. If you hadn't come along, I don't know what we would have done."

The faint breeze, cool and refreshing, fanned the flames to stronger light. Looking at her, he thought again how like Lucy she was.

"Forget it," he said. "And don't worry. Everything will work out right."

He glanced about, drawn by some small sound. Chick Adams was standing behind them, having come into the fan of light silently and unnoticed. He was looking over Ruby's shoulder at the map.

"Does that show the way to water?" he asked.

Banning got to his feet, his hand at Ruby's elbow, assisting her to rise, also. He nodded to the cowboy's question. "All set so's you can start in the morning. You'll do the driving."

"What about you?"

"I'll be moving out. It'll be up to you to see these folks get to the water hole."

Adams said: "Good enough." He extended his hand for the map. "Reckon I ought to study it some, get it straight in my head."

"No need," Banning replied coolly. "Missus Simmons will take care of it. All you have to do is drive. She'll keep you moving in the right direction."

Adams stared at Banning, his features stiff with suppressed anger. He shrugged. "Just as you say."

Ruby folded the map into a small square. Reaching up, she tucked it inside the bodice of her dress, down into the hollow between her breasts. Smiling at Banning, she turned and walked quickly to the wagon.

VIII

"Will, oh, Will, we're going to be all right. We have a map showing the way to water."

Will Simmons heard the sound of his wife's voice and caught the note of gladness and relief in it. He stirred. With an effort he pulled himself to one elbow and forced a smile to his pinched lips. Now, if only the damned coughing wouldn't start. Let Ruby have a few minutes of hope and happiness. God knew she had seen mighty little of either since their marriage.

She appeared at the end of the wagon. The fire threw its flickering glow against her, shadowing and highlighting her lovely features. He realized again in that moment, just as he had always known, that she was the most beautiful woman he had ever seen.

"We're going to make it now," she murmured, crawling along the pallet to his side. "Our worries are almost over."

"Of course," he said, patting her shoulder tenderly. "It will all work out, just as we planned."

"John . . . John Banning has to ride on in the morning. He is a lawman or something, and is hunting for some men. But he drew us a map that will take us to water."

"I heard most of what he said," Simmons told her. "What about the horses? Can they stand the trip?"

"He thinks they will if we're careful with them. You should see them, Will. He worked so hard over them. Rubbed them down like Father used to do. And cleaned their hoofs. They're like a new team, almost."

"Banning seems to be quite a man," Simmons murmured, unable to keep the slight edge out of his voice. "What about that other fellow . . . Chick, or whatever his name is?"

"He will stay with us and do the driving. I'm not to let him see the map. John says it's the only way we can keep him with us."

Simmons nodded. Evidently this Banning was no fool. He swallowed hard, feeling the beginning of another coughing spell. "Call your new friend. I'd like to express my thanks."

He felt, rather than saw, Ruby's eyes searching his face. She had detected the irony in his voice. He had not meant it to be there; it was only—well, he was so damned helpless, so utterly dependent here in this huge land of strong men. Ruby pulled away silently to the end of the wagon. She called to Banning, and a moment later he was there, his wide shoulders nearly blocking the opening.

Get it over with . . . before the coughing starts. Simmons swallowed again. "Banning," he said, "I'd like to shake your hand. My wife tells me you've solved our big problem. I want you to know I'm grateful."

Banning ducked his head. "I don't know as I've done that, but I'm glad I can help. Once you reach the Whitetails, I figure the most of your problems will be licked."

Simmons said—"A great favor."—and settled back on his pad. He closed his eyes. "Now, if you two will excuse me. I seem a bit tired."

Banning murmured—"Good luck."—and left the end of the wagon. Ruby still hovered about Simmons, worrying and fussing over him, as a woman will do. He was torn between two desires—to keep her there with him by his side, but also to have her leave and be away from him when he got another bad coughing seizure.

"I feel like sleeping," he said, watching her through half-shut eyes. It was hard to talk. His throat was so terribly dry. That last swallow of water from the canteen Banning had given Ruby had helped. But this was no ordinary thirst burning through his body, he knew. "No use staying in here, Ruby. Go outside where it's cooler."

"But, you. . . ."

"I'm all right."

He felt her lips brush against his forehead, no longer on the lips, as once it had been. The doctor in St. Louis had cautioned them on that. Never again on the lips. He heard her make her way from the wagon and listened while she said something to John Banning.

His voice was solid and deep. "I think I'll take a walk to the top of the sand dune. I'd like to look around a bit."

Simmons waited out the minute, wondering whether Ruby had accompanied the big man. A twinge of jealousy ripped at his heart. Damn John Banning! Damn all the tall, wide-shouldered, animal-healthy men who showed up to help Ruby! Did she often wish she had someone like this Banning for a husband instead of a sickly, wasted invalid such as himself? He had been of no earthly good to her for over two years now—not to her or himself. And day by day he had grown worse, turning thinner and weaker until he was scarcely more than a skeleton.

Could he blame her for thinking of another? Ruby deserved better. She was a beautiful girl, with the natural, normal desires of all women. She wanted a home, to have children; she needed a strong, whole man for a husband, to love and take care of her. He had given her none of those things. His dowry had been worry and grief and bitterly hard work. A man ought to die before allowing himself to drag his woman down to such slavery.

Someone was moving about outside, near the wagon. Probably that shifty-eyed fellow, Chick. Simmons had decided, in that sudden, impulsive way of the very ill, that he did not like Adams. He was sorry the cowboy was to be a factor in their journey to safety. But a beggar could not be a chooser.

"Ruby?" He placed his question, half hopefully.

She replied at once, sending a stream of relief through him. She had not gone to the top of the dune with Banning, after all. When, oh, when would he learn to trust her? Why couldn't he admit, and believe, she could never do anything cheap and common and wrong? He groaned; it was only because he was so helpless that he often thought of her doing things she would not want him to know. And he could not blame her if she did. He punished himself with that thought. After all, she was still young, and only human. But to think of her in the arms of another man nearly set him wild.

"What is it, Will?"

"Nothing," he replied, coughing a little now. "Just wondered where you were."

"Would you like for me to light the lantern and read for a while?"

"Not tonight. Plenty of time for that when we are waiting at the water hole."

He heard her resume whatever task it was she had been pursuing. It would be different when they reached his brother's place in Nevada. She wouldn't have to do all this hard work then. They all said he could get well there, too. And that was what he wanted most—to get his health back and live a man's life again. In his own mind he believed it, and he knew Ruby believed it, but lately a new question had been posing itself before him with each succeeding sunrise. Could he hold out that long? Could he muster enough strength to stay alive until the journey was over?

He hoped so, and each day he girded himself for the fight to accomplish that end. He had to make it. For Ruby's sake as well as his own. The thought of her stranded there on the unfriendly desert, alone, prey for any passing outlaw or depraved scoundrel, nearly drove him out of his mind at times. He couldn't let that happen to her! But deep in his mind persistent, grave doubts had begun to settle there. A man could be determined, but there were always other, powerful factors to be considered.

Lately his coughing had seemed different—more submerged and wracking. Sometimes he felt as though he were on the verge of heaving up everything inside him. And there were those times when his mind wasn't exactly right. Some sort of fever, he guessed. But it was welcome. It acted as a kind of anesthetic, obliterating the dull, gnawing pains in his chest and filling his head with all manner of strange but good memories.

At times he saw himself walking down the brick-paved streets of St. Louis, feeling the rain beating lightly at his face, so cool and refreshing. And there was always the smell of lilacs, sweet and heady on a spring night. Now and then he would hear the clang of a horse car's bell or the lonely hoot of a steamboat carving a furrow up the thick, lazy Mississippi. Always such dreams ended the same. He became abruptly and cruelly aware of his actual whereabouts. He was once again facing reality in the wagon, with the pitiless heat pressing him down, constricting his throat and draining his wasted body of its meager strength. Ruby would be there watching anxiously over him, and beyond her, beyond the arched end of the canvas cover, would be the same empty, brassy sky in which no cloud ever appeared. And, as the dream came and went, he found himself each time more reluctant to return to reality. It was strange.

Hell! A man would be better off dead! He ought to dig down under his pallet and pull out the old ten-gauge shotgun Ruby's father had given him for the trip and blow his damned head off. That would solve his misery, put an end to all pain and worry. He groaned softly, thinking of that. But to do so would leave Ruby at the mercy of the desert and its brutality.

Banning climbed the slope with one purpose in mind—to take a long look at the desert for the sign of a campfire. A glow somewhere out in the night could mean the location of the outlaw camp. In the morning he would saddle the buckskin and be on his way. He would now, of necessity, have to swing by the water hole, but that would not cost too much time. The need for water was urgent. He and the buckskin were good for one more day, perhaps. After that it would be dangerous.

He should make the Whitetails by night, if he got away early. It would be a long, full day's ride, traveling slow, but it would be foolhardy to press the little horse. Once he was down he would never get up, and Banning's hopes for catching up with the outlaws would be lost. Of course, there was always the chance the outlaws knew of the water hole and also were heading now for that same point. If so, it would be a fortunate break. But John Banning had learned long ago that few things came so easy, and that depending upon good fortune generally produced only disappointments.

He gained the top of the dune and stopped. The inside of his mouth was like cotton; the long hike up through the loose sand had whetted his thirst to greater intensity. He reached down, plucked a small stone from the sand, and thrust it into his mouth, doing what he had done many times before to ease a craving for water. The pebble would start a flow of saliva and bring some relief.

Sitting down on the rim of the dune, he began a long, probing search of the widely flung desert, darkly beautiful now under a shroud of night. Faint star shine illuminated the land, lending it a weird, magic glow that turned the harsh browns and bleached grays of the sunlit hours to pale silvers and dull golds.

He remained there on the ridge for some time, probing the dark world before him. He saw no signs of a camp, near or distant. The outlaws were keeping themselves well hidden. But they were out there somewhere, he assured himself again. And he would find them, bring them to an accounting. After that, what? Stay in Yucca Flats? Continue to be the lawman for a town that cared little for his problems or whether he lived or died? There was little reason to do so now, with Davey gone, too.

Ruby Simmons had stirred his thoughts of Lucy. She had awakened all the old, long-reaching hungers inside him that had, for so many years, remained silent. He was glad he was to move on with the sunrise. When he was near Ruby, he found it hard to keep his thinking straight, harder still to keep from reaching out, touching her. He was a strong man, of this he was fully aware, but he also knew he had possessed little strength where Lucy had been concerned, and with Ruby Simmons it was no different. He was thinking of that when her scream, racing up the slope to him, brought him to his feet and sent him plunging off the ridge.

IX

John Banning went down the grade in lurching, ten-foot strides. Loose sand clutched at his boots, threatening to trip him up and set him to staggering like a drunken man, but he plunged recklessly on. Ruby's screams were continuous, and that spurred his heedless, stumbling pace.

When he drew nearer, he made out two figures struggling in the fire's half light. One was Ruby. Her hair had come down and was streaming out behind her. The other form was that of a man. Sudden fear clawed at Banning. *The outlaws!* was his first, impulsive thought. They had come across the camp and, finding Ruby unprotected and seemingly alone, were taking their ruthless advantage of her. A curse ripped from his lips. If they had harmed her, he would make them pay doubly. That they outnumbered him did not enter his mind; that there would be four guns to his one found no consideration. His head was filled only with the girl's cries for help.

"Ruby!" he yelled as his feet struck the more solid earth at the bottom of the slope.

The figure of the man pulled free of the girl. A flare of fire struck across his face. Chick Adams! Banning lunged straight for him, a furious anger lashing him to blindness. Ruby, disheveled, dress ripped, staggered off beyond the fan of light and fell.

From inside the wagon Will Simmons was calling out hoarsely: "Ruby? Ruby? What's the matter?"

Banning closed with the weaving shape of Adams. The cowboy darted to one side, seeking to drive a down-swinging blow to Banning's head. Banning saw it coming and lurched away. His clawing fingers snatched at Chick, caught the man's shirt front, and dragged him off balance. Banning spun on a heel and drove his right hand, wrist deep, into Chick's belly. The man buckled, and wind exploded from his flared lips. Banning straightened him up with a left and folded him back over with a whistling right.

Adams, sucking loudly for breath, flung both his arms about Banning. They went off balance together and crashed to earth.

Locked tightly, they rolled back and forth, Banning endeavoring to break the powerful clamp binding his arms to his sides. He butted with his head, but Adams jerked away, protecting himself. Banning brought his knee up, aiming for the cowboy's groin. Adams twisted aside and took the wicked blow on his hip.

Then Banning felt the hot coals of the fire against his neck and shoulder. The pungent odor of singeing hair curled into his nostrils at the identical moment flames licked at his bare skin. He howled, and with a mighty heave broke Adams's locked hands apart and rolled away. Chick was after him like a silent cat, reaching for his legs. Banning lashed out, a wide-swinging, backhanded blow. It caught the cowboy across the bridge of his nose, stalling him momentarily. Banning, again rolling, bounded to his feet and whirled.

Adams was already there. He caught Banning by one foot and pulled back hard. Banning went down once again. In a flash Adams was upon him, pinning him flat with his weight. Both men were gasping for breath, mouths opened wide, eyes bulging from the strain. Adams, one arm free, struck with deadly regularity at Banning's exposed jaw. Banning wrestled the cowboy and tried to overturn him, but failed. A solid blow caught him on the ear. Lights danced before his eyes, and his head rang. He realized his strength was fading fast, that he could not take many more such blows. He must act quickly or Adams would have him out of the fight. He sucked in a deep breath. With all the strength he could gather in his straining body, he twisted himself under Chick's weight. He managed to roll to one side. Adams, feeling the taste of victory, hammered away. Reaching up, Banning grabbed for the cowboy's long hair. His fingers found purchase, and he closed them tight and pulled hard.

Adams yelled and toppled. Banning, spinning, was on his

knees and out from under the cowboy almost before he had stopped falling. From that crouched position, Banning drove a knotted right fist into Adams's face, then saw him go back and out to full length. Banning lunged forward, across Chick's prone body. He drove the cowboy flat again as he tried to rise. Adams groaned and tried to crawl away.

Banning flung a glance at Ruby. She was near the end of the wagon, just beyond the sputtering fire's glow. Will Simmons had ceased his frantic calling, the sight of her at the end of the vehicle having apparently eased his mind. Her face was set, intent, as she watched the fight.

"John! Look out!"

Her voice brought Banning wheeling about to meet Chick Adams again. The cowboy was crouched, both hands still on the ground, like a runner beginning a race. Banning moved toward him, ready to finish the fray, once and for all time. Adams's hands came together, palms outward, in a scooping motion. Banning checked his forward movement and staggered back, his eyes blinded and suddenly burning from the fine sand that had been thrown into them. His mouth was full, his sweaty face and neck plastered over. He brushed at the gritty particles angrily, cursing himself for having been caught unaware. He should have expected some such trick from Adams. A wild yell erupted then from the cowboy, now little more than a vague shadow weaving across his hampered vision.

"No!" Ruby screamed, jarring him badly. "No!"

Immediately there was a blast of gunfire, a bright orange explosion only steps away. Banning felt the heat of the bullet graze his thigh. He hurled himself away, instinctively going down to lessen the target area he was presenting. His eyes were clearing, although each felt as though it were bedded in flame. He focused them on the dim shape of Adams, who was crouched just beyond the smoldering embers. Banning heard the overly loud click as a gun's hammer came back to cocked position. He dug into the sand and around in the brush, seeking a weapon of some sort—a rock or a length of wood, anything. There was nothing.

He continued to move, knowing his only hope for safety lay in offering the cowboy no target. Yet at such close range the man could scarcely miss. The deeper shadow of a larger and thicker clump of brush loomed up a dozen steps away. He dodged toward it.

Chick's voice came to him through the darkness. "Maybe you thought you had me, Marshal, but you're mighty wrong! You're a long ways from it. Ain't you nor nobody else ever taking me in. I'll stop you right now. . . ."

He never finished the sentence. A rifle cracked through the night. Banning twisted about and looked at the wagon. Ruby was holding the heavy gun Banning had seen earlier in Adams's hands. She levered another cartridge into the chamber and moved nearer to him. She was no more than an arm's length away.

The cowboy yelled as the bullet caught him somewhere in the body. His dim shape staggered back a long, awkward step. He spun halfway about and went down to one knee. He was up almost at once, cursing and screaming in a wild voice. Banning saw him level his gun at Ruby. He yelled a warning at the girl, leaped to his feet, and threw himself against her. They went down together into the brush, just as Adams's gun roared again.

Banning disengaged himself from Ruby. He was still searching for his pistol, lost sometime in the fight. But there was no time to look then. He seized the rifle she had used and levered it, making certain it was still loaded. He crawled to one side, getting Ruby out of the line of fire. Adams was a faint, weaving shape a dozen yards away. Banning fired hastily. The bullet missed, ricocheted against a stone and sang off into the night.

Adams sent his answering shot as he lurched for the safety of the wagon. The bullet struck flat against the metal body of Banning's gun and slammed the weapon with shocking force against his head. Banning saw the angry explosion of sparks—and then the impact plunged him into complete blackness.

X

John Banning opened his eyes to the soft, indefinite profile of Ruby Simmons. She was on her knees beside him, her face like a delicately carved cameo in the starlight. She was watching something beyond the camp, off in the desert. She held the rifle ready in her hands, apparently unaware its mechanism had been damaged by Chick Adams's lucky shot.

Banning allowed a space of time to slip by. Cobwebs were still clouding his brain, but as the seconds passed and his senses once again became keen and alert, she continued to hold his attention. Her likeness to Lucy was startling; she was so calm, so capable, yet so beautiful. Will Simmons was fortunate to possess her love.

She glanced down and, seeing his open eyes, smiled and sighed deeply. Her shoulders relaxed their tense rigidity, and relief flowed through her like daylight spreading over night's shadows.

"Thank heaven, you're all right. I was afraid you were badly hurt."

Banning grinned and rubbed the side of his head ruefully. "I'm fine. That rifle really handed me a wallop when Chick's bullet hit it. I expect the rifle is a lot worse off than I am."

He pulled himself to a sitting position, setting off a momentary spinning in his head. He glanced at Ruby. She was staring at the weapon, not thoroughly understanding what was wrong.

"The bullet jammed the action," he explained. "No use to anybody now. What happened to Chick?"

"He took one of our horses and rode off into the desert. He was having a bad time of it. I think he was seriously hurt."

Banning thought for a moment. "How long was I knocked out?"

"Only a couple of minutes."

"He might still be near here. Reckon I'd better have a look around."

At once she touched his arm, delaying him. "Please . . . don't go far. Don't try to find him tonight. He could be out there, just waiting for you in the dark. And you wouldn't have a chance." She paused and shook her head slowly. "Anyway, I don't think he will hang around now. He got what he wanted."

Banning looked at her quickly. "What?"

"The map you drew for us. That's what he was after. When you left, he waited until you were on top of the hill and then asked to see it again. I refused, and he grabbed me. He tried to take it. That's when I started screaming. I tried to save it, but he was too strong for me."

Ruby trembled, filled with the frightful memory of those moments while she had struggled in the hands of the cowboy. Banning placed his arm about her shoulders and drew her close, comforting and quieting her as best he could. She remained that way, head touching his chest, breathing rapidly.

"Forget about it." He spoke gently. "Like you said, he's got what he wanted. He won't bother us again." She did not reply at once, but after a moment she said: "You were right about him, John. He wanted only what he could get from us. He didn't really want to help, just stay around as long as it suited his needs. And he left without giving us a thought." She began to tremble again. "What would have happened to Will and to me if . . . if that bullet had struck you instead of that gun . . . had killed you?"

"Don't you be thinking of that now," he said softly.

In his own mind he could not justify the actions of Chick Adams. Why had the cowboy been so anxious to possess the map immediately? What made it so important, so imperative, that he would manhandle a woman to get it—even resort to gun play? All he had needed to do was bide his time and soon he would find himself at the water hole. Was it the fear of a desperate fugitive expecting arrest at the hands of Banning, who he assumed to be a lawman? Was that his only reason?

It was the only one that made any logical sense to Banning. Adams, believing him to be on his trail, apparently thought he was being drafted into aiding the Simmonses, only to be taken into custody when the party reached the Whitetails. He had merely made his escape before that time arrived.

"Things are so different, here on the desert," Ruby was saying in a low, distant voice. "Nothing seems to have any value . . . not even life. I don't think I shall ever get used to it."

"You will in time," he replied. "And it won't seem so bad." Then, wishing to channel her thoughts into a different vein, he asked: "Was the map and a horse all Chick took?"

Ruby pulled away from him, her brow knitting into a small frown. "That was all, I think. Everything happened so fast. I saw him sort of stagger by the wagon. He was holding his saddlebags in one hand, the gun in the other. He crawled onto one of the horses and started off. He was having a hard time staying on."

Banning nodded. "Hit in the shoulder, I'd guess. Maybe even in the chest. Doubt if he will go far." He swung his gaze to the long reaching, shadowy depths of the desert. "Not much use looking for him. We'll wait until daylight. We've got to get that horse back."

He heard her soft sigh of relief and knew he had been right; she was afraid to have him away from the camp, afraid the cowboy might return while he was gone. It made him feel good, somehow, just being needed and wanted again. Will Simmons's cough came from the wagon, hard and prolonged, the man sounding as though he were strangling. Ruby arose and at once hurried to the vehicle. Banning watched her slight figure climb in under the canvas arch and then, tossing the useless rifle aside, went to get his own. He found it leaning against a stand of greasewood where Chick had placed it. He checked its chamber and, finding it loaded, moved to the edge of the camp.

From a slightly higher point, where a yucca plant thrust its needlepoints upward, he began a slow, sweeping search of the land before him. He strained his eyes for any signs of movement and listened carefully for sounds—the rattle of dry brush, the click of a horse's metal shoe against a stone, the groaning of a wounded man. The desert was deathly quiet. There were only the small, hollow clacks of insects brought out by the starlight.

He returned to camp. Ruby was still within the wagon with her husband. Banning could hear his labored breathing, even at the distance where he paused. He shook his head, having his doubts about the man, and walked to where the horses were picketed. Ruby had been correct. Adams had taken one of the Simmonses' blacks. The cowboy, in his frantic haste to escape, had chosen a poor mount, one that would not carry him far if pressed. Not that the buckskin was in much better condition, but he excelled the blacks in many ways.

Restless, disturbed unduly for a reason he could not exactly put his finger on, he returned to the center of camp. He started to rebuild the scattered, nearly dead fire but thought better of it. He was thinking then of Adams. And of the outlaws. The gunshots could have been heard a considerable distance, too. A fire would reveal the location of the camp to anyone endeavoring to determine the source of the shooting.

He remained motionless there in that small, cleared area, a tall, lean figure silhouetted against the faint silver glow of the desert. Thirst was nagging at his throat now that the excitement of the last few minutes was over. The strenuous efforts he had put forth had increased his need for water. And that brought him face to face with the problems of the coming day. What of the Simmonses now? They could not continue on, as planned, with one horse to draw the wagon. Chick Adams, in stealing the black, had ended their hopes for that unless. . . . Banning's thoughts came to a full halt. He knew the answer to the question, but he would not permit himself to recognize it. He swore softly. It was exactly the thing he had promised himself would not happen. Nothing would swerve him from his determination to settle his score with the outlaws.

But what was a man to do? He asked himself the question desperately. Unless he hitched the buckskin in with the remaining black horse, the Simmonses could not move. They would have to remain there, without water, hoping for another passer-by, who likely would not come for weeks. Will Simmons's death would be a certainty. And Ruby's only a matter of time. He should not take this into consideration, he told himself. It was really no affair of his. The Simmonses should never have attempted the journey without being prepared for the worst. He had already spent far too much time over their problems—had almost got himself killed, in fact. It was asking too much of him, of any man. But a man just didn't ride off and leave a woman like Ruby Simmons, or any woman, with the troubles she faced. No matter what his own particular needs and desires happened to be. He admitted that without second thought. Maybe he had told her things were different here on the frontier, that people had to look out for themselves or take the consequences. He still could not walk out on her. He would have to arrange things somehow. He would have to gamble on the outlaws getting beyond his reach. The welfare of the living came before the avenging of the dead.

He swore again, softly, dissatisfied with himself, with his own decision, but knew it could not be otherwise. He remembered then his lost pistol and prowled about the camp until he located it, almost buried in the sand. He cleaned it and thrust it back into its holster. He heard Ruby climb down from the wagon and watched her walk slowly up to him.

"Will is much worse," she said, her voice ragged with worry.

Some of his frustration and impatience got into his voice. "What did you expect?" he demanded harshly. "You folks should never have started this trip, no better prepared than you were."

She lifted her glance to him, disturbed by his tone. "We thought we. . . ."

"You think you can travel right now?"

She stared at him for a long moment. Then, dropping her eyes, she said: "I don't think it would matter one way or another. He's too sick to notice."

"I'll hitch up the horses and we'll pull out," he said. "We gain nothing, sitting here."

"The horses . . . are they in condition to travel?"

"They'll be all right. They've had a few hours rest. It won't hurt them any."

"Just as you say," she murmured, and began to collect the cooking equipment scattered near the dead fire.

"Don't take time to pack anything," he said. "Just throw that stuff into the chuck box. We'll straighten it out next stop."

He moved off to harness the team. He felt her eyes upon his back, knew she was wondering about him. He was already sorry he had spoken so roughly, but the unreasonable anger within him would not let him apologize.

XI

Chick Adams threw his arms about the horse's neck, clamped his legs against its ribs, and hung on. He was giddy from the loss of blood, and he seemed to have little strength left in his body. The horse, badly frightened, was stumbling along over the uneven ground, but running his best. Chick rocked from side to side as the black swerved and dodged both real and fancied obstacles looming suddenly in his path, and several times the cowboy came close to losing his perch. But somehow he managed to stay on.

He had no idea of direction. He thought they were heading into the deep center of the desert, but he had no way of knowing for certain. A stranger to the country, he knew none of the distinguishing landmarks that might serve as guideposts. It mattered little. The important thing was that he had gotten away from the Simmons party and that lawman, Banning, who'd kept watching him with those cold eyes of his. Banning knew the truth, Chick was sure. But, in the end, he was having the last laugh; he had fooled the marshal. He still had the money taken from the bank at Yucca Flats. And now he had a map showing the way to water.

The horse began to blow, to slacken off. The loose sand and outcroppings of rough rock and hindering brush had taken quick toll of his meager strength. The black dropped to a walk, and Chick could feel him trembling from his labors. He did not attempt to speed up the horse. Common sense told him it would be useless, and, besides, it was easier to stay on the black when he moved at this more deliberate pace. Anyway, they should, by now, be far enough from the Simmons camp to take it slower.

Although there was some moonlight and the stars were fairly bright, it was too dark for tracking at any degree of speed, if Banning had decided to follow. Chances were he would wait until daylight. By then, Chick figured, he would have put enough miles between them to allow him to escape with little difficulty. Come to think of it, Banning likely wouldn't try to follow at all, not so long as he had the Simmonses on his hands. He was the sort who would overlook his own problems to help somebody else. He would go right ahead and finish the drive to the water hole for Ruby. It was easy to see how the big lawman felt about her. Too bad she already had herself a husband, otherwise she could probably have Banning mighty quick. But that could all change powerful fast. Will Simmons wasn't going to last much longer, sick as he was. That would make it fine for Banning then. He could have his Ruby and there would be no guilty consciences to plague anyone. Couldn't really blame Banning. Ruby was quite a woman, all the things a man wants, and she was hungry as hell for a strong man's attentions. Simmons must have gotten sick soon after they were married. Likely he had never been able to take care of her in the way she needed.

Chick shook himself violently. He realized suddenly he had been talking aloud. *I must be out of my head,* he thought. *Lost more blood than I figured.* He guessed he ought to haul up and see what he could do about plugging that bullet hole. The bleeding sure needed to be stopped. Damn that lucky shot the woman had got in, anyway. One chance in a hundred of her hitting him—and she had.

On the other hand, maybe it wouldn't be so smart to halt just yet. Wouldn't pay to underestimate this John Banning. He just might be out there in the dark right at that minute, prowling about, looking for a trail. Chick reckoned he'd better keep on moving, however slowly. He maybe should get as far from the Simmons camp as possible before he stopped to lick his wounds. The saddlebags moved heavily to one side at that moment, sliding down the black's withers. Adams clutched frantically at them and tugged them back into place. The leather felt greasy, slick from blood, his blood. Best he'd fix them so they wouldn't drop off and get lost. He grasped a handful of the horse's coarse mane and twisted it into the lacings that held the bags together. No chance now for the bags to get away.

He tried to straighten up and get his bearings. He hoped to see something, anything, he did not exactly know what. But there should be something around that would give him an idea of where he was. The effort had sent his head into a sickening spin. He pulled his hands from the black's neck and pressed his fingers against his throbbing temples. If he could just stop the damned dizziness that kept sweeping over him! He would soon be over that, he told himself. It was only because of the hard fight he had had with Banning and, of course, the blood he had lost. Soon he would stop and take care of that. No use to worry about it. Come daylight, he would locate the water hole from the map he had taken from Ruby. Then he would push on to it, getting there well in advance of the Simmonses and Banning. They would be moving slowly. That would give him a chance to rest for a spell and soak up all the water he needed. Then he would be off to Mexico.

From then on the world was his own little red apple. A man with $15,000 could live like a king in Mexico for a mighty long time. He could do what he pleased, have all he wanted of everything. Of course, he would have to be on the watch for Groth and Hondo and old Coaley. They, all three, would now be gunning for him since he'd given them the slip with the money. But they would have to find him first, and Mexico was a big place. And, if and when they did—well, that could be handled, too. If he didn't feel like meeting up with them, face to face, why, he'd just step out and hire a gunslinger to do the job for him. That was the good part of having plenty of money; you need something done, go right ahead.

He was talking aloud again. That knowledge jarred him, set up a small, ragged worry in his mind. He felt for the saddlebags, assuring himself that they were still there, that the money was safe. He should be moving south, he suddenly decided. The water hole was south. He remembered that from overhearing

Banning talk about it. Which way was south? He glanced upward to the vast, dark canopy of velvet sky, speckled with its millions of diamonds. If he could locate the Dipper, he could then find the North Star. South should be in the opposite direction. He'd sure be glad when it got light enough to look at the map.

He felt the horse veer sharply. The black reared and came down solidly on stiff knees as something catapulted from the ground and whirred off on broad wings. Chick felt himself leaving his uncertain seat as the horse spun wildly around. In the next fragment of time he was sailing through space, clawing frantically at the empty air. Then came a jolting impact that sent pain flashing through his body as he piled up against a clump of brush.

He came to his senses slowly. There was a lightening in the sky, and he knew it was near sunrise. He had lain there for hours, apparently. He struggled to a sitting position, his entire left side throbbing with the monotonous regularity of a clock. His head was still whirling, and this infuriated him unreasonably. He managed to get to his feet, legs quivering beneath him. He had to do one thing—find his horse and keep going. He took half a dozen faltering steps, his eyes eagerly searching the slowly brightening desert. But the black was not to be seen.

"God-damned horse!" he screamed in a wild, cracked voice. "I catch you, I'm sure goin' to peel the hide offen your back!"

He pulled up short, weaving unsteadily. The horse was gone—and so were the saddlebags containing all the money. This realization brought forth another torrent of profanity from his swollen lips. It would be hell to find that horse now. And the bags might not even be on him. They could hang on ten feet—or ten miles. Anybody's guess which. And the fool horse might have headed off in any direction. He came slowly, uncertainly around, anger and disappointment slogging through him. All that hard work, all those chances on getting killed, all this misery from Ruby Simmons's bullet—for nothing. It was that goddamned black horse that had caused it. It was. . . .

He was no longer alone. Three dark-faced riders, still in their saddles, were lined up a dozen yards away, watching him with cold detachment. Their presence, at first, startled him, then filled him with a flood of joy as he envisioned rescue. But all washed quickly away when, at last, he recognized the trio. He stared at them for a long minute. He swayed drunkenly on his feet, a foolish grin stretching his lips.

"Hey there, Hondo. Groth . . . Coaley. Where the hell you jaspers been? I been hunting all over this here desert for you."

"I'll just bet," Groth answered.

"Got myself winged back there a piece. Sure glad you all showed up. You got some water?"

Groth, his heavily seamed, broad face crushed into a black scowl, spat. "Where's the money, Chick?"

Adams took a hurried, uncertain step forward. He tripped and went to his knees, clutching at his bloodstained shoulder. "I don't know. I sure don't. There any water in your canteen, Coaley?"

Groth came slowly down from his saddle. The other men did not move. Groth moved up to Adams, grasped the cowboy by the shirt front, and dragged him to his feet. Drawing back his huge, ham-like hand, he cracked Chick viciously across the face. Adams's head wobbled and his eyes rolled. Groth glared at him for a moment, and then allowed him to fall, full length, to the ground.

"Where's that money, Chick?"

"I ain't got it," Adams whimpered. "I'm telling you I ain't got it. Search me, you'll see. But for God's sake . . . give me a drink of water! And help me with this here arm, one of you."

"You had the money," Groth pressed in a deep, unrelenting voice. "You cut out with it when we got separated. What did you do with it? Hide it somewhere?"

Chick Adams stared up at Groth's hulking shape. His eyes slid to the others, Hondo and Coaley. They were watching with no particular interest—or pity. A faint spark of cunning began to glow within him.

"Well, now, maybe I do know something about that money, after all. You give me a drink of water and help me patch up this bullet hole first. Then I'll do some talking."

"We ain't got no water either, kid," Coaley said. "Been clean out ever since we hit this danged desert. We been looking for both you and a water hole. Right now I'd fork over my share of that bank money for a canteen full of fresh water."

"We don't get some soon," the bronze-faced Hondo observed sourly, "that money ain't going to do any of us much good."

Adams's gaze swung from one to the other. The truth was plain on their haggard faces. They were every bit as bad off as he. He thought of the map he'd taken from Ruby Simmons.

"Supposing I tell you I could take us to water. Would you be willing to help me then? You give me your word you'll help me plug up this bullet hole and not leave me here on this desert, and I'll sure do it."

Groth had not moved. He still stood before the cowboy, a sullen, threatening brute. "What about the money, Chick?"

"You give me your promise first. Then I'll do my talking."

Groth said: "All right, you got your promise."

Adams managed to get to his feet. He kept one hand over the steadily bleeding wound in his shoulder. It had started afresh when Groth slammed him to the ground.

"I didn't hide the money," he began. "I was riding a horse I borrowed last night after I got plugged. Damned marshal mighty near got me. I rode this far, and the horse spooked and threw me. He's out there somewhere on the desert with the money slung across his back, in the saddlebags."

Adams suddenly felt very weak, as though his legs were paper. His head was whirling madly. All that talking had overtaxed him, he realized. He must be worse off than he figured. He sank to a sitting position.

Groth eyed him coldly. "What horse you bleatin' about? What happened to yours?"

"Broke his leg," Chick replied wearily. "How about one of you helping me with this shoulder?"

"Whose horse was you riding?"

"Belonged to some people named Simmons. Wagon I joined up with after I started walking."

"Where's the wagon now?"

A look of worry and desperation crossed Adams's face. "Ain't you going to help me, Groth? You going to stand there and let me bleed to death? Tell Coaley to get down here and give me a hand."

Groth repeated his question. "Where's the Simmons wagon now?"

"Oh, back there somewhere," Chick said, with an indefinite wave of his hand toward the desert. "Reckon that would be sort of northeast."

"Sounds like a team horse," Hondo remarked from his saddle. "Critter probably headed straight back for that wagon. Even if he didn't, it sure ought to be easy to spot him out there on the flats."

"Maybe," Groth murmured. "We didn't do so good spotting Chick. It was his crazy yelling that helped us."

"He took off to the east," Hondo replied stiffly. "We was looking in the wrong direction all the time."

Groth shrugged. "No matter now. We found him. Next thing is to find that horse. I expect he'll head for the wagon, like you say. But Simmons will be hunting for him, too. We got to find him first."

Groth pivoted on his heel and walked to his horse. He was a big man, thick through the shoulders. When he moved, he carried his bullet-like head thrust forward.

Chick Adams watched him depart with rising alarm. "Hey!" he yelled. "What about me? You said you'd help me. You give me your promise."

Groth settled himself in his saddle. He turned his small, hard-surfaced eyes on the cowboy and grinned bleakly.

"Why, we aim to do just that, Chick," he said, and, drawing his pistol, fired pointblank at the cowboy.

Adams's body jumped from the bullet's force. He went over backward and struck the ground hard, sending up small spurts of fine dust.

Coaley eyed the lifeless shape unfeelingly. "Did he say something about there being a lawman with this Simmons outfit?"

Groth prodded the spent cartridge from the cylinder of his gun and replaced it. Sliding the weapon into its holster, he studied Adams's contorted face. "Reckon we got us only a three-way split now."

Coaley repeated his question. "Didn't he say something about a lawman?"

Groth half turned to face the outlaw. "So? You getting worried about one lousy lawman? Three of us to him and this Simmons. Figure that's pretty good odds, even for you, Coaley."

"I was just thinking about it," the sharp-featured outlaw mumbled.

Groth grunted. "Let's go," he said, and prodded his horse into motion. The others followed, neither of them glancing down at the dead outlaw.

"We better be finding us some water soon," Hondo said after a time. "Me and this nag can't go much farther."

"We'll make it through today," Groth replied. "Probably be

water at the Simmons wagon. We ought to run across it before dark."

They rode in silence for several more minutes. Coaley spoke up. "What do you reckon Chick meant by saying he knew where there was water and he'd take us there? You figure he did know?"

Groth wagged his head. "Another one of his damned lies. If he knew, you think he'd be needing some himself? You think he'd be out here drying up if he had some idea where it was?"

Coaley said: "No, reckon not. Just him talking."

"Now, keep your eyes peeled for that horse. Watch for tracks. Ain't been no wind, so we ought to see them easy."

"I still figure he'd head straight for the wagon," Hondo said. "A team horse will do that every time."

"That'd sure suit me," Coaley remarked feelingly. "I'm going to get me a swallow of water, first off."

Hondo lifted his bloodshot eyes to the eastern horizon. The first blaze of sun was making its appearance. "Going to be a hot one again. Ain't so sure I can make it."

Groth laughed. "You can make it. Just you keep thinking about all the women your share of that money is going to buy you. That'll keep you alive when nothing else will."

XII

Near midmorning, John Banning drew the Simmons wagon to a stop. He had followed his plan to push on until noon and then wait out the balance of the blazing hours until dark before continuing on to the water hole. In that way, giving the team a break during the hottest part of the day and traveling at night, he could conserve their rapidly diminishing strength. Following such a schedule, he estimated they would reach the Whitetails around sunrise that next morning. It was only a guess, however. He could not recall how far it was to the low-piled formations. He hoped he was near right, for one thing was certain—they could not last much longer.

The horses were suffering terribly, Ruby had taken on a parched, feverish look, and his own body felt as though there was not one drop of moisture left within it. And, in the sweltering depths of the wagon, Will Simmons lay as though dead. His coughing had ceased almost entirely, and he was mostly quiet, his abnormally bright eyes upon Ruby when she was near or reaching out past Banning on the seat, to the empty sky, when she was absent.

At the start Banning had planned no morning stops at all. But he had overestimated the team, even with the buckskin replacing the lost black. It had become quickly evident there would be many periodic haltings. Now, at this pause, the third since daybreak, he drew the vehicle up beside a fairly thick stand of yucca that afforded no shade at all but did, somehow, break the vast, monotonous sameness of the land. Anger still rankled faintly through him, and, when he turned to the Simmonses, his voice was curt: "We'll rest an hour."

He climbed down from the seat, accidentally brushing his hand against the iron tire of the wheel. It was hot as fired metal, and he jerked violently, an oath exploding from his lips. He moved forward to the team, easing the harness and dropping the tongue to allow them as much rest and comfort as possible. There was little else he could do for them. Their great need was for water.

Standing there in the broad, streaming sunlight, Banning rubbed the buckskin's sweat-plastered neck in thoughtful silence. As each hour dragged by, during which the Simmonses' outfit crawled slowly southward, he knew his chances for finding Hondo and his two companions grew smaller. The wagon's tortoise-like pace was maddening at times. More than once he wished he had ridden on alone, had cast the Simmonses and their troubles from his shoulders and looked after his own interests. But always there arose good reasons why he could not.

The off horse, the black, lifted his head and nickered plaintively. Banning pivoted about to the direction in which the black was looking. A single horse was plodding wearily toward them. Banning wheeled, intending to reach for the rifle lying on the floor of the wagon. He saw then that the horse was riderless. It was the one Chick Adams had stolen. Somehow it had gotten free and returned.

Elated, Banning waited quietly beside the buckskin, not wanting to spook the horse by moving out to meet him. The black was coming in of his own accord, as a teammate in a pair will generally do. Banning wondered briefly about Adams. The cowboy either had carelessly allowed the horse to get away from him or else had fainted from his wound and was lying somewhere out in the desert. Possibly he was dead. Even a well man could not live long under that merciless sun without some manner of protection.

The black drew nearer. There was something draped across his withers, entangled somehow in his long mane. Saddlebags. That proved one thing to Banning—the horse had done little running since he'd escaped from Adams; otherwise, he would have shaken loose the pouches. Therefore, he had not been pursued. Considering that, Banning concluded the cowboy was dead.

The black halted beside his partner and brushed at his shoulder with a quivering muzzle. Sweat and dust had caked his coat thoroughly, and he looked as though he had come a long distance since Adams had stolen him. Banning eased slowly toward him, quickly fastened a lead rope to his halter, securing him. He then disentangled the saddlebags. They were stained and heavy, and they clinked when he dropped them to the ground. Frowning, he squatted down, unbuckled the straps of one, and looked inside. Besides several packs of currency money, there was a large quantity of gold and silver coins. The other bag contained the same. The stolen bank money.

Banning sat back on his heels, understanding coming to him in a tumbling flood. Chick had been one of the outlaws, the one who had held the horses. It explained why he had been so disturbed at Banning's presence; it was the answer to why he had been in such great haste to reach the water hole. He must have double-crossed his three partners and was trying desperately to escape. A strong current of triumph flooded through John Banning. Since Chick was a member of the outlaw gang, the others would at that very moment be searching for him. They would not be trying to cross the desert and escape into the hills. They would want Chick Adams—and their share of the stolen money. It was logical to believe that, in their quest, they would soon discover the Simmonses' wagon. It would draw them in and they would halt to ask their questions about a lone rider heading for the border. And then he would have them. The chase would be over. He would take them in, alive if they put up no fight, dead if it came to resistance. He hoped it would not be necessary to use his gun. It would not be a pleasant thing for Ruby to witness, but there was no help for it. He had not asked her to be present.

He should hide the money. It was the sugar that drew the flies, and, besides, it would be better if Ruby knew nothing of it. The Simmonses could not tell of something they knew nothing about. He should take the money from the pouches, which surely belonged to one of the outlaws, and put it in a safe place. Then get rid of the saddlebags.

He set about the chore at once. He emptied the money into a flour sack he found in the chuck box. Tying it securely about the neck, he suspended it from the wagon's rear axle, alongside a similar bag containing extra hub nuts and other small, spare parts. This done, he stepped back and critically examined his work. The sack was too clean. He rubbed a bit of grease from the wheel onto it and tossed a handful of powdery dust over that. It looked, then, exactly like the one hanging next to it; a casual observer would think it had hung from the axle all those many miles from St. Louis.

That off his mind, he heaved a sigh. He brushed at his face. The heat was breathless, constricting. He no longer sweated, only seemed to dry out more and more with each passing minute. His skin felt as though it had shriveled and was drawing tighter by degrees across his bones. But he felt good inside. Now he had the outlaws coming to him. He moved closer to the wagon, seeking a few moments in the scant shade laid down by the vehicle. From inside he heard Ruby saying something, followed immediately by Will Simmons's petulant complaint.

". . . necessary you spend so much time with him? After all, you are my wife . . . he's no more than a stranger . . . hardly a close friend. . . ."

"Not too good a friend now," Ruby answered in an exhausted voice. "We've forced him to help us. Against his will."

Banning pulled away from the wagon, unwilling to be a witness to their private quarrels. Jealousy on the part of Simmons was a natural and expected thing, he guessed. Lying flat on his back, helpless all those many weeks, while his wife was thrown closely with other men, would make any husband think deeply about such matters. But Will Simmons need not worry. Ruby was safe with John Banning. Not that she was no woman fit to tempt any man. Were she not already married, Banning would have thought much about her and the possibility of a life together for them. But she was another man's woman, and that changed the picture. Ruby could stop fretting about one thing, though. Helping them no longer was a hindrance to him. It was, instead, an aid, a great help. He was sorry he had been a little sharp with her. He would tell her so.

When he strolled back toward the wagon some time later, Ruby was outside. She was standing near the horses, staring at the returned black. She made a fetching scene posed that way, her profile etched against the cloudless sky, her slender, well-shaped figure molded by her thin dress. She heard him and turned.

"Our horse . . . he's come back."

"A few minutes ago. He must have got away from Adams and headed straight for his partner."

She thought for a minute. "What about Chick? Do you think that he's . . . dead?" She hesitated over the final word, seemingly reluctant to speak it.

Banning nodded. "Most likely he is. I guess he was pretty hard hit by that bullet of yours."

Ruby shuddered visibly, and a spasm of pain crossed her face. "Then . . . I've killed a man. It's a terrible thought."

"You only did what had to be done," Banning said. "Don't blame yourself. And don't think about it. It never helps."

"But to shoot a man . . . a human being . . . and kill him . . . I'll remember it all the rest of my life."

"You would have shot a rattlesnake if he was about to strike you, wouldn't you? And you wouldn't have given it a second thought. There's little difference in this case."

She shook her head. "There's a world of difference. He was a man, a person. Nobody has the right to take human life."

Banning said quietly: "If you hadn't, I reckon somebody else would have shot him soon." He wanted to say more, tell her about the killings in Yucca Flats, but to do so would only lead into further explanations and revelations. He remembered then his intention to apologize. "I just wanted to tell you I'm sorry if I was a bit short with you. Guess I really didn't mean it. Things sometimes get under a man's hide and put him on edge."

"It's all right," she said listlessly.

"Reckon we'd better be moving out. We can do a little better now, with three horses changing off."

She helped him harness up, and then climbed to her place on the wagon seat. When he was beside her and they were once again in forward motion, she asked: "Is it much farther?"

"Quite a piece," he admitted. "But we'll make it by morning."

"I hope so. I don't think I can stand it much longer."

He reached over and patted her hand, seeking to comfort her. "Is your husband worse?"

"I think so. He just lies there, staring at me. His eyes look so empty and have sunk way down in his face. He doesn't cough hardly any now, and that worries me, too. It's like everything has just stopped inside him, even the sickness. I'm afraid, John."

"It's been a hard row for a woman to hoe," he said. "Try not to fret over it. Like worrying, it helps none. And if things go bad, I'll be around to help."

She looked directly at him, her face grave and sad. "Without you, John, I don't know what I would have done. You are all I have between me and this terrible country. The only thing I can trust."

XIII

It was as though the desert sensed an escape was near, and had redoubled its efforts to thwart it. They had pulled up beside a low butte. At first, when they stopped around noon, the sun beat directly down upon them, mercilessly broiling them with its brilliant, relentless rays. Their skins had taken on a shriveled, old-parchment look, and their lips had cracked and dried and peeled in minute patches. The horses, although coddled by Banning and their strength hoarded all that morning, were scarcely alive. Studying them, he wondered how they could go any farther.

Inside the wagon was an inferno of trapped, dead heat. Banning had again lifted the sides of the canvas, hoping to create better air circulation for the sick man. It helped little. Over the vast desert not the faintest breeze stirred. Only the static, breathless heat.

The midday hour dragged by with the Simmonses and John Banning unmoving. They were figures of wood, unable to move about, pinned motionlessly in the clutches of an all-powerful master. But, at last, a small and narrow band of shade began to form, to spread slowly outward from the butte as the sun began its long, arcing descent. Starting first at the foot of the lava bluff, it widened, climbing with maddening deliberation, as though taunting the suffering travelers and their worn beasts. It finally reached the top of the wagon's dusty cover, and was of some help. At least the driving, burning shafts were shielded, turned back. But there was no surcease in the heat itself. Shimmering layers, piled one upon the other, lay across the copper-hued country, all but melting the glistening particles of gypsum.

Ruby, who had been inside the vehicle spending those terrible hours fanning Will with a yellowed newspaper, came out and crossed slowly to where Banning was resting. His back was propped against the rough surface of the butte.

"Might be some cooler out here now," he said, glancing at her flushed face. "I'll carry him out, if you like."

She brushed a lock of dark hair from her eyes. She was near to total exhaustion, driven to that point by care for her ailing husband and the sapping, sucking heat. "I suggested it, but he said no. He said he didn't really feel the heat any more."

Banning nodded. "Not moving about, I guess a man doesn't work up much of a sweat." It was a poor answer to the worry and doubt in her voice, but he was reluctant to say more.

"If only we had a little water. He is so thirsty. I know a drink and a wet compress on his head would do so much for him."

Banning rolled a cigarette. He lit it, took a puff, and cast it aside. With a mouth dry as dust, he was learning that a smoke held no attraction. "I've been thinking about that. It might be a good idea for me to ride on ahead to the water hole. I could fill up a couple of canteens and bring them back. I'd meet you coming."

She made no comment, but waited for him to finish.

"I figure I could start soon as it's sundown. You won't have any trouble driving. Mostly flat land from here on in."

She read the meaning in his proposal. "You don't think Will can last out until we get there?" When he did not immediately respond, she leaned forward and added: "Please, John, the truth. I want the truth."

He met her eyes squarely. "His chances are pretty slim, Ruby. No two ways about that. He might make it because sick people fool you sometimes. But, if things go wrong, I wouldn't want to think we didn't do everything we could for him."

She held his gaze for a moment, then dropped her eyes. "Thank you," she said quietly. "But don't blame yourself if things do go wrong. You've already done more than I should have expected. Going miles out of your way, neglecting your job when you should have ridden on."

"Sometimes things don't always work out the way a man figures them to."

"How well I know that," she said, her voice lifting a little. "When we left Saint Louis for Nevada, we thought it would be great fun. All that traveling across the new West. It sounded like a thrilling, wonderful adventure. I think Will was almost happy his health broke, because it forced us out of the old life, started us into a new one."

The conversation had brightened her, momentarily removing

the deep shadows from her eyes. He said, prompting her to continue: "Saint Louis was always your home?"

"Most of our lives. We both were born in smaller towns, but our families moved in to Saint Louis later. We went to school there, met at my high school graduation, in fact. Oh, Will was so handsome then. He was in his first year of college . . . I was the envy of every girl in my school."

Unaccountably she began to weep, the tears rolling slowly down her cheeks, carving small trails through the dust. It was something she had to do, had to say, Banning realized. She needed to unburden herself, release all the pent-up emotions and fears that were bottled so tightly within herself, even if upon so frail an excuse as remembering the way of things, long past.

"We married a year after that and stayed right there in Saint Louis. Will had a good job. Then he broke down. His lungs, the doctor said. He would have to go and live in a high, dry climate. That's when we wrote his brother in Nevada. He answered us right back, told us to come on, and, if we needed money, to let him know. We had a little saved up, so we didn't need his charity. We just sold our furniture, bought this wagon and team, and started out. It was great fun at first. On the move all the time, seeing new places, new towns, meeting people and making new friends who were also traveling West like we were doing. But after a few weeks I could see Will was tiring. He grew thinner and began to cough terribly hard. I wanted to stop and rest for a while, a month, if need be. But he would not hear of it. We had started for Nevada and that's where we were going, he would say.

"We fell in with some other wagons. It wasn't a regular train, just some folks, like ourselves, moving out to find a new home. But none of them was going as far as Nevada, and finally we were alone. Will was really sick by then, spending most of his time on the pallet in the wagon. I didn't mind the driving. In fact, I got to like it. What worried me most was that I couldn't always be with him when he was having a bad coughing spell. Sometimes it would happen in a place where I couldn't stop the team but just had to keep on driving. I would sit there and listen to him coughing his heart out and pray for the moment to come when I could pull up and go back to him. That's when it seemed to me that I failed him. My not being there, at his side, helping him when he needed me so. It could have been that, during one of those times, the turning point came, and had I been there, making it easier for him, he would not now be so sick."

Banning closed his big hand about hers, pressing it reassuringly. "You didn't fail him, Ruby. Don't ever believe that you did. You were doing what had to be done, and, even if you weren't right there at his side, he knew you were close by. And that's what counted to him."

"And then to make it all worse," she continued, as though she hadn't heard, "I got us lost. And we ran out of water."

"It happens pretty often," Banning said with a shrug. "It's big country, and it all looks alike. As for running out of water, it happens to most everybody one time or another. Take a look at me . . . I'm an old hand around the desert, but I wound up with an empty canteen."

From beneath the brim of his hat he studied her calm features. She seemed relieved, relaxed now. The talking had done her much good. He saw then, looking beyond her to the desert, that it was drawing near to sundown. The last bright rays were touching only the sky.

"About my going after water . . . you feel all right about it? I won't go unless you are agreeable."

"If you think it's best, John. How long will you be gone?"

"I should get back some time after midnight."

She raised her gaze to his. He saw then the faintest glimmer of fear and doubt in her eyes.

"If you think there's a chance I might not come back, forget it," he said, instantly injured. "I could have pulled out a long ways back, was I that sort."

At once she turned to him and placed her hands upon his wrists. "Oh, John, I'm sorry. I know you wouldn't do such a terrible thing. You couldn't, not to anybody. It's only that I'm not thinking straight. I'm at my wits' end. I keep remembering the things you said about Chick Adams. And how they all came true."

He got to his feet, took her by the hands, and pulled her up, also. "Forget it. How about fixing us a bite of supper while I get the horses ready?"

"Some for you," she said. "I just can't eat. I don't want anything."

"You try. There's a long night ahead of you, and you'll need all the strength you can muster."

She nodded woodenly and started for the rear of the wagon. Then Banning heard a cry of surprise burst from her lips. He wheeled about.

Three riders, with drawn guns, watched them from the end of the butte. Hollow-eyed, dirty, dust-covered, he knew them, nevertheless. The outlaws.

XIV

"You got some water?"

Banning ignored the question. A dull anger moved through him. Here were the men he was seeking. Here were the ruthless outlaws who had killed Davey, had shot down Gordon Campion, old Horace, the bank teller, perhaps killed Abel Moss; here were the remnants of the wild Wind River gang, drawn into his net as he had hoped and planned—and they had taken him unawares. Inwardly he cursed his own stupidity, his carelessness.

"You hear me, mister? You got some water?"

The voice was a hoarse croak, the speaker a thin-faced, turkey-necked man with sunken, colorless eyes. All three men were in bad shape, Banning saw. The mark of the desert lay upon them, upon their beat horses. He stared at them, endeavoring to assess his chances for drawing the pistol at his hip. One of the three, a thick-set, broad-featured man, dismounted stiffly. He moved forward slowly, his small, brown eyes burning fiercely. He came to within an arm's length of Banning, reached out, pulled Banning's weapon from its holster and thrust it into his own belt. He backed away. "You Simmons?"

His voice, too, was a grating rasp. Banning knew he had to think fast. He had to hold these killers, keep them around until he could get his hands on a gun. His chance would come. It had to. "No."

"Reckon you're the marshal, then. Where's this Simmons?"

Marshal! They had seen Chick Adams then. Only he could have given them that information. And Chick was not with them. Banning ducked his head at the canvas arch of the wagon. "Inside, sick. Leave him alone."

The broad-faced outlaw's steady expression did not relent. "Coaley," he called over his shoulder to the man who had asked for water, "get down off that horse and take a look inside that wagon!"

"All right, Dan," the man groaned, and came off his horse.

Banning watched Coaley shamble over to the wagon in a loose-jointed, aimless fashion. He reached into the seat and picked up Banning's rifle.

"Here's a gun, Hondo," he said, and tossed it to the red-haired one.

Hondo caught the weapon neatly, looked briefly at it, and

slid it into the scabbard hanging from his saddle.

"See if there's any water in that barrel," the big man said to him then.

"Yes, sir, Mister Groth," Hondo replied, his voice faintly sarcastic. He swung down and swaggered toward the wagon.

Banning saw his plan for getting his weapon fade when Coaley found it. But his hopes did not lower. He would have another chance, if not with his own gun, with one of theirs. He swung his glance to Hondo. The outlaw was thumping at the water cask. Not satisfied with that test, he took it between his broad hands and shook it violently.

"You're Simmons's wife, I take it," Groth said to Ruby in a harsh voice.

"I am. Please don't let your friend disturb him. He's very sick."

"Coaley won't hurt him none, lady. Just wants to be sure he is sick. And that there ain't nobody else there in that rig with him."

Hondo walked up to where Groth was standing. He was a well-built, wide-shouldered man who, Banning thought, could be considered handsome were it not for the cruel twist to his mouth. His face was covered with a fine, golden beard, which gave him a sort of rakish appearance. He brought his thrusting eyes to a stop on Ruby and swept her appreciatively.

"Barrel's empty, sugar. Where you got the water?"

Under his bold, raking gaze, Ruby moved closer to Banning's side. Hondo would have to be watched. The way he was eying Ruby meant sure trouble.

"No water," Banning said. "We've been out for days."

Groth swore gustily and rubbed at his cracked lips with the back of his hand. "Give Coaley a hand there, Hondo."

Hondo did not move. He remained where he stood, legs spread apart, thumbs hooked onto his gun belt. He had not taken his eyes from Ruby.

Groth glared at him hotly. "Forget that! We got more important things to be thinking about."

Hondo grinned, his lips pulling back over broad, white teeth. Coaley climbed down from the wagon, his inspection completed. "Nobody in there but a sick jasper. And I reckon he's some sick." He leaned against the wheel. "Mighty close to cashin' his chips, I'd say. You find the water, Hondo?"

The dark outlaw shrugged. "No water, Coaley. Not a dang' drop. Reckon you'll just have to do without a while longer."

"I can't!" the older man wailed. "I purely can't go no farther without me a drink of water!"

"Shut up," Groth snapped impatiently. "Bound to be some around that wagon, somewheres. You two look again. And, while you're at it, keep your eyes peeled for that there money."

"Money?" Ruby echoed. "If that's what you're looking for, there's none around here. We had only a little to start, and it's almost all gone now."

Groth shook his head. "Don't be telling me that, lady. There's a saddlebag full of. And it's right here. Maybe fifteen or twenty thousand. We didn't have much time to do any counting. But we've come after it now."

Ruby, amazement blanking her face, turned to Banning. "What is he talking about? Is it stolen money?"

Banning said: "Yes. Let them look for it. They won't find it."

She did not take her eyes off him, still not fully understanding. "What makes them think it's here?"

"Chick Adams was one of their bunch."

"But he left us. Stole one of our horses and left. The horse came back, but he didn't."

"We saw old Chick," Groth said dryly. "Talked to him for quite a spell. He said the money was on that horse and the horse came back to you. Now, the saddlebags sure didn't drop off along the trail. We was watching for them."

Again Ruby's eyes searched John Banning's face, her question unspoken but plainly there. Inside the wagon Coaley was duplicating his search. Outside, Hondo prowled like a hunting cougar. Banning smiled at Ruby, endeavoring to put her at ease. But it belied the worry digging into him. The outlaws were merciless killers. They would not hesitate to kill again and again if the time came. With or without the money, they could not afford to leave anyone alive who might later identify them. Banning was thinking fast, knowing he must come up with an idea quickly. Even if he passed up his need to settle his own score with them and gave them the bank's money, they would not ride out and leave the Simmonses and himself alive. They would cover their tracks—and cover them well.

A glimmering, a faint inkling of a plan, came to him in that next moment. It took shape slowly, reluctantly. Nothing definite and concise but at least a means, perhaps, for delaying them until the coming morning. That would give him more time in which to think. He threw a glance at the wagon. Wait until Hondo and Coaley were finished, were thoroughly satisfied there was neither water nor money to be found. Then he would spring his plan.

His attention came to abrupt halt upon Hondo. The outlaw had completed his search of the chuck box, was now staring at the two flour sacks hanging from the wagon's rear axle. If Hondo examined them both, the problems of the future would quickly resolve themselves. What came next would be immediate action. Groth still stood before them, his pistol never wavering from Banning's breast bone. Hondo dropped to his knees, and tension began to build inside Banning. He would act at once if the outlaw discovered the money. Groth's attention would shift momentarily, and that would be the moment for him to make his play. He would have to leap across the distance that separated him from Groth, knock his gun aside, and try to get it into his own hand. It would be a long chance, but it would be his only one.

He watched Hondo reach out and wrap his fingers about the bag, probing its contents carefully. Feeling the square, hard corners of an axle hub nut, he spat in disgust and moved back. Banning breathed deeper. Hondo had fingered the sack with the wheel parts—and, assuming the other alongside it contained the same, did not bother further.

"Nothing around here I can find," he said, removing his hat and running his fingers through thick, oily hair.

Will Simmons groaned from the interior of the wagon. Ruby whirled and ran quickly toward it. As she moved by Hondo, the outlaw reached out and grasped her by the wrist. Like a dancer spinning his partner, he swung her up against his body.

Banning, suddenly infuriated and blind to his own danger, lunged across the narrow, intervening space. Groth's gun sounded through the twilight. Dirt spouted at Banning's feet, but he ignored it and rushed on. He reached past Ruby's struggling shape and closed his fingers about Hondo's throat. The outlaw yelled and released the girl. She fell back against the side of the wagon, breathing heavily. Banning, a savage hatred turning his muscles to steel, slammed Hondo's head against the unyielding wood of the vehicle. He lashed out with his left hand, and the blow caught the outlaw on the jaw, driving him hard against the rigid boards a second time. Completely aroused, Banning struck again. His fist drove into Hondo's slack face, and the outlaw's knees buckled. He sagged downward, catching himself by clawing at the water-keg platform.

Hondo drew his gun, only faintly conscious. He thumbed back the hammer, his slitted eyes hazy and flat. As Banning stared at the muzzle of the pistol, the wild fury began to fade. It came to him that he had pulled a foolish stunt; if Hondo pressed that trigger, Ruby would be at the mercy of the outlaw.

Groth's rough voice rapped through the tight silence. "Put that iron away, Hondo. And, dammit, leave the woman be! You hear me? Time enough for that later, after we get away from here."

Hondo, his senses recovered, remained poised. He didn't seem to be listening to Groth. For a long minute he did not move, and then the points of his shoulders went down as he relented. He released the hammer of his pistol and slid it back into its holster.

"Sure, sure," he murmured softly. "You never was much of a one for fun, Dan."

"Time sure ain't now when there's a posse out there somewhere, riding our tail," Groth snapped.

Hondo only grinned. He cocked his head, looking at the wagon into which Ruby had disappeared. "Lot of woman under that old dress. Just found that out for myself."

Anger roared through John Banning again. His arm came up, cording the thick, rolling muscles of his shoulders, and his hands clenched into rock-hard fists. But before he could move, he felt Groth's gun barrel jab deeply into his spine.

"Don't try it, lawman," the outlaw warned. "Not that I give a damn, but I need you alive right now. Just you stand easy. Hondo," he added to the redhead, "go fetch some rope. We'll spread-eagle this saddle warmer to the wagon wheel and find out where he stashed that money."

Hondo moved off toward the rear of the vehicle. Groth, laying a heavy hand against Banning's shoulder, pushed him up against one of the rear wheels.

"Coaley, build up that fire. And put one of them butcher knives in it. I got an idea a little hot steel will make the marshal open up."

Hondo returned with a length of rope. He cut it into four

pieces and, with Groth still holding his gun on Banning, bound the big man to the wheel, arms outflung, legs spread. Finished, he stepped back. A sardonic grin on his face, he slapped Banning hard across the mouth.

"That's for buttin' in when I'm busy with a lady."

Groth shook his head in disgust. "Cut that out, Hondo. Let's just find out what he's done with that money. Then you can take your cut and damn' well do what you want to with him and the woman."

Banning's head rang from the blow. He shook it, clearing it, and glared at the outlaw. "Manhandling a woman seems to be your style. Comes to a man, you need some help . . . like right now."

Hondo's expression tightened. His heavy lips drew down into a curling sneer, and his eyes narrowed. "No need to go to a lot of bother, Dan," he said softly to Groth. "Just you give me a few minutes with this bird. I'll make him talk."

Groth grunted. "Yeah, he'd probably be in fine shape to talk, once you got done with him. I saw you trying to make that rancher talk up Wyoming way. You didn't have much luck."

Hondo made no reply to that. A smirk had come to his lips. "I was just thinking," he said. "It's been pretty cozy for the marshal around here. Sick husband and that woman all alone like she is."

"Don't you never think of anything else?" Groth demanded, and shouldered him aside. To Banning he said: "You'd save us a lot of time, was you to do your talking now."

Banning shook his head. He had decided he would hold out, delay as long as possible. Then he would offer his bargain, his deal. Groth shrugged and turned to the rising fire. The desert was almost in full darkness now, and soon there would be only the faint star shine and light from a weak moon. And it would be cool, even cold. He could hear Ruby inside the wagon behind him, murmuring to her husband, striving to comfort him. He hoped she would stay with Will Simmons, under the canvas and out of sight. She would need protection, once darkness fell. The minutes moved slowly by. His arms began to numb as the ropes binding his wrists cut into the flesh and throttled blood circulation. His feet and legs were all right, his boots having given them some degree of protection.

"God!" Coaley yelled unexpectedly. "I just got to have some water. Mouth of mine feels like it's full of thistles!"

Groth, startled, stared at the man and muttered something under his breath. He walked to the fire, staggering slightly as he brushed at his eyes. Banning watched with satisfaction. All three of the outlaws were near to caving in. The days and nights on the desert with no food and water were taking their toll. That was good. That would aid his plan.

"That knife hot yet?"

Coaley leaned over the fire and fumbled with the handle of the blade, trying to pick it up without burning himself. Hondo observed the man's awkward efforts for a moment and impatiently pushed him aside. With gloved hand he pulled the knife from the fire and held it aloft. It glowed brightly in the half light.

Groth crossed to Banning, Hondo and Coaley at his heels. The outlaw reached out, grasped the two edges of Banning's shirt and ripped them apart, exposing the browned expanse of his thick chest.

"Lay it flat against him," Groth directed, stepping back. "Right across the nipples."

From the end of the wagon Ruby Simmons's scream shattered the quiet. She leaped to the ground and rushed to Banning's side. Groth caught her by the shoulders and pushed her into Coaley's hands.

"Hold her back. Keep her out of the way."

"No!" the girl cried, struggling against the outlaw. "Don't hurt him! He doesn't know anything about that money!"

"Put it on him, flat," Groth said, ignoring her. "Cut out the stalling. We're using up good time."

Inside the wagon Will Simmons, aroused by Ruby's shrill pleas, was calling her name. She seemed not to hear. Her attention was upon John Banning.

"Please . . . please don't! Tell them, John! Tell them you don't know anything about that money!"

Banning watched Hondo step up close, and then he felt the heat of the knife's broad blade against his chest. His skin flinched instinctively. He shifted his eyes to Groth. "All right, you win. I'll talk. I'll make you a bargain."

XV

"Bargain!" Hondo echoed the word with a loud laugh. "Somebody else wanting to make us a bargain, boys!"

"One you better listen to," Banning said coolly, "unless you don't figure to live long enough to spend that money."

Ruby had ceased her struggling against Coaley's firm grasp. She watched Banning intently, a strange, disbelieving look on her face. The fire, licking out farther, caught the pile of brush Coaley had gathered and burst into higher flames, illuminating the area brightly.

Ruby's voice was low when she spoke: "You mean you have that money yourself? That you hid it here . . . knowing they might come after it and cause trouble?"

Banning nodded slowly. He saw the flare of anger in her face and then the resignation and faint despair that replaced it. He had deceived her, she thought. He had used her, and as a consequence greater trouble had piled upon her already weary shoulders. Probably she thought of him now as little better than Chick Adams or any of the outlaws. He should have told her about the stolen money, of how he would use it as bait to catch the killers. Only it was too late now.

Ruby turned away, moving dispiritedly to the front of the wagon. Coaley had released her willingly enough; there was no fight left in her now. Groth, grinning, reached over and plucked the lawman's badge from Banning's shirt pocket. He flipped it to Coaley.

"You was always hankering to be a big marshal," he said, laughing. "Reckon this is your chance. Just might come in handy, having a lawman around later on."

Coaley, grabbing for the star, missed. It fell to the ground, a shining bit of metal against which the firelight flickered weakly. The outlaw picked it up and hung it on his greasy shirt front, his narrow, whiskered face cracking into a pleased grin. "Once was going to be a lawman," he cackled.

Groth glanced at the outlaw with an expressionless face. He swung back to Banning. "What's this here bargain you're talking about. Make it quick. I ain't got much time to fool around."

Banning, his eyes following Ruby's dejected figure, came back to the outlaw. "Not much time left for living, either, unless we get to water."

"Don't need you to tell me that."

"By this time tomorrow we'll all be dead unless we get to that water hole. And so will the horses."

"All right, all right," Groth said, angered and impatient. "So we need water bad. What's that got to do with the money?"

Banning, building his case with deliberate care, said: "Have you got any idea how far it is to water? A night's ride is all . . . if you go in the right direction. A week or better, if you head out wrong."

"So?"

Hondo suddenly pushed the knife closer to Banning's chest. "What the hell's he yappin' about? You was in such a blasted hurry, what are you holding back for?"

Banning looked squarely into Groth's eyes. "That money's not going to do any of you much good, if you're laying out there on the desert, dead from thirst. I'll make you a deal . . . I'll turn the money over to you and take you to water. My price is your word that you won't harm the Simmonses or me."

Banning paused, studying the outlaws before him. He knew in advance what their reaction would be—accept, but not for a moment entertain any plans for going through with their end of the bargain. The danger lay in that Groth might figure it too simple, not really believe Banning would fall so easily into the trap, and suspect he had some other idea in the back of his mind.

Coaley nodded vigorously, working his dry lips eagerly. Coaley was the weak link in the outlaw's chain, the one who would break first. Banning had to remember that. Hondo lowered the knife, the heat of its broad surface having diminished considerably by this time. A half smile was on his lips, and he could not hide the cunning in his dark eyes.

"Why, sure, I don't see no reason why that kind of a deal wouldn't work out, do you, Groth? All we want is the money. And some water so's we can keep traveling."

Groth, his gaze riveted to Banning's, said nothing. He was not fully convinced of Banning's intentions, and he was going over the idea, step by step, seeking a flaw. But after a time he nodded. "All right. But you sure you got the money?"

Banning said: "I've got it."

"Then how come Coaley and Hondo didn't find it? They pulled this outfit apart and didn't find a thing. Be mighty hard to hide something around a wagon a man couldn't find."

"Maybe the woman's got it hid on her," Coaley suggested. "Once knew me a woman who was always hidin' her money inside her dress and things."

Immediately Hondo's face brightened. "That's a fact, Groth. Only place we didn't look. I'll bet she's got it on her. By God, I'll strip her jay-bird naked and see!"

Banning, keeping a tight rein on the fear that rocked through him, said: "It's not on her. She didn't even know I had it up to now. You saw that yourselves."

Groth nodded. "Reckon that's right." He threw a side glance to the outlaw. "Hondo ain't half so anxious to find the money as he is to pull all her clothes off."

"They could be lying about her knowing," Hondo persisted.

"Forget it," Groth snapped. "It ain't on her. You can bet on that. She'd have forked it over when we was about to brand her friend here." He came back to Banning. "Anyway, I can't see it makes any difference now. It's no good to us unless we get to water . . . and we'll get it when we do. But"—he added, shoving up against Banning threateningly—"you try crossing us up, friend, and you and your lady partner are dead."

"That ought to prove I'm telling you the straight truth," Banning countered. "I'm buying our lives with that money and the trail to the water hole. I fail to come through with either one, I know you'll be on my back."

Groth said: "You got it right. And you can sure figure on it."

"And, when we get there, I'm expecting you to live up to your end of the deal."

Groth nodded, grinning faintly. "You got my word, ain't you?"

"Then cut me loose from this wheel. We've got to get moving."

"What's to keep him from taking us on a regular snipe hunt?" Hondo demanded. "He could just lead us out there into the desert, figuring we'd soon drop."

Groth snorted his disgust. "You're as feather-headed as Coaley. Can't you see they're needing water bad as us? Maybe even worse. He won't be taking us anywhere except straight to that water hole. Cut him loose."

Hondo, saying nothing more, moved up beside Banning and, with the still-warm knife, sliced through the ropes that bound the big man to the wagon. Free, Banning rubbed at his wrists, relieving the cramped, numb feeling.

Groth grinned in friendly fashion. "Now that we've set us up a deal, any reason why you can't turn the money over to us now? You still got the big ace up your sleeve, the water hole."

Banning shook his head. "Let's keep it the way we spelled it out at first. I'll give you the money when we get there and you're ready to ride out."

Hondo glanced toward the wagon. "I still got a hunch the money's on the girl. She could've been putting on a show to fool us. I'm for finding that money now and taking our chances on the water."

Groth favored the outlaw with a slanted look. "Like I said, you just want to have yourself a time taking the clothes off that girl. Anyway, suppose you did find the money . . . what direction would you start in for water?"

Hondo shrugged and examined the knife in his hand carefully. He reversed it, took the point of the blade between thumb and forefinger and raised it above his shoulder. With a quick, downward motion, he sent it spinning through the air to drive deeply into the side of the chuck box. "We'd reach it, sooner or later," he said.

"Later would sure as hell be too late," Groth observed. "We're going to have to get water and plenty soon. No, I reckon this deal with the marshal is the best way. We can't lose."

"One thing more," Banning said, breaking in. "Any reason why I can't have my gun back?"

"You bet," Groth said flatly. "What you need a gun for, anyway? We'll give you all the protection you'll be needing."

"I've got one reason only," Banning said, looking straight at

Hondo. "He lays a hand on Missus Simmons one more time, I aim to kill him."

Groth gave him a twisted smile and nudged Hondo. "What you think, Hondo? Reckon it would be a good idea?"

"Give it to him," the outlaw said, his dark face a blank mask. "I can take care of myself."

"Maybe so," Groth observed, no longer smiling. "Far as I'm concerned, it wouldn't make no difference to me if he did put a bullet in your hide. But it might turn out the other way around, and I don't want him dead. I've got to keep him alive for two things . . . money and water. Once that's done, you can settle your private argument any way you please." Groth swung around to Banning. "How soon before we're pulling out?"

"Quick as I can harness up. We've got to travel all night while it's cool." He started for the team, then halted and turned halfway around. "This is no one way set-up now, Groth. I've got your promise you'll live up to your end of the bargain."

"You got my word," Groth replied. "And Hondo's and Coaley's, too."

"Which are about as good as a Confederate dollar," Banning murmured under his breath as he continued on toward the horses. But that was the way he wanted it. He had to keep the outlaws believing he trusted them and their promise. He had to keep alive somehow, until he could get the Simmonses off his hands and out of danger. Then he could think about his own problem—about the duty that must be fulfilled, the obligation that must be met.

XVI

The problem was simple to understand, not so easy to solve. Alone on the seat of the wagon, Banning thought about it—get the Simmonses and himself to the water hole, but keep the outlaws from it. He racked his brain for a solution as the horses plodded wearily onward through the night. It seemed an impossible task, but he knew he had to come up with the answer. The bargain he had made with Groth and the other two outlaws had purchased only a few hours of life for Ruby, Will, and himself. Once they reached the water hole, the outlaws would toss all considerations to the wind; they would be interested in one thing only—the money. And they would be pulling out fast, leaving no witnesses behind.

He glanced at the sky. Near midnight. They should be about one third of the way, he judged. He swung his gaze about the wagon. It was flanked by the outlaws, Groth on the right, Hondo to the left, and Coaley somewhere at the rear. The two visible to him were slumped in their saddles, near exhaustion. Only the coolness of the night was keeping them going. They would never make another full day under the blazing desert sun without water. *Nor can we!*

Banning admitted that truth to himself. Ruby and Will had to have water, as well as himself. Thinking of the girl, he looked back over his shoulder into the shadowy darkness of the wagon's interior. Ruby's slender shape was huddled beside that of her husband. She had not changed position since they had departed the lava butte. Seeing her there sent a twinge of loneliness through Banning. He wished she would come forward and take her customary place beside him on the seat. There were so many things he needed to explain—about the money and why he had not told her of it. And he would tell her, too, of Lucy and the lonely years since her death. And now of Davey. But she had turned her back on him, shut him out of her thoughts. She was Will Simmons's wife—he was not forgetting that—but it did not alter the fact that she had carved a definite place for herself in his life. She had filled, for a time, that great chasm of emptiness left by his loss of Lucy and Dave, and for all those hours, good or bad, they had been thrown together, there was a pleasant recollection in his mind. He would like to put things right with her before they parted. He would not want her to leave him, either of her own accord or at the violent hands of the outlaws, thinking him completely black.

All this passed through his mind in its slow way, disturbing him, grieving him, leaving him at loose ends. He was, basically, a methodical man, one who restlessly sought the correct answer to every problem he faced, who never left any task half finished but always saw it through to final completion. Now, here in this star-flecked desert night, all things were wrong. Nothing was working out right. And there appeared little likelihood they would.

He stared straight ahead. The horses were moving slowly, their heads rising and falling mechanically as they trudged on. Banning shrugged, throwing off the feeling of despondency that clouded him. He was still alive, still able to fight, even though he was unarmed and the odds against him were high. Actually all he needed to do was get Ruby and her husband to the water hole, then they were off his hands. He would be free then to deal with Hondo and Groth and Coaley. But how does a man lead a thirsting party to a water hole, allow half to take its fill, and keep the rest from even knowing of its existence?

Banning shook his head; it was a tough situation. But it had to be met. He glanced ahead, beyond the team. They were nearing the crest of a long and sandy slope. The team was blowing hard from the pull. They should take a rest, an hour at least. He allowed the horses to complete the climb and pulled them to a halt. A seemingly endless, gently flowing mesa stretched out below them. It was a good place to stop, for the team, once rested, could then make excellent time across the downgrade plains when they resumed their traveling.

Groth had come awake as the wagon ceased its rattling progress. He wheeled about and rode up. Hondo closed in swiftly from the opposite side.

"What's the trouble?" the outlaw leader demanded suspiciously.

Banning looped the reins about the brake pedal. "The team needs a breather. We'll lay up for an hour."

Coaley came up from the rear, starlight glinting against the badge on his shirt. "We here, Groth? Where's the water?"

Banning glanced at the outlaw. Coaley, he had noticed, had an odd, childish manner about him. "Long way yet before you get a drink," he said, and watched the man lower his head in disappointment.

A half sob came from Coaley's parched throat. "Just got to have some water," he moaned, and turned away. A dozen steps, and he stopped. "Groth, you want I should still stand guard back here like I been doing?"

Groth gave the man a puzzled look. He shrugged his massive shoulders. "Sure, Coaley. You just keep right on standing guard."

"What the hell's got into him?" Hondo asked wonderingly, staring after the outlaw.

Groth rubbed at his whiskered chin. "Being thirsty is addling his head, I reckon. It'll be doing the same to us if we don't get some water soon."

"We'll be there," Banning said, seeing Groth's hard, threatening eyes upon him.

The outlaw said no more but wheeled away, pointing his horse for a clump of brush. Dismounting, he tied the animal and motioned for Hondo to do the same.

"Better save up on that nag. Once we pull out in the morning, we won't have time to be stopping along the way."

Hondo grinned his understanding and kneed his horse up alongside Groth's.

Banning waited until they had strolled off beyond earshot. Then he called to Ruby. "How's Will?"

"No better, no worse, I guess," she replied in a dragging tone. "Just lies there, not seeming to know at all what is happening."

Her voice, reluctant and weary as it was, sounded good to Banning. At least she had finally spoken to him. Later he would try and persuade her to listen to his side of the story.

"We'll be reaching water in another four or five hours," he said, keeping his words low. "A drink will make a big difference in Will's condition."

"Do you really think . . . ?" she began, then stopped, some strange fear closing off the rest of her question.

"Don't worry about Groth and the others," he said, guessing at her meaning. "They're my problem. You sound very tired. Are you all right, otherwise?"

"I suppose. I've reached the point where there is no feeling, only a numbness. Even if someone offered me a cup of water, I doubt if I could drink it. My throat seems to have closed up."

"It won't be too much longer," Banning assured her, having no idea, however, how he would fulfill the implied promise he was making. As he climbed down from the wagon, a sudden giddiness swept through him. He grabbed at the wheel to steady himself. After a moment he shook his head and swore softly. That was all he needed now—to have thirst and the lack of sleep knock him off his feet. "Think I'll take a little walk," he said, covering up. He hoped Ruby had not seen him falter. It would only add to her worries. "I need to stretch my legs a bit. One thing, stay inside the wagon while I'm gone. Don't get out unless I'm around. Understand?"

"All right," she replied.

Banning walked out beyond the horses, along the rim of the slope, heading for a slightly higher knob rising some hundred yards or so to his right. Groth and Hondo, squatting on their heels in the coolness, immediately rose and fell in behind him.

"Just taking a look around," he explained.

"Sure, and we'll do a mite of looking with you," Hondo said. "Wouldn't want you getting any ideas about burying that money up here somewheres."

"It'd be a fool thing to do," Banning said scornfully. "I'm using that money to pay for the Simmonses' lives and my own. What good would it do me buried up here?"

"Never know what a man's thinking," Hondo answered.

On the hilltop Banning halted. The desert was in the deep hush of night, and the far-flung flat plain was indistinct and ghostly in the pale starlight. For a brief moment his troubles were forgotten as he was caught up by the magnificence of the scene and, like countless travelers before him, the inconsistency of how a land so cruel and pitiless by day could be so utterly beautiful at night. But a man, if he wished to live, could not be influenced by the land's breathtaking enchantment. Rather, he had to recognize it for what it was, a heartless and uncompromising enemy, and warily lay his plans for survival. Somewhere beyond that velvet darkness were the Whitetail hills. They could not be far distant now.

Banning's thoughts came to a sudden, complete stop. Something deep inside his mind was prodding him, pushing at his consciousness. It clamored for recognition, demanded to be remembered. Systematically he sorted through his knowledge of the country, of the desert and the low-piled Whitetails where the water hole bubbled from the rocky earth. The water hole—that was it! A plan for salvation, for the safe escape of the Simmonses and the opportunity to complete the capture of the outlaws, burst full-blown upon him in that next fleeting instant. It was the answer he had sought, water for the perishing Simmonses and himself, none for the outlaws. Why hadn't he thought of it sooner? He wheeled about, keeping his face tipped down to hide the elation he knew it betrayed.

"Ready to pull out?" Groth asked, coming to his feet.

"Any time," Banning answered, then stopped short.

Something was wrong. He stood dead still there on the crest of the hill, trying to think, trying to put his finger on the cause of the fear that was gnawing at him. And then realization came to him. "Where's Hondo?"

XVII

"Hondo." Groth echoed the red-bearded outlaw's name in genuine surprise. "Was right here a few minutes ago." He swung about. "That danged fool . . . he's after the woman again, sure as the devil!"

Banning scarcely heard. He started down the ridge at a fast run. Ten yards later he was sucking frantically for breath, and his body had begun to tremble like a leaf in winter's first storm. There was little strength in his legs. He had not realized how weak he had become in those last days. But, spurred by thoughts of Ruby in the brutal hands of Hondo, he drove himself on. Behind him he could hear Groth in stumbling pursuit. The outlaw was having the same difficulties, and the rasp of his breathing was a loud sawing sound in the night.

"Wait . . . dammit . . . wait, or I'll shoot!"

Banning heard the words, but they meant nothing to him. Groth would not use his pistol. Groth needed him alive, could not afford to let him die. It came to him then why the outlaw was trying to stop him. He was afraid of a fight between Hondo and Banning, fearful of the possible result. That thought lent new strength to Banning. He reached the edge of the ridge. The wagon top loomed up whitely a dozen yards to the left. He rushed on, tripped and went to one knee, striving for breath.

"Ruby!" he gasped.

He regained his footing, listened for her reply above his ragged breathing. He gained the wagon, caught himself against a rear wheel, and rested his heaving body. "Ruby!"

He heard it then, a half-strangled cry off in the shadows beyond the wagon. Ducking by Groth, he lunged across the loose sand. Two indistinct figures were dead ahead, struggling, swaying from side to side. Heedless, seething with a revived, raging fury, Banning hurled himself at the taller shape.

The impact knocked Ruby clear of Hondo's clawing hands. She staggered off and fell to the ground. Banning and the outlaw went down in a tangle of threshing arms and legs. Both men were gulping for wind, striking out with their fists, trying to regain their feet, all at one and the same time.

Hondo broke away and rolled to one side. He came to his knees, then to his feet. He was like a cat, and he crouched there, ready to spring. Banning, a yellow film veiling his eyes, lunged. He scarcely heard the blast of Hondo's gun. The breath of the bullet upon his cheek went unnoticed. He struck the outlaw straight on, his knotted fists, like battering rams, catching Hondo on the jaw and in the face. The outlaw went over backward. His gun flew from his stiffening fingers and buried itself in the sand. He was stunned, and Banning, new strength coming from some untapped reserve in his tremendous animal system, hurled himself against the man. Astride him, he began to hammer him mercilessly about the head and neck.

"I'll kill you . . . I'll kill you!" he raved, his voice pitched to an unnatural level. "With my bare hands . . . I'll kill you!"

Someone was dragging at him from behind, trying to pull him off the nearly unconscious Hondo. Banning lashed out with one arm, backhanded, seeking to ward off the interference. Something solid and heavy struck him across the head. His senses reeled briefly, and then a voice got through to him—Groth's voice.

"Get off! Let him be, you crazy wild man! You want me to bend this gun barrel over your head?"

A measure of rationality returned to Banning. He dragged himself off the groaning outlaw and allowed himself to sprawl full-length on the cool sand. His lungs felt as though knives were pricking at them, and his head was spinning from the exertion. He was conscious, then, of someone bending over him, of fingers stroking his face.

"John. John, are you all right?"

It was Ruby's anxious question. He managed to nod. "Are you?"

"Yes . . . you got here just in time. I didn't have much strength left to fight with." He said nothing, and she, reading his thoughts, continued: "I'm sorry I got out of the wagon. I wasn't thinking."

"Forget it," he said, beginning to feel better. "It's all over and done with now."

"What's going on here?"

It was Coaley. He was astride his horse, sitting very erect and stern.

"Little fracas between Hondo and Banning," Groth explained. "Nobody hurt."

"I heard a shot," Coaley went on. "Now, I want it plain understood . . . there'll be no gun play in my town!"

Groth and Hondo swiveled their startled attention to the man. Ruby and Banning stared at him.

"What's that?" Groth demanded.

"You heard me! I said I'd put up with no shootin' in my town. And I mean it. Either check them irons at the saloon or ride on out."

"He's gone loony!" Hondo exclaimed in an awed voice. "Thinks he's a regular lawman."

Groth walked slowly toward the outlaw. Instantly Coaley's gun was out, the hammer cocking loudly in the strained hush.

"Hold up right there, mister. Don't come no closer. I'm on

to your smart tricks."

Groth hesitated. He glanced at Hondo and grinned helplessly. "All right, Marshal," he said softly. "Have it your way."

"Reckon that's better," Coaley muttered, his manner relenting a little. "No need of us having trouble. You all just better mount up and line out."

"We're going, Marshal," Groth assured him, ducking his head at Hondo. He made a similar motion to Ruby and Banning. Under his breath, he added: "Better humor the old fool, leastwise until I can get that gun away from him."

Coaley sat stiffly on his horse, a thin-faced picture of stern authority, while Hondo pulled himself to his feet. As a group, they started for the wagon.

Hondo moved to Banning's side. Blood streaked the corner of his mouth, and a purplish welt was lifting beneath one eye. "You and me ain't finished yet," he said to Banning. "We'll take this up later."

Anger still glowed within Banning. "You can bet on it, friend. And any way you want it . . . guns, knives, or fists."

Ruby and Banning climbed into the wagon. Will Simmons was fretful, muttering unintelligible, barely audible words. She went to his side while Banning took up the reins. He glanced about. Groth and Hondo were in the saddle. Coaley, presumably, was also, having never dismounted.

Coaley had cracked. He fancied himself a real lawman, a bona-fide town marshal. Banning thought about that, the hope within him building higher. If he could keep Coaley thinking along that line, he perhaps would have an ally when the showdown came. He would need to convince the man that Groth and Hondo were dangerous killers, outlaws, and that it was their combined duty to capture them or even kill them. A minute later he brushed the idea aside. Dependence upon Coaley, even for just a brief time, would be risky and most foolhardy.

At any moment the outlaw could snap out of his illusion.

They moved out, rolling easily down the long slope. The night had grown cold, with a slight breeze coming in from the west, and Banning wished he had his brush jacket. But it was hanging at the rear of the wagon, out of reach. He cast a glance at Ruby. Will had quieted down under her ministrations. She was sitting behind him now, in her usual place, and Banning could see the slow, tireless motion of her arm as she stroked the sick man's forehead.

"When you get a moment, come up front," Banning said in a low voice. "We need to do a bit of talking."

At first she did not appear to have heard. Then he realized it was reluctance on her part. She was back inside the shell into which she had drawn when she first learned of the money and the deceptions she believed he had played upon her. A few minutes earlier she had been grateful—he had been her good friend, for he had saved her from Hondo. But that was over with now. She had given him her thanks, and it ended there. He guessed he should not blame her. Things did look bad—and maybe it was better that way. Once they reached the water hole and he successfully carried out his plan, they could part with no regret. Likely he would never see her again.

"It's about tomorrow," he said. "I need to tell you what we've got to do if we're to come out of this alive."

She came forward at once and settled herself on the seat beside him. She brought an old comforter with her, and this she drew about her shoulders to ward off the chill.

Banning regarded her pale, sober face for a time, a touch of pity for her going through him when he thought of the troubled hours she had seen and was yet to experience. It was not right that a girl such as Ruby should be forced to cope with brutal realities. She had no background, no experience that would aid her in the grim battle for survival. But she had not flinched. She had kept going, wavering sometimes when the burden on her shoulders became too great. But she never gave in. *Enough woman for any man, and more,* Banning thought. *One to be proud of.*

"You wanted to talk about tomorrow?" she prompted.

Banning shrugged away his thoughts of her. He had not been wrong. She was all business, and, he decided again, that was the way he would keep it, too. It would make the coming day easier. "We'll be reaching the Whitetails a little before daylight," he said, keeping his gaze straight ahead. "When we stop, we'll be at a dry water hole."

It took a moment for his words to register with her. Then she whirled to him, surprise and alarm contorting her features.

"But you said we. . . ."

"Keep your voice down," he ordered roughly. "I told you we'd have water, and we shall. The main thing is I don't want Groth and the others to know about it. I want them to think the spring has dried up."

"But . . . how? Won't they see the water?"

"I'll drive this rig into a cañon where there is a dry spring. It's been that way for years. When we get there and you learn that, go all to pieces. Put on a big show, crying and blaming me. We've got to make them think we are at the real water hole, only that it has gone dry."

She said: "I understand. After that, what?"

"I'll explain when the time comes. No chance to now."

She nodded and said no more. He was aware that she was sitting quietly beside him, her eyes upon him, studying him for some time. He did not turn to face her. It was better for both of them that matters be kept on the impersonal plane they so recently had reached. It would be easier. He heard her wheel about on the seat, heard the dry rustle of her clothing as she crawled back into the depths of the wagon. Or would it be easier for him? He wondered.

XVIII

The Whitetail hills loomed mistily in the distance. Low, flat-topped, covered with rock and scrubby vegetation, they were even less impressive under the feeble light of the stars than during the day. Formed by some prehistoric upheaval of Nature, eons past, they were an odd, cañon-scalloped blight on the otherwise clean horizon to the south. Banning had watched for them steadily. He saw them finally and glanced quickly at Hondo and Groth. He wondered if they were awake, and hoped not. They weren't; both men were riding with chins sunk deeply into their chests, their shoulders slung forward. Banning was thankful for that bit of luck. He needed a little time to study the hills, locate the one cañon in which water was to be found—and point the weary team for the next, adjoining slash.

There was also the matter of approach. He would have to come in upwind so as not to excite the horses. Once they smelled water, his entire plan would miscarry, for there would be no holding them back. He removed his hat and felt the breeze riffling gently in his hair. What wind there was came from the west. He would have to take the party in on that side of the water hole.

A short hour later he had his bearings. The cañon in which the spring lay, marked by a slab of chalk-white shale near its mouth, became distinct. He checked the breeze again. It had not changed. Accordingly he began to curve the wagon gently to the right, pointing for the larger opening in the hills. He had matters timed well. When they were no more than a hundred yards from the entrance, Groth awakened. He dropped back immediately to Banning.

"This where we get water?"

Banning said: "Cañon right ahead."

Hondo, aroused by the talk, rode to Groth's side. The pair conversed in low voices for a few moments, after which Hondo swung about and waited for Coaley. Shortly afterward, the three outlaws had joined together and were moving on forward.

Banning grinned in the darkness. They were in for a surprise, a cruel one, to be sure, but one that was necessary. Now, if he could just carry off what he had in mind, all would work out well and as he hoped. The wagon, creaking and popping over the rougher road, began to enter the cañon proper. The trail sloped only slightly upward from the desert floor, and the horses were having no unusual difficulty. Banning turned and called softly to Ruby. She awakened and came at once to her place on the seat.

"We're here," he said. "The others are up ahead of us. Just about time now for them to discover we've come to a dry spring. You remember what you have to do?"

"Be upset. Put on a good show."

"Right. Make it look real. Soon as I've convinced Groth and the others that we'll have to move on, we'll get that water for you and Will." He looked beyond the horses. "Reckon they know. Here comes Groth."

Banning watched the outlaw approach. It was a tense moment. It was too dark to see the man's face clearly, and he did not know what to expect. The condition they all were in made it difficult to predict reactions. They could explode in anger, become infuriated at his failure to lead them to water and vent their rage upon him and the Simmonses. Or they could accept it rationally, admitting the truth that water holes quite often go dry in the desert country and rely upon him to guide them on to another.

Banning drew the team to a halt. Groth eased in beside them and stopped. "No water in that cañon." The outlaw's face looked pale in the starlight. "You sure this is the right place?"

"That water hole dry?" Banning asked, frowning.

"Like dust. Been that way for a hell of a long time."

Ruby suddenly burst into tears. "We've got to have water!" she sobbed. "You said we would find some here . . . but you weren't telling us the truth! You've just brought us here to die! You want us to die!"

"I'm thirsty as any of you," Banning snapped. "You think I brought you here, to a dry spring, on purpose?"

Groth stared at him for a long minute. He removed his hat and mopped at his face with a trembling hand. "No, I reckon not. Wouldn't make sense. What's the next move?"

"Groth!"

Hondo's urgent summons came from up the cañon. "Come here, quick!"

The crash of a gunshot ripped through the early morning hush, setting up a rolling string of echoes. Groth leaped from his saddle and started up the ravine, Banning not far behind.

"Look out!" the outlaw leader yelled, and threw himself to one side.

Banning plunged into the brush. A horse thundered down the trail. It was Coaley, hat gone, eyes wild, bent forward in the saddle. His mouth was flared open, and he was shrieking some insane gibberish. His arms lifted and fell methodically as he whipped his animal mercilessly. He passed only a few steps from Banning.

"Grab him!" Hondo shouted, coming from the cañon at a stumbling, uncertain run. He was having a bad time keeping his footing on the uneven, rocky surface. "Soon as he saw there wasn't any water," he continued, "he went off his head. Started to yell and even took a shot at me when I tried to settle him down. Then he took off. Said he was going back to town and get himself a drink of water."

"We'll just let him do that little thing," Groth said calmly, getting up.

Banning watched the crazed outlaw disappear into the dim, grayish haze of the desert. Coaley would not live long, once the sun came out full strength. He was living his last moments on earth, but Coaley did not realize that. He knew only that he must have water.

John Banning was realizing something, also; now he had but two of the outlaws to deal with.

Hondo said: "Old Coaley always was sort of loco. But that's a mighty rough way to cash in."

"Could be he's better off than us," Groth replied. "Leastwise, he won't be choking up for a drink of water, not after a little while, anyway."

Hondo chuckled, a low, knowing sound. "And I reckon it changes your arithmetic some, too. Makes for a two-way split. First it was four. Now it's down to two."

Groth's gaze was on the desert, where man and horse had vanished. "What good would money be to a loony?"

Banning listened in silence. If there had been any doubt in his mind as to the death of Chick Adams, it was clearly established now. Add to that the end of Coaley. Life was a cheap item to Groth and Hondo, even the lives of their own partners. His plan for saving the Simmonses and completing his own chore had better work. Otherwise, they would be quickly joining Coaley and the others.

Hondo moved away from the boulder against which he had been leaning. He came toward Banning. Some of the iron-hard confidence had gone out of the outlaws, Banning saw. The breaking down of Coaley had shocked them considerably, despite their outward callousness—not because they knew he soon would be dead, but because they realized that their own desperate need for water could affect them the same way.

The outlaw halted before Banning. "Well, Marshal, you got any more good ideas about water?"

"On farther west," Banning replied coolly. "Couple more places where there ought to be springs. But don't blame me if we find them dry. Water holes dust over mighty fast in this country."

"How far to the first one?" Groth asked. He had his hat off again, and was rubbing nervously at the back of his bull-thick neck.

"Half a day, more or less."

"Half a day," Hondo muttered, "and he ain't even sure there'll be water. Hell of a note, this."

"One thing you can't bank on around here is water," Banning said.

Groth sank slowly onto a flat ledge of rock. He began to brush at his eyes and to dig his knuckles into their sockets. His face was gaunt and gray-colored, and the cheek bones stood out bleakly. He ran his tongue over his swollen lips.

"By God! I just got to have a drink of water pretty soon! Ain't you got no ideas about a for-sure water hole, Banning? Don't know if I can stand another five or six hours. 'Specially after that sun gets out and starts beating down."

"You'll make it," Hondo said, his deep voice tipped with sarcasm. "Just you keep thinking about all that money. That'll keep you alive and going."

First Coaley, now Groth was beginning to show signs of cracking. That was a mild surprise to Banning. He had figured Hondo would be the most likely to break after Coaley. The dark outlaw was made of much better stuff than he had anticipated.

"How about the horses? They able to go on?"

"Not without a couple hours' rest," Banning replied. A thought came to him. "You want to ride on ahead and look for that water hole? Just head on due west, keeping along the edge of the hills. We'll be waiting here."

Groth lifted his shaggy head and glared at Banning. "Maybe I'm in pretty rough shape, but I ain't that far gone. When we move, we'll move together. But I've about run my string with you, Banning. You better be finding water for us and finding it soon! Understand?"

The outlaw's voice had risen to a shout. He swayed slightly on his rocky perch, and his hand trembled as he pointed a thick finger at Banning. Hondo had stepped away from his partner and was regarding him intently.

"All I can do is take you where there ought to be water," Banning said with a shrug. "If it's dried up, you've got no call blaming me."

He pivoted on his heel and moved back to the wagon, straining to hear if the outlaws were following or had elected to wait out the prescribed two hours in the cañon where they were at the moment. He could detect no sounds of footsteps behind him.

Reaching the vehicle, he glanced to the eastern horizon. It was still a heavy, leaden gray, but soon it would be paling and daylight would be upon them. There was no time to waste.

"Ruby," he called in a whisper. "Come out the back of the wagon."

He moved slowly to the rear, making it look natural in the event the outlaws had moved in closer and were watching. Reaching the corner, he shuttled a glance in their direction. Hondo and Groth were not in sight; apparently they were still where he had left them. He heard Ruby making her way over the items inside the wagon, heard the scraping sound her shoes caused when she came over the tailboard. A moment later she was beside him.

Before he could speak, she asked: "Are you all right? I heard a shot. I was afraid they. . . ."

"That was Coaley. He went crazy when he saw there was no water. Took a shot at Hondo when he tried to stop him."

"Stop him?"

"He took off into the desert. Said he was going back to Yucca Flats for a drink of water."

He heard her catch her breath. "Poor man. He won't get far, will he?"

"No, once that sun gets up it will be all for him. But we better get things started. We've got to get this done while it's still dark, and while Hondo and Groth are away from camp. Take this canteen with you. Follow along the foot of this slope, keeping to the right. It will take you to the water hole. About a half a mile, maybe a little less."

"I can carry more than one canteen. . . ."

"One you can hide, in case they should see you coming back. Two you couldn't. Now, I don't think they'll miss you while it's still dark. It's me they're keeping an eye on. If they happen to be watching when you get back, just act easy. Like you've been out for a walk while it's still cool."

She murmured her understanding. "When I do get back, then what?"

"I'll be waiting right here for you. Main thing is to get that one canteen full and inside the wagon without them knowing about it. Think you can manage it?"

"I can," she said confidently, and slipped softly, like a slender shadow, from the wagon.

XIX

Ruby moved swiftly along the base of the hill, the thought of fresh, clean water lending wings to her tired feet. Earlier she had been weary, about ready to drop, but that was forgotten now. Soon there would be water. Cool, precious water for them all. Water to ease poor Will's suffering, water to slake her own burning thirst, water for the horses and for John Banning, who was making it all possible.

She was having a hard time understanding him. That he had not placed enough faith in her to tell her about the stolen money he had hidden somewhere about the wagon, or wherever he had put it, had hurt her deeply. It appeared he did not trust her at all. Did he think she would tell anybody about it, somebody like the outlaws, if she had known he wanted her to remain silent? Or did he think she might try and keep it for herself—steal it? There really was nothing wrong with him hiding the money, using that as bait for the outlaws. But he should have taken her into his confidence and told her about it.

She had never before known a man like him—so big, so quiet and sure. And decent. Never once during the hours they had been together, alone, you might say, had he made the slightest advance to her. Always so formally polite. Once in a while impatient, perhaps, but never insulting or lustful, like that Hondo. Yet he was deeply interested in her. Her woman's keen insight for such things assured her of that. It was simply that she was married, another man's wife, and that he respected her status and kept his distance. He was kind and gentle; she had learned that from watching him tend the horses and help with Will. Yet he was savagely brutal if need be, like when he returned to the wagon and found Hondo trying to drag her off into the darkness. Had not Groth sprung to the aid of his partner, Banning would surely have killed the man.

Thinking of Hondo sent a chill up her spine. He was the only man she had ever met that she wholeheartedly feared. To have him rake her with those evil, wanting eyes made her blood run cold. It was a horrible experience, just having him look at her. Like being undressed and standing naked before him. Groth and Coaley and even poor Chick Adams had not worried her any, even when Chick nearly ripped her dress off getting the map. But Hondo—she had but to think of the man to start trembling.

She reached the furthermost point of the slope and began the inward swing for the cañon proper. She could almost smell water. First thing she would do would be to take a drink and ease that terrible craving. Then she would wash her face and hands; surely she could spare a minute for that. Then she would fill the canteen and hurry back, run all the way if necessary. John said she ought to try and be back before it became light.

Back, somewhere behind and above her on the slope, a small rock clattered hollowly. She froze at once, fear clutching at her. She remained motionless, scarcely daring to breathe, listening. A long minute dragged by. She heard no more. She moved on then, stepping softly, straining to hear further noises. But all was quiet on the side of the hill, and she pressed on. Likely a bird or some small animal foraging for food.

She thought of the coming day. The water would help Will, oh, so very much. He should begin to improve at once. After they rested up a few days, they could move on toward Nevada. John said there likely would be other wagons passing by and they could join with them.

What was Banning going to do? It was strange, now that she thought of it, but he had never spoken of his plans. Was he married? Did he have a wife, a family somewhere? Or was there a girl he loved and hoped someday to make his wife? If so, she would be a lucky girl. A faint twinge of jealousy passed through her. She brought her thoughts to a sudden, abrupt halt. Jealousy. What right had she to be jealous where John Banning was concerned? She, a married woman with a husband of her own. Yet, to think of him, with a wife. . . .

A darker patch of brush appeared ahead. Trees—low, scrubby things, to be sure—but real trees. She heard the distinct, pleasant sound of water bubbling over rocks. Immediately she began to run. The sound grew louder, and the soft reflection of the brightening, faintly starred sky on water caught her anxious eyes. She was there—she had found it! A small prayer of thankfulness broke from her lips.

She dropped to her knees beside the pool and plunged her arms, elbow deep, into its thrilling coolness. She lifted her cupped hands, brimming over, to her parched lips. Nothing in the memory of her lifetime had ever tasted or felt so good as that first drink. And she knew if she lived a hundred years more, nothing ever would. Being careful not to drink too much at first, she lowered the canteen into the water, hooking its strap over a partly exposed root close by. While it gurgled and filled, she washed her face and dampened her hair. As further luxury, she unbuttoned the top of her blouse and, with her handkerchief, bathed her neck.

The stealthy crunch of gravel brought her to her feet. She whirled about, eyes wide as fear gripped her. Hondo!

Her hand flew to her throat and her heart seemed to stop when she beheld the man standing before her. He was no more than a stride away. Hands on hips, elbows jutting out, legs spraddled, he was watching her through half-closed lids. A smile creased his dark face, and there was an oily glisten to his skin. He scoured her with his glittering eyes, bringing his hungry gaze to a final stop on the white area of her neck and breast, revealed by the unbuttoned blouse. He licked his lips, making a dry, popping sound.

Seemingly for the first time, he became aware of the spring. His glance went beyond her to where it bubbled from the rocks, traveled a short distance to form the pool, and then disappeared into the ground a few yards away.

"Water, by jeez!" he said in an odd, hurried voice. "That Banning was fooling us all the time! Groth's going to be mighty pleased when I tell him about this."

He took a step toward Ruby. She moved quickly back, one foot going into the soft mud at the edge of the pool.

"Keep away from me!" she cried, the words quivering with the fear that racked her.

"Well, now, that's no way to talk, honey," Hondo said in a husky, breathless voice. The fixed grin never left his face. He lunged suddenly, his reaching hands catching her by the arms. He whirled her about, his strength lifting her clear of the ground, dragging the hem of her skirt through the water. She screamed once, then began to fight, using her small, clenched fists, kicking at his legs with her feet. He laughed at her efforts.

"What I sure like," he rumbled, "is a woman that gives a man a bit of a tussle. One with some fire in her."

Ruby, tired, ceased her struggles. She was desperately seeking some avenue of escape. "The water . . . don't you want a drink of water?" If he would relax his grip for only a second, she might be able to break free and run.

He crushed her against his body, the stale, sweaty stench of him almost overpowering her. Lowering his head, he sought to press a kiss upon her mouth, but she twisted away and he found only her soft cheek.

"Man can always find a drink somewheres," he said thickly. "Don't often catch himself a pretty little filly like you off in the woods."

She began to struggle again, pitting all her strength against his two hands. It was hopeless. She was like a small child in his grasp.

"Might just as well make up your mind, girlie. You ain't getting away from me this time. Nobody around to get in the way."

"Let me go," she pleaded. "Please let me go!"

"Not for a spell. Not till I'm done with you. Don't know what you're raising such a ruckus about, anyway. You and that Banning've been carrying on for days, and I sure didn't hear you hollering for help. What's the matter with me? You figure I ain't as good a man as him?"

"John didn't . . . ," she began, then halted. The mention of Banning's name seemed to bring a measure of sanity and calmness to her. She quieted in his hands, fear ebbing slowly from her as she sought to think straight, to reason. The heaving of her breast lessened.

"Let me go," she demanded in a nearly normal voice. "If you don't, I'll tell Banning. He'll kill you. You know that."

Hondo chuckled. "Don't you go figuring on him doing much of anything, 'cept maybe furnishing breakfast for the buzzards. After I tell Groth about this water hole, and how Banning kept us from it, he ain't going to be much pleased." He paused, leering down at her. "Now, honey, this ain't the kind of talk we ought to be making. We ought to be cozying up, having us a real time. What do you say, you ready to be good?"

She allowed her breath to go out in a long, relenting sigh. "I guess I don't have any choice."

"That's right," he said quickly. "No use you wearying yourself down for nothing. All this kicking up a fuss ain't going to change me any. Ain't no woman ever got away from me yet, once I set my mind on having her."

He dipped his head suddenly and placed a bruising kiss fully upon her lips. She turned her face away, the fetid odor of his hot breath sickening her. Immediately the steel-like fingers tightened on her arms.

"You're hurting me," she said, striving to keep her voice from breaking, from revealing the revulsion that was almost turning her stomach over. "Just take your hands away. I won't run. I promise."

"Now you're making good sense," Hondo said, relaxing his fingers. "No reason why me and you can't have us a time before we go back to the wagon."

He let his hands slide down her arms, to her waist, about her hips. She stepped back. Instantly he seized her again and slammed her tightly against him. "Don't you go trying anything. . . ."

Ruby shook her head, hanging onto her screaming nerves. "Just . . . thought . . . maybe you wanted a drink of water first," she managed to say. "I know you're thirsty."

He stared at her, baffled. He grinned. "Dang! You women sure can surprise a man sometimes." He released her once again. "Drink's just what I can use. Now you stand right there, honey. Take me just a minute."

He swung about and dropped to his knees beside the pool. Going out full-length on his belly, he buried his face in the cold water. Coming up, he shook his head violently, sending a spray of drops in all directions. Ducking once more, he began to drink, sucking in the water in long, noisy drafts.

Ruby, clinging to her courage, stooped quickly. Taking up a rock several times the size of her two hands, she lifted it over him. With all her strength she smashed it against the back of his skull. His long body convulsed and went slack. His head, neck, and the tops of his shoulders sagged and went below the surface of the pool.

For a long, dreadful moment Ruby stood transfixed with horror. Then, remembering, she snatched up the canteen and started for the wagon at a run.

XX

Banning cast a worried glance toward the trail. Ruby should have returned by now. It was steadily growing lighter, and, if she did not soon put in an appearance, there was a good chance her absence would be noted. He could, of course, explain it away if questioned by the outlaws, but he wanted no doubts placed in their minds.

He turned his attention to Groth. The outlaw leader was squatting on his haunches, morosely smoking a brown cigarette. Hondo was not to be seen. That set up a slight worry in John Banning, too; if the red-haired outlaw was out prowling, he might accidentally stumble into the adjoining cañon where the water hole lay. And he might see Ruby. Banning tried to map out a course of action should something go wrong with his plans. Without a gun, and against the two well-armed, ruthless killers, he would have small chance in a straight showdown. He needed to think of something else, to improvise a weapon or a means. His eyes fell upon the chuck box. The broad blade of the butcher knife, used earlier by Groth to threaten him, caught his gaze. He took it up quickly and thrust it inside his shirt, anchoring it under his belt. It was a poor substitute for bullets, but he might get lucky enough to use it.

He looked again to the slope, growing more uneasy with each passing moment. Inside the wagon Will Simmons stirred restlessly and muttered in his fretful way. Beyond the eastern rim of the desert it had grown lighter. Sunrise was not long off. And then at that moment he saw Ruby at the foot of the hill.

She hesitated, waiting for his signal to come in. He assured himself that Groth had not changed position, and Hondo was still not about, and motioned for her to enter. She did so at once, running lightly with the canteen tightly held in her hands. When she was again at his side, he reached out and impulsively took her by the shoulder, a sigh of relief slipping from his lips.

"Had me worried. Thought maybe you'd run into trouble. Hondo's out there somewhere."

A tremor shook her. "He's dead."

"Dead?" Banning echoed blankly.

"He followed me to the water hole. I tried to get away from him but couldn't. Then I pretended to give in, and, when he got down to get a drink, I smashed him on the head with a rock."

Suddenly she was in his arms, pressing her head against his chest, weeping brokenly. The trials of the past days, climaxed by her experience with Hondo, had shattered her fragile reserve. She had given way at last. Banning held her close, comforting her as best he could, stroking her hair and whispering his reassurances.

"All done with and over now," he said. "You're back, safe and sound. Hondo won't ever trouble you again. Soon as I get the chance, I'll make sure."

She shuddered. "It was terrible . . . having to hit him with that stone. It made an ugly, soft sound. I'll hear it the rest of my life."

He kept on soothing her. "Just remember you didn't have a choice. Like I've said before, in this country you protect yourself against all comers, the best way you can. It was you or him. You only did what you had to do."

"So terrible . . . so savage. It's not even civilized out here. I've killed two men . . . two men."

"Forget it now," he said, and took her firmly by the shoulders. He held her away from him, looking intently into her eyes. "We still have Groth to deal with. Get inside the wagon. Give some of the water to your husband, and then come back out. I've got a hunch we'll have plenty of trouble explaining Hondo's disappearance."

She recovered her self-control and smiled feebly at him. She offered him the canteen, but he shook his head.

"Later. Take care of Will now."

He helped her into the wagon. She squeezed into the back and worked her way along the narrow space left by the chuck box. Banning heard her pour a quantity of the water into some container. The sound seemed overly loud to him in the predawn hush. He glanced to Groth, fearful that the outlaw had heard. The man was nervously plucking at a branch of mesquite, stripping the small twigs from the main stalk.

The odds were down now, Banning thought, watching Groth closely. Hondo was out of the picture. Chick Adams and Coaley no longer had to be considered. He would not be taking them back to face justice, but they would never rob and kill again. Groth was the last of the Wind River bunch.

Banning calculated his chances for rushing Groth, for overcoming the outlaw. Very small, he finally decided. Too small, and there was too much at stake. He would play out the hand the way he had planned it. With Hondo out of the way, the problem of staying alive and protecting the Simmonses did not seem so insurmountable to him. Of course, there was still the difference the gun made, a vast one, any way he figured it. He wished Ruby had thought to take Hondo's, then the question would be solved. He considered the advisability of going to the water hole himself and getting the weapon. Once he had a gun in his hand he could settle with Groth and do so quickly. He concluded it was the thing to do. He would wait for an opportune time and then go for the outlaw's pistol. That would end it.

But there was no time now. Groth would be clamoring to move on in a few more minutes. What would his reaction be when he learned his partner was no longer around? Would he accept it as desertion on the part of Hondo or would he become suspicious and blame Banning, believing he had something to do with it? In the man's present state of mind, he could come to any number of conclusions and, flying into a senseless rage, take bloody revenge. Tight moments were ahead for Ruby and himself, Banning knew. The bright promise of violence was as certain as the rising sun. He felt the cool blade of the knife inside his shirt, pressing against his skin. The odds were down now, a long way down. Groth might get him with his first bullet, but the knife would have its taste of blood, too.

He heard a slight sound at his shoulder. Ruby was descending from the wagon. He lifted her down, her weight light as thistles in his powerful arms. She handed the canteen to him. He tipped it to his long lips, filled his mouth and held the water there for several seconds, savoring its refreshing qualities. It was difficult to swallow, but the second mouthful went down easier. Immediately, it seemed to him, he could feel the change within his body.

"Will acts much better already," Ruby said, placing the canteen inside the chuck box. "He had two good drinks, and I left another cupful beside the pallet for him. I put a wet cloth on his head, and I know it helped. His eyes opened, and he actually smiled."

"Good," Banning said. "I figured he needed water about as bad as medicine. I'll try to get that other canteen filled before we pull out. And I've got to get my hands on Hondo's gun. I sure would like to figure a way to get water for the horses. I guess they can last through the day. I don't believe it will take any longer than that."

"For Groth to drop . . . to die of thirst?" she asked.

He met her gaze steadily. "Yes. That's the plan. We go on, like we still were looking for water." He half expected her to make some protest, decry the inhumanity of his methods, but she said nothing. It came as a relief to him. At last she was accepting things for what they were, reality for reality's sake. No longer was she the naïve young woman believing completely in the goodness of all men, in the sanctity of honor even among outlaws. It had been a bitter, brutal awakening for her, but she would be better off for it.

"Couldn't I go back for Hondo's gun?" she suggested, the idea of seeing the outlaw's body again chilling her visibly. But she was willing to bear it if it would help.

"Too late," Banning whispered. "Here comes Groth."

"All right, Banning . . . let's get moving."

The outlaw's voice was a hoarse croak. He walked unsteadily toward the wagon, his weapon in his hand.

"Whenever you say," Banning answered. He moved to the front of the vehicle, Ruby at his side. "Horses ought to have more rest, but, if you say so, we'll pull out."

"The horses are in better shape than I am," Groth snarled. "You seen anything of Hondo?"

Banning shook his head. "Last time I looked, he was with you."

Groth swore. He pointed his pistol skyward and fired twice, rapidly. When the echoes had died down, he shouted: "Hondo! Hey, Hondo! We're pulling out!"

In the subsequent silence, the outlaw replaced the spent cartridges. Thrusting the weapon into its holster, he again called out his partner's name.

Banning began to line up the horses, Ruby helping with the harness. "Looks to me like Hondo's run out on you, Groth," he said over his shoulder.

The outlaw snorted. "On foot? His horse is standing up there in the draw right where he left him. You think he would take off walking?"

Banning lifted his shoulders, then allowed them to fall. "Could be he went off his head like Coaley. Maybe you ought to ride out on the desert a ways and see if you can spot him."

He backed the team into place, waiting for Groth's answer. If the outlaw rose to the bait, he would have time to recover Hondo's gun. He reached for the traces and hooked them into the trees. He began to fiddle about the collar of the horse nearest him, adjusting the rein, straightening the pad. Why didn't Groth say something?

"Here, you, girl. Come here."

Banning wheeled about at the outlaw's harsh command.

Ruby threw him a frightened look and moved up to Banning's side.

"What do you want with her?"

"What's that there on her shoes? And on her dress? Looks mighty like mud. You been in water somewhere, girl?"

Before Banning could frame a reply, Groth had dipped forward. With his gun pointed at Banning, he hunched down and grasped Ruby's skirt. He ran his fingers over the dark splotched areas of the hem and rubbed at her shoes.

"Wet, by jeez! You two got some water around here, somewhere! You've been holding out on us!"

Groth backed away, his face livid with fury. His eyes blazed with an insane light.

"You've done something to Hondo, too! That's why he ain't around!"

Banning had eased slightly ahead, putting himself before Ruby, shielding her with his body. He watched Groth narrowly, seeking to anticipate the man's intentions, his next move. He lifted his right hand slowly and moved it toward the knife inside his shirt. He was no expert at throwing a blade, but, with luck, he might destroy the outlaw's aim with the pistol, even knock him down.

Groth's gun suddenly roared, and a bullet dug sand at Banning's feet. The outlaw had seen his furtive movements and guessed at a hidden weapon.

"Put your hands up . . . over your head!"

Banning complied. Groth cautiously moved in. The cocked pistol needed only the slightest pressure from his finger to send a bullet plowing into Banning. Groth reached out, and then his fingers brushed aside Banning's shirt and found the knife. He pulled it free and tossed it angrily into the brush a dozen yards away.

"You're a fool," the outlaw said, and backed off. "Think you could stand me off with a knife? Now, I want some of that water. I'll give you ten seconds to get it. You don't, this next bullet goes into your belly. The one after it hits your lady friend."

Banning had no choice. His plan had failed, just when he was so near to winning. He could refuse to give Groth the canteen—and both he and Ruby would die. And Groth would find the water himself. Or he could turn the container over to the outlaw and postpone death for a few more minutes. Either way, they were lost. But to comply now would at least give them a little more time. To Ruby he said: "Get it."

She was back in a moment, and pressed the canteen into his hands. The outlaw watched with feverish eyes. He licked his lips like some hairy-faced, starved animal.

"Hurry it up! Hurry it up! No, don't bring it. Stay where you are. I don't trust you none, Banning. Just you toss it over."

Banning, another faint hope of using the canteen as a weapon blasted in that instant, did as he was directed. Groth caught the container neatly. He removed the cap with his strong teeth and spat it out, then tipped the canteen to his lips and began to gulp down the water, never once taking his eyes off Ruby and Banning. He drank his fill noisily. Finished, he placed the container on the ground, wiped his mouth and glared at Banning.

"Tricked me good, didn't you, Marshal? You had water all the time while me and Hondo was needing it bad. And poor old Coaley. He's dead because you held out on us. But I reckon I got the last say-so after all."

"You still don't have the money."

Groth nodded. "Sure, but I ain't worrying none about that now. You say you hid it somewhere around this rig, and I believe that. You wouldn't have been fool enough to leave it back along the trail. Too easy for it to get lost, covered over by the wind, say. So it's got to be around that wagon."

He reached for the canteen and took another half a dozen

swallows. “No hurry about things now. Long as I got water, I can spend all the time I want taking that rig apart, piece by piece. Sooner or later I’ll find that money.”

“I could save you all that trouble,” Banning said, clutching desperately at last straws. “My deal still stands. I’ll turn the money over to you if you’ll let us alone. All you need do is throw down your gun where I can keep an eye on it until you ride out. Take the shells out of it, if you think I won’t keep my word.”

Groth wagged his head slowly. “A man needs a gun when he rides this country. And me with all that money, I’d sure need one.”

“Hondo’s over in the next cañon. Dead. You could pick up his when you ride by.”

Groth’s face hardened. “So you went and killed Hondo, eh?”

“He asked for it,” Banning answered. “You know that. He had it coming. We got a deal?”

“No deal,” the outlaw answered flatly. “I figure I owe you plenty, Banning. All that time without water, just plain sweating blood for a drink. And there’s Coaley and now Hondo. I got to square things for them. I never would feel just right if I didn’t.”

“You might not have as much time as you think,” ’ Banning said then, trying a different tack. “The posse can’t be too far off now.”

Groth chuckled. “Know something, Marshal? You’re that posse. All that’s left of it. There won’t be nobody along here for days. Maybe longer.”

The outlaw lifted his pistol to a higher level, pointing it directly at Banning’s chest. The hammer came back, the click of it loud in the hush.

“*Adiós,* lawman. Better tell your lady friend good bye.”

“No use harming her,” Banning said desperately. “She only did what I told her to do. She’s got plenty of troubles of her own, Groth. Let her be."

"And have her running to some John Law about me? You think I'm loco?"

Banning studied the outlaw's hard-surfaced eyes. There was no hope there. He turned slowly to Ruby. Her face, pale and sweet, was tipped up to him. Her lips parted slightly. He leaned over to catch her words.

"I love you, John. . . . Good bye."

XXI

Something was terribly wrong, more so than the usual, ordinary problems that had beset them. Will Simmons, lying on his pallet, realized that as he watched Ruby pass beyond his range of vision and on out the rear of the wagon where John Banning, presumably, awaited her. It was written on her face, reflected in her troubled eyes, and he wished again, as he had for the thousandth time, that he might be of some help to her.

The water had done marvelous things for him. His throat no longer felt like age-old parchment, and the fire in his stomach had lessened considerably. He had taken on added strength, but there was no change in the strange emptiness that was his chest. Since yesterday—or was it the day before—when that harsh, dragging pain had suddenly vanished after a bad siege of coughing, he had experienced little sensation of any sort. He had just lain there in a kind of lethargy, an odd feeling of being there in the canvas-covered wagon and yet not being there at all. Actually thirst in those hours had troubled him less and less. Nor had the aches and pains from lying for so many endless days in the wagon bed. If he had developed bedsores, as he once thought, they were now gone, for there was no more of that itching irritation along his back that, at first, had almost driven him mad. There was now only a vague airiness, a sort of suspension about his entire self; the only thing positive was a difficulty in drawing breath.

Lying there, he heard Ruby and Banning conversing in low voices. By raising his head he could see one of the outlaws, the heavy one they called Groth, sitting on his heels some distance in front of the wagon. There was a second outlaw somewhere, or rather, should be. The third one, Ruby had told him, had gone mad and run off into the desert to die. He was the hawk-faced one who had come poking about inside the wagon that first day. When he saw Simmons's emaciated figure lying there, he had pulled hastily back, refusing to touch anything or any part of the sick man, apparently fearful of contamination. But he had made it sound, to his friends outside, that he was doing a thorough job inspecting the wagon. Perhaps the second outlaw was who they were talking about. It was possible he had deserted Groth, or followed the hawk-faced one's example and rushed off to die alone. Or maybe Banning had killed him. He'd needed killing, judging from what Ruby had said about him. Odd how people talked so casually about death here on the desert. It was so commonplace, of such small consequence, it seemed. The first one—Chick Adams, or whatever his name was—Ruby said was dead, too. He did not know the exact circumstances, although she had told him. Funny, he didn't seem to have much of a memory any more. Anyway, Chick was dead. *Just as I soon shall be.*

He considered that thought calmly, wondering why it did not disturb him. Once the idea of dying had horrified and appalled him. Of course, every man had to die at some time or another, but usually it was expected of the very old, the badly injured, or severely ill. But to think of himself no longer living in a wonderful world of sights and smells and sounds, of being unable to see people, feel gay, think, understand, work, and have Ruby for his very own had repelled and shocked him. Now it no longer affected him at all in that manner. His mind, in its mysterious processes of preparation, had come to accept the inevitable. And possibly that had, in turn, been brought about because of Ruby.

He had loved her more than he thought it possible for a man to love a woman. From the day they had met—and it would continue until the moment the last strained breath departed his tortured lungs. He wished he had been able to give her more, that life could have been easier for her. But he had made it difficult. He had waited too long to see that doctor; delayed too long before starting for Nevada. A trip they never should have begun, he saw now. It was his fault Ruby had been forced to bear the load on her small shoulders. And each small line of care and worry marking her lovely face was of his doing. Now he had brought her to this, to a vital crisis, in which she was at the mercy of desperate outlaws, in a wild and terrible land that showed mercy to nothing alive.

There was one consolation. John Banning. He was big, strong, a whole man who had the strength and courage to fight for Ruby and look out for her. And she loved him. Will had seen it in her eyes when she spoke of him, watched it light up her features when she heard his voice. Hour by hour he had witnessed her wage that inner battle with her conscience; she had clung tightly to her loyalty for her husband, as any good wife would. But it was a losing fight, and Banning, without being aware of it, had won. At first Will Simmons's jealousy had known no bounds. It had raked through him like a barbed scourge, taunting him, mocking him, disparaging his hopes for one day regaining his health and winning back Ruby's love. He'd hated John Banning then, just as he had hated all men who looked at his Ruby with admiration in their eyes. But all that had passed, going with the pain. Some sort of emotional change had taken place during those long, dark hours, and now, instead of the bitter hatred searing his soul, he found himself thankful for the man's great strength, his complete courage and dependability. He did not understand this change, nor did he attempt to. He was aware only of an inner tranquility because of it.

Gunshots suddenly crashed through his consciousness. Raising his head, he could see Groth standing a short distance from the wagon. The outlaw's blocky shape was darkly etched against the gray rocks behind him.

"Hondo! Hey, Hondo! We're pulling out!"

Simmons lay back. It was an effort to hold his head off the pillow. He readjusted the wet cloth Ruby had draped across his forehead. Odd how good it made him feel. There were a few minutes of quiet, broken only by the faint jingle of harness metal. Banning was hitching up the team. There was a low run of conversation, but he could not make out what was being said. He reached for the cup of water Ruby had placed beside him and took a swallow. Groth's voice came to him again, harsh and demanding as he yelled at Ruby.

He lifted his head again that he might see. Groth was fingering the hem of Ruby's dress. Then he stepped quickly back, shouting something about water. Simmons understood then. They had not shared the canteen with the outlaws; they had kept it secret from them.

Groth, his gun out, was threatening. A few moments later he had the container in one hand and was drinking from it while he kept his pistol pointed at Banning. Nearly exhausted from the effort of watching these proceedings, Simmons sank back to the pallet. Groth was plainly angered beyond reason by what had taken place.

Will waited a long minute, gathering strength. He again pulled himself up to one elbow. Groth was still leveling his pistol at Banning. Ruby now stood beside the big man. There was no doubt the outlaw intended to shoot them both where they stood. A thought moved through Will Simmons's mind—perhaps there was one thing he could do for Ruby after all, one final thing to atone for all the care and grief he had put her through these last months. And repay, in part, some of the happiness she had given him.

Digging down beneath the pallet, he felt the cold steel of the shotgun Ruby's father had given him. It was a heavy, long-barreled weapon used mostly for hunting water fowl. A Long Tom, he thought they had called it. It required every ounce of his strength to drag it clear of the mat and work it up to where it lay along his wasted body, the muzzle propped on the edge of the wagon bed. The stock would not reach his shoulder in that position. He braced it against his right breast and aimed it at the outlaw as best he could.

He saw Groth prepare to shoot, saw the almost maniacal look that flooded the man's gross features. With his left hand Will pulled back one of the shotgun's rabbit-ear hammers. He tipped his head and sought to look down the twin cylinders. Then, with the forefinger of his right hand, he pulled the trigger.

The blast deafened him. The monstrous recoil of the weapon jarred him and drove the steel butt plate of the gunstock into his body. It seemed to be severing him into separate pieces. A great flood welled up within him, and his head began to spin and whirl as his breath closed off.

At the shocking blast of the shotgun, Dan Groth spun around. The charge had passed over his head and missed him. But it seized his attention and threw him off guard. In that split second of time John Banning acted. He hurled himself forward. The outlaw, realizing his error, whirled back and fired hastily. The bullet went wide of its intended mark, and Banning crashed head-on into the man. They went down in an explosion of dust,

Banning straining to wrench the revolver from the outlaw's vise-like grasp.

They rolled over and came to their knees, locked together in struggling effort. The harsh sound of their breathing was like a rasp being drawn across rusty iron. Groth drove his elbow into Banning's throat and twisted away. The lawman recovered, grabbed at the outlaw's hair, and dragged him back. They fell again, going prone into the dust and sand—writhing, kicking, rolling over and over. Banning felt the smooth roundness of the gun's barrel tear from his sweaty fingers. He was suddenly aware of it pointing into his face. He knocked it aside, seized it again, and twisted it downward. The gun's blast was muffled. It slammed up against him, driving what little breath he had from his heaving lungs. He felt the hot, searing flare upon his body—but there was no sickening impact of a bullet. Groth went limp against him. The outlaw's fingers loosened their hold, and his shaggy head sagged forward. For a long minute Banning lay still, waiting, and then he rolled free of the man. Groth was dead.

He came to his hands and knees, head hung low, as a long-reaching exhaustion overtook him. Faintly he could hear Ruby sobbing. He turned his eyes toward the wagon. Will Simmons was dead, too; he knew that without being told. He drew his weary, trembling legs up beneath himself and prepared to rise, to go to Ruby and comfort her as best he could.

The sharp crack of a gun split the hush. Dust spurted upward, spraying Banning's sweaty face with a fine, dry talcum. The bullet had missed only by inches. It had come from the edge of the camp, from somewhere in the rocks. Banning reacted instinctively. He lunged forward, plucked Groth's pistol from the outlaw's lifeless fingers, went full length onto the ground, and began to roll, all in one fluid motion.

The pistol in the rocks cracked spitefully again—and again.

Bullets smacked into the sand and clipped into the low brush around Banning, but the lawman kept moving fast, offering no target. He was trying to reach a mound of rocks near the mouth of the cañon. Once there he would be out of reach of the bushwhacker, could pause and fight back. And perhaps he could see who it was.

The safety of the rocks was yet a long ten feet distant. Bullets continued to buzz angrily by him, plucking at his clothing, thudding into the sand or the brush, always uncomfortably close. But he had to reach the rocks. The man doing the shooting undoubtedly was Hondo, not dead from Ruby's blow after all. And, being Hondo, he must be stopped at all costs.

Banning spun, rolled and dodged as the bullets sought him mercilessly. His breath, never fully recovered after the fight with Groth, was gone again, and he was sucking desperately to fill his lungs. He flung a quick glance at the ridge where the gunman was hidden. It was Hondo. And now, sure of himself, he was standing upright, his mouth twisted into a cruel leer. He had a bandanna around his head, covering the wound Ruby had evidently inflicted at the water hole. Banning, a wild anger flooding through him, snapped a quick shot at the outlaw and dashed for the shelter of the rocks.

His bullet had missed, of course. He had not bothered to take close aim, had intended only to distract the outlaw long enough to reach the mouth of the cañon. He dropped into a crouch behind the pile of boulders and peered around the edge. Hondo instantly fired. The bullet smashed against the rocks and set up a shower of fragments at the impact. Banning returned the shot. He saw Hondo jerk to one side as the slug beat into the sand nearby.

At that moment Banning saw movement in the end of the wagon. Ruby, alarmed and drawn by the shooting, had crawled forward and was now leaning over the seat backrest.

"Keep inside!" he shouted. "Don't come out!"

Hondo drove a shot at him. The bullet struck a flat surface near Banning's head, sprayed him with slivers of stone and screamed off into space. Angered again, the lawman flung his reply, but he could not manage to aim with any degree of accuracy and his bullet missed once more.

A sobering thought moved into his mind. How many cartridges were left in the gun? Had that one, fired so hastily, been the last? If so, he and Ruby were in a bad position. He settled back against the rocks, well out of Hondo's reach. He flipped open the loading gate of the pistol and methodically punched out the bullets into the palm of his hand. One shot left. Not much to fight a kill-crazed gunman with, not much to save Ruby and himself from death. Thoughtfully he replaced the remaining cartridge in the cylinder and turned it to where it would be in line for the next firing. This last bullet would have to count. When it was gone, if Hondo still lived, they would be at the man's mercy. He glanced toward Groth's body. A nearly full cartridge belt encircled the dead outlaw's waist. But to try and reach it would be suicide.

He looked again toward the wagon. Ruby was not in sight. Evidently she had heeded his words and gone back inside. He raised his head slightly and swung his attention to Hondo. Instantly the outlaw fired, and that bullet, striking the curved crown of a rock, ricocheted off into the cañon. Hondo had not changed his position. Banning turned about and concentrated his attention upon the brush- and rock-cluttered floor and walls of the cañon. If he could, somehow, make his way up the narrow slash, then circle around. . . .

"Hey, lawman!" Hondo's scorning voice thrust through the hot, still air. "Reckon you ain't much better off than you were! You're about out of cartridges, I figure. Maybe you got only a couple more. How about us finishin' this up, man to man?"

"Meaning what?"

"Meaning you just step out from behind those rocks. Then we'll start even."

"Got no holster," Banning replied, stalling for time to think. He did not believe one word of the outlaw's proposal that they face each other for an equal showdown. He knew the moment he showed himself he was a dead man. But he needed time to think, to perfect some plan. He still feared Hondo might remember Ruby and make his way to the wagon. Then, with the girl as a shield and hostage, he could accomplish anything. It had not occurred to the outlaw yet, but in time it would.

Hondo said: "Never mind the holster. Just you stick the gun in your belt. Or hold it, if you want. Anyway you figure's best is agreeable with me."

I'll bet on that! Banning thought bitterly. A man holding the big hole card can afford to be generous. He again looked up the cañon. It would be slow going. He would have to be careful and make little noise. Otherwise, Hondo would grow suspicious. As it was, much more stalling was likely to turn the outlaw restless and unpredictable.

"How about it, lawman? You brave enough to have a showdown?"

"Brave enough," Banning replied, "but I got a little thinking to do."

"Make it quick," the outlaw said. "I ain't goin' to set out here in this sun all morning."

"Five minutes!" Banning called, and immediately moved away from the rocks and started up the ravine.

The brush was dry from the desert's intense heat and the lack of rain, and Banning was compelled to make his way painfully slow to keep the noise down. He was on all fours, and in this manner he covered the first fifty yards. Then, at a point where a lesser wash cut in from the left, he turned inward, able now to straighten up and walk at a crouch.

The slope was steep. Each foot of progress, it seemed to him, was achieved with far too much noise. Hondo was bound to hear, to become suspicious. But he pressed on. Sweat poured from every bit of his body. He went back to hands and knees when the brush started to thin out and began to crawl through scrub oak. He could see nothing, and figured it could be working both ways; he was not visible to Hondo, either.

The brush ended. Again he was in a field of stones and short weed growth. He raised his head carefully to get his bearings, to ascertain his position in relation to that of Hondo. He saw the outlaw at the same instant the man saw him. Hondo had moved. He now was farther up the cañon, squatting along the rim of a rocky ridge that crowned the east wall. He was not over forty yards away.

Banning ducked back quickly, but Hondo had seen him as he rose out of the rocks and brush. The outlaw fired. The bullet seared through Banning's left arm, furrowing through the fleshy part just below the point of his shoulder. It had been a fortunate shot, almost a miss, but it caught the lawman off balance, spun him half about, and sent him sprawling.

He lay there, gun ready, hoping the outlaw would think his bullet had gone true and would come to investigate. But Hondo was a cautious man. He remained on the ridge, his pistol poised, ready. Brush was apparently hiding Banning, and Hondo was taking no chances.

Banning's arm was bleeding steadily, but it did not pain too much. He could not see Hondo from where he lay, but the outlaw's position was now well fixed in his mind. If he could manage to keep the man's attention for another few minutes, he might still be able to work around and come in on him from the side. Both would thus be out in the open and the odds would be even. It had to be that way when a man had only one bullet left in his gun.

He laid the weapon down beside him, moving carefully so as not to disturb the brush and reveal his exact position. He pulled off his shirt, a slow, painful process, sprawled out as he was. Draping it over his shoulders, anchoring it securely by looping the arms of the garment about his neck, he picked up his pistol and began to worm his way back toward the heavier stand of brush.

He made it without incident, and, once there, he cut back again toward the ridge. Sweat was standing out on his body again, but it was some relief to have the shirt off. Rocks and dry brush, however, scraped and dragged at him, scratching him deeply now and adding to his discomfort.

He reached the edge of the brush, this time some distance farther below than he had the first time. He was only a few feet below the ridge. He lay flat on his stomach and looked to his left. Hondo was still crouching on the rim of the cañon, his eyes fastened upon something down the slope that had caught his attention. The outlaw still believed that Banning was lying along the trail somewhere below.

Banning looked about and located a rock of suitable size. He removed the shirt from his shoulders and wrapped it about the stone until it was firmly in place. Then, rising to his feet in a crouched position, he half turned. Like a man playing ten pins, he sent the rock with its colored wrapper hurtling back down the trail.

Hondo rose to the bait at once. From where he stood it would appear that his intended victim was racing down the slope below him. Instantly he was on his feet, his gun cracking. Banning, bending low, leaped across the narrow space separating the edge of the brush and the ridge. Hondo, intent on his target in the rocks and brush, was half turned away. Banning reached the ledge, breathing hard from his efforts. He halted and straightened up, his bare torso brown and glistening in the sunlight from its coating of sweat, his left arm stained with crusted blood. The outlaw was only yards away.

"Hondo!"

The outlaw whirled. His eyes flared with surprise, with hate. He brought his gun up in a blurred arc, but Banning matched the move. He had but one bullet. He could not afford to miss. His shot was a fraction of time slower than the outlaw's, but it was accurate. He felt the hot brush of Hondo's bullet against his side. In that same instant he saw the outlaw go taut and lift himself to his toes. He hung for a moment in that strained position, like a man trying to withdraw into his own body, and then he toppled over the ridge, rolled down into the rocks and brush.

John Banning stood quietly on the rim of the cañon, his gaze upon the outlaw's crumpled, still shape. He let his trapped breath run slowly out, easing the pent-up tension that had built within him. He shook his head savagely, trying to throw off the sickness that threatened to engulf him.

"John! John! Are you all right?"

It was Ruby's voice. Lifting his weary gaze, he looked down the slope to where she stood. He sighed again, his shoulders sagging with relief.

"I'm all right. Everything's all right," he said, and started toward her.

XXII

They buried the three men there—Will Simmons on a short hill that overlooked the trail, the two outlaws a short distance away.

When it was done and they stood in the shade of the wagon drinking the last of the coffee Ruby had made, Banning pointed to a low roll of dust in the east.

"Wagon train," he said, "headed on West."

She studied the pall for a long minute. Then: "What will you do now?"

"Go back to Yucca Flats. This job's not finished until I turn in the money. Then maybe stay, maybe push on."

"Alone?"

"Alone," he replied. "There's nobody left now, not since the boy was killed. That is . . . ," he added uncertainly, haltingly "unless you. . . ."

"Unless what?"

"Unless you meant what you said back there when we thought Groth had us for sure."

She turned to him at once. "Oh, I did mean it, John. I tried not to let it happen . . . with Will lying there so sick, but I couldn't help it."

He tossed his cup aside and took her into his arms. "I had hoped . . . only hoped," he began, then stopped short. He glanced again to the eastern plains of the desert now stirring with the rising heat. "Reckon we won't need to wait for that wagon train," he said softly. "We best get started for Yucca Flats."

ABOUT THE AUTHOR

Ray Hogan was an author who inspired a loyal following over the years since he published his first Western novel, *Ex-Marshal,* in 1956. Hogan was born in Willow Springs, Missouri, where his father was town marshal. At five the Hogan family moved to Albuquerque where they lived in the foothills of the Sandia and Manzano Mountains. His father was on the Albuquerque police force and, in later years, owned the Overland Hotel. It was while listening to his father and other old-timers tell tales from the past that Ray was inspired to recast these tales in fiction. From the beginning he did exhaustive research into the history and the people of the Old West, and the walls of his study were lined with various firearms, spurs, pictures, books, and memorabilia, about all of which he could talk in dramatic detail. "I've attempted to capture the courage and bravery of those men and women that lived out West and the dangers and problems they had to overcome," Hogan once remarked. If his lawmen protagonists seem sometimes larger than life, it is because they are men of integrity, heroes who through grit of character and common sense are able to overcome the obstacles they encounter despite often overwhelming odds. This same grit of character can also be found in Hogan's heroines, and in *The Vengeance of Fortuna West* (1983) Hogan wrote a gripping and totally believable account of a woman who takes up the badge and tracks the men who killed her lawman husband by ambush. No less intriguing in her way is Nellie Dupray, convicted of rustling in *The Glory Trail* (1978). One of his most popular books, dealing with an earlier period in the West with Kit Carson as its protagonist, is *Soldier in Buckskin* (Five Star Westerns, 1996). Above all, what is most impressive about Hogan's Western novels is the consistent quality with which each is crafted, the compelling depth of his characters, and his ability to juxtapose the complexities of human conflict into narratives always as intensely interesting as they are emotionally involving. *Apache Basin* will be his next Five Star Western.